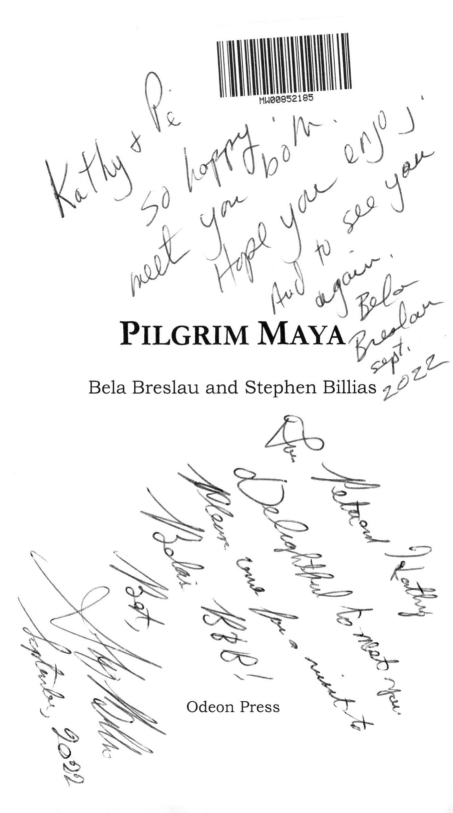

PILGRIM MAYA

Bela Breslau and Stephen Billias

Odeon Press

Printed in the United States of America

ISBN 978-1-7335750-4-1

Published by Odeon Press
www.Odeonpress.com

Every journey has a secret destination of which the traveler is unaware.

Martin Buber *The Legend of the Baal-Shem*

for all the pilgrims

BOOK I   THE LOST TRIBE 11

Chapter 1   Blackness 13

Chapter 2   Leaving 19

Chapter 3   San Francisco 25

Chapter 4   Meeting the Tribe 35

Chapter 5   Jane's Story 45

Chapter 6   Dinner with the Tribe 53

Chapter 7   Saturday in the Park with Sajiro 63

Chapter 8   The View from the Top of the World 71

Chapter 9   Oregon, Washington, Change 85

Chapter 10   Japan 111

BOOK II   THE BON VIVANTS 159

Chapter 11   The Bon Vivants 161

Chapter 12   The First Party 189

Chapter 13   Surfing 209

Chapter 14   Kumiko 219

Chapter 15   Endless Summer 231

Chapter 16   Taisha's Class 239

Chapter 17   "A Change Is Gonna Come" 251

Chapter 18   The Abyss 269

BOOK III   BUDDHA 277

Chapter 19   The Beginning of the Way 279

Chapter 20   In Deeper 303

Chapter 21   Zen Body, Zen Mind 321

Chapter 22   I Meet the Buddha 335

Chapter 23   The Cloud Nine Ball 347

Chapter 24   Gone Beyond 367

BOOK I   THE LOST TRIBE

Chapter 1   Blackness

For a long time, I see only the headlights rearing over me like a monster, two high-beam lights for eyes. Everything after that is darkness, blackness, emptiness.

I close my eyes tightly. *I will not cry*, I tell myself. I realize where I am, on an overstuffed red velvet couch, flowers, filtered light coming through the shades, in the office of my therapist, Sarah Altmere.

Sarah's voice breaks through my mind's haze and tells me—no, wait, that's not right. Sarah hardly ever says anything; she just sits there and listens. This time she makes a suggestion.

"Why don't you keep a journal?"

"I'm not a journal writer, not a Facebook poster. I don't share my life anymore."

"A private journal."

I'm lying on my back. She's sitting in a straight-backed chair. There have been times when I just lie there the whole fifty minutes and say nothing at all. Sarah also says nothing. Then I get up and leave.

I half-sit up and look over at her: Sarah is short, full-bodied, her graying dark hair in an uncomfortable-looking tight bun. Probably in her early fifties. She looks like the kind schoolteacher in a Disney film, but to me she is severe and remote. I know she is smart and a good listener. How would I know anything else? Maybe her friends would say she is bubbly, has a big laugh, and is kind and giving.

"No, that's not me. I don't want to catalogue and document my existence."

"Is that what you think a journal is for?"

She has that crooked half-smile that is her neutral mode.

"What is it then?"

"It's a place to talk to yourself."

I pull myself up to hug my knees. "I do that all the time."

"Talk to yourself in private. Say things you can't say to me."

This gets my attention, because over the last year I've said more intimate, personal, revealing, shocking things to this austere woman than to anyone else in my life, ever.

"I'll think about it," I say.

The rest of the time goes by uneventfully. I think the word "unhelpfully." Sarah ends the session in her usual way. Spot on time. She summarizes and says something bland like, "We've gone a bit deeper and covered a lot of territory." She stands up and smiles her stupid half-smile and starts to walk to the door. Keeping everything on time. As she opens the door, she adds: "Think about the journaling not just as a way to dig deeper and discover and explore your pain, but as a way to open a door."

Whatever, I think but I say nothing. *Why do I even keep coming?*

As I leave, I see my reflection in the full-length mirror in the waiting room. Thank god there's no one there. I stop and stare at myself. My eyes are red even though I didn't cry much this time. How can I look so unkempt, so pathetic, so too-thin? My pale skin is ghostly. I used to pride myself on my looks. I was considered beautiful. Will I ever look at myself again and see the tall Maya, who liked to shake her dark, almost black, wavy, shoulder-length hair and smile? Will I ever smile again when I see my reflection?

I clomp down three flights of stairs to the street and sit under the red umbrellas at the café. It's cold. The November wind rips through me even though I'm sitting next to an outdoor café heater. Almost all the leaves are brown or gone and the sky is a dull grey. Maybe my soul is dead. Newbury Street is bustling with shoppers, happy people. I never drink, but I order a vodka tonic and some greasy fries. I never eat greasy fries. Who cares? I sit alone for an hour, hardly tasting what I am eating and drinking. The vodka is swirling in my head as I walk back to my apartment.

The door to my apartment clicks closed behind me. For a flash moment, I want to call out to Dan and see him walk into the living room holding Ella in his arms—Ella holding one bright blue rubber marimba mallet. Dan Brown with his gentle bright smile, full lips, beautiful teeth. Ella Rosa, our baby, lighter skinned than Dan, with curly brown hair.

I sink to my knees on the brightly colored oriental rug.

A year has gone by since the accident. I will give up all this, I will go back to being a miserable daughter, a miserable childless mother. I've alienated all my friends with my grief. No one wants to be with me, and why should they? I'm filled with darkness. Dan and Ella are dead. I'm in the deepest, blackest hole in deep space. I suck the energy out of everything that falls into my gravitational pull.

Before I shut down my computer, I deactivate my Facebook account. I was never that active anyway and certainly not since the accident. I'm not much of a social media person anyway—no Twitter account, and LinkedIn only when I needed to find a job. I want to disappear altogether from the online universe.

I'm outside walking. I've thrown on the light coat that I used to wear at the law firm and my good running shoes. I walk along the river. Over the bridge and into Boston. More than an hour later, I'm standing outside of One Boston Place, where I worked in a law firm on the thirtieth floor until the time of the accident. My body is shaking. I go in and up.

Standing outside Melissa's office, I see she's at work and on the phone, her red hair pulled back in a no-nonsense ponytail. As I turn to walk away, she sees me. She comes quickly to the door and pulls me in. I'm still shaking. Melissa twists the blinds so others can't see in. She holds me by the shoulders and looks into my eyes. I am tall, five eight, but she's inches taller, angular, but with a fullness to her body at the same time. I loved working for her.

"How are you?"

"I can't find any—" I drift off.

"Maybe go up to Maine, to see your mom?"

"Maybe."

"I can't talk right now. I have a meeting with the big guys and I'm late. Come have lunch next week?"

"I'll call. Hey, is the roof garden still open?"

"Sure, they have heaters there this time of year."

Melissa looks alarmed.

I see her look. "Don't worry. I used to go there to be by myself when things got crazy. I'll call next week about that lunch. You're buying."

Up on the roof garden, I look over the city streets. Dan and Ella are gone. I grasp the rail and the shaking gets stronger. My hair is blowing. I'm so terribly frightened. I take out the engraved bronze locket that Dan gave me when Ella was born. My hands shake so much that I can barely open it. I see Dan's gentle smile on the left and baby Ella's brown eyes and curls on the right. Is there a place, a heaven? Will I see them there? My shaking stops and everything is quiet, calm. Should I tumble over headfirst or move one of the chairs to stand on the rail and dive? I look down for the last time. A man, a woman, and a baby carriage have stopped right below me. There's a bright red blanket over the baby. If I land on them my fall will kill them. I could wait until they pass. I wrap my arms around myself and instead of crying I breathe deeply. It always helps, but will it save me? Ten minutes later, I am still standing at the rail. I lift my arms to the sky and bring them down to eye level, palms extending outward. A gesture of prayer? A silent plea? Not sure why I added this movement to my breathing. I'm calm. I will go on, at least for now.

Chapter 2   Leaving

I'm sitting at my desk staring at papers. I'm waiting for my insurance settlement. It's going to be a hell of a lot of money. What is it worth—Dan Brown's life, the life of our precious baby Ella Rosa? Today I walked and walked the streets of Cambridge. I'm a zombie, crazed, the apartment drives me out early every morning. Ella's room is still filled with toys, tiny cute outfits, goofy mobiles hanging over the crib that will never again hold her warm infant body, so pale and delicate. It's the smell that drives me away. I smell her or perhaps I just imagine I smell a combination of my milk and talcum powder. The nights are the worst. I get into the cold bed and drift off. Where is Dan, where is the tall, lanky, brown body, that welcomes me as I cuddle against him, my back-side curling, seeking his warmth, fitting perfectly against him, his strong arms holding me as I drift off to sleep?

The phone rings. It's a friend from college, asking if she can come stay. She has a new job in Boston. She can pay the rent until she can find her own place. I tell her I am taking a long trip and will sublet to her. She's thrilled. When I hang up, I sit still. My office chair armrest bumps against the keyboard, creating random letters on the computer screen.

My life has no rhythm, no cadence, no meaning. I must go, I have to abandon this apartment that is so me and so Dan and so Ella. None of that anymore. All the love I put into making it our home is dead for me.

I pack randomly, taking things I don't need (a baby rattle for god sakes). I put all the things I want to keep separate and safe in Ella's room, otherwise untouched. I run out to the hardware store near Central Square and buy a lock. I install it and lock the door to Ella's room. I'm gone. I have no plan.

My first stop is right near Sarah's office, under the same damn red café umbrella. It is late afternoon, and it is even colder and bleaker. There is a freezing drizzle. I call Sarah's office thinking I will leave a message. She is there and she takes my call. She listens politely. I tell her I'm leaving for a while. She gives me her cell number, something she's never done. "Call me if you need to talk." After a minute she says, "Where are you?" I tell her. Next thing, Sarah is standing in front of me. No crooked half-smile. She looks at me intently. She takes in my huge backpack and equally huge suitcase.

I laugh, a first laugh in what feels like years. It's a bitter, guarded laugh. "Did you leave your client upstairs in the lurch?"

"Here, take this with you. I was going to give it to you at our next session." I take the package and stuff it in my already overflowing purse. It's wrapped, I recognize the paper is from Trident bookstore, my favorite on Newbury Street. She doesn't ask where I am going, which is a good thing. I couldn't have told her. As I stand up, Sarah takes me in her arms and hugs me hard. I think I see tears glistening in her eyes. Now the crooked half-smile has reappeared. She turns silently and walks back to the door to the building, never looking back.

In a sudden mood of almost absolute freedom, I head toward North Station. "The change is going to do me good," is my mantra. For the first time in a long time, I can almost breathe without a heavy weight on my chest. Almost. I'm walking slowly and dragging ridiculous amounts of stuff in my suitcase and backpack. But I'm moving. "Plane, train, or automobile?" I say to myself, although I've made the decision already because I'm heading toward North Station just blocks away. I can make it. I've carried heavier burdens in my life. I'm walking as fast as I can. One of the wheels on the suitcase is broken and it makes a horrible scraping sound as I drag it along. I'm moving. What am I moving towards? A young Asian woman throws herself in front of me. She's at most five feet tall, with short cropped hair, dark eyes circled with black kohl and wearing dangling earrings that are bright gold and in the shape of Japanese characters. She's so tiny that if I'd had a bit more steam up, I would have run over her. Even though she is so small, she effectively stops me in my tracks and smiles at me. "So sorry. Would you like to meet Jesus?"

"Excuse me, please," I say. She's blocking my way. I'm in no mood to meet Jesus. I might say something offensive. My heart is failing me. I'm gasping for breath. "Look, I don't have any money," I start to explain, but the young woman cuts me off peremptorily.

"We don't want your money. We want to bring you to the light."

I groan audibly.

"Come, he's right over there." That gets my attention. Usually the meet-Jesus people are speaking metaphorically. I see a knot of people gathered around a speaker. No, that's not right, he's not speaking, he's leading them in some kind of exercise. They're swaying, ignoring the rain. Their movement is strange, writhing, but beautiful. The first image that comes to my mind is of an Indian fakir with a flute and a blind cobra. They are making a guttural, chanting sound that matches their movement, awkward yet somehow free.

"Sajiro! Sajiro! This person wants to meet you!"

I thought you said his name was Jesus, I want to say, but it's too late. Sajiro is right in front of me. I stop in my tracks and am almost swallowed up by his smile. If I were going to be honest with myself, and I am not ready to be honest in this way, I would note that he is one of the handsomest men I have ever seen.

"These people," he says, gesturing at the small group of worshippers that surround him, speaking as if they can't hear him, "think that I am the latest living descendant of our Lord and Savior, because my family is one of the last true descendants of the Lost Tribe of Israel." He speaks softly, and I'm hanging on his every word. Not only is his voice soft, his character is also soft, graceful, somehow gentle.

Even though I'm being subsumed and enveloped by his personality and force, I blurt out: "That's the craziest thing I've ever heard."

"Oh, yes," he says. "Crazy that we traveled all the way from the Middle East to Japan—"

"You've got to be kidding me!"

"—and that for a hundred generations and more we have practiced in secret, but now it has been decided that I am come as the Jewish-Japanese Messiah to reveal all." He gives me a sly smile that could be anything from Son of God to saint to wise man to clown to homicidal maniac.

"Look, Sajiro, I've got a train to catch—"

He places his hands on my shoulders and looks deeply into my eyes. "You have such beautiful green eyes," he says. "But you are hurt. I can help you. I can heal you." And he gives me a look that goes right to my heart as if he'd opened a door behind his eyes and invited me in. I must have either blushed or blanched, not sure which.

The young Japanese woman is still standing next to me. "Come with us. We have a bus!"

"No, no!" I say too quickly. "I'm late for a train." She hands me a flyer, the one they are handing out on the street.

I need to keep moving and I really need to get away from her and especially from the Sajiro-Jesus character who is pulling me in.

"You will find us," Sajiro says. A cleansing wave washes over me. My rational mind tells me to run, get away as quickly as possible.

Chapter 3   San Francisco

I am not sure how I got myself to where I am now.

The train ride was a four-day blur of weary nights sitting up because I didn't want to pay for a sleeper, mingled with occasional flashes of distant white and sometimes pink-tinged brilliance as we crossed the snowy mountains of the West. I have almost no memory of the endless plains of the Midwest. Now I'm sitting at a table at the Cliff House looking out over the Pacific Ocean. Earlier, I walked up and down the beach. It was warm enough to take off my shoes and let the bracing water of the Pacific Ocean play over my feet and legs. I ventured into the ruins of the Sutro baths. I sent Instagram pictures of the iconic ocean views to a couple of East Coast friends. When there were almost no people walking in the fading light, and I really needed food and warmth, I came inside the Cliff House.

Now the sun is setting. A hush has fallen over everyone in the room as we watch the grand solar performance together. Just as the light flattens out and the bright orange band fades away, everyone claps. How strange we all are. How strange this place. How strange that I'm here. I've been in the city for less than twelve hours. I know no one. I don't know why I'm here. My backpack and suitcase are stowed in a locker at the Amtrak train station in Emeryville, a bus trip away across the Bay. It's going to be a pain to retrieve them, but I needed freedom. Freedom to walk around the city. Freedom from my few belongings.

The train had arrived at dawn. I'd taken the day to do some of the tourist things I'd read about—a stop at the City Lights bookstore in North Beach, lunch at Joe's, a wander through Golden Gate Park still heading West, and finally ending up here above Ocean Beach at sunset. It's wildly impractical not to have found a place yet, at least for the night, but I don't care. All I have with me now is the new satchel I bought at City Lights. I'm like a beatnik or a hippie, but I'm not one. I'm lost. In search of a future, any future. Is it even possible? I eat an over-priced meal of "Cliff House Cioppino" at the Bistro. It's getting late and I'm exhausted. There's no way I'm going all the way back downtown and across the bridge by bus to get my stuff. I've screwed up again. What a loser I am! Can I sleep in the park or on the beach without getting run over by park rangers or the police, or being raped and beaten by strangers? The Bistro is closing. It was warm enough during the day but now the fog is blowing in and I'm freezing almost as soon as I step outside.

A couple of taxis are parked near the entrance. I slip in the back of the first one and the driver asks the traditional, "Where to?"

"I don't know. I just arrived in San Francisco and I need a not-too-expensive place to stay. Can you help me?"

I see the driver's dark, almost black eyes in the rearview mirror. He's about twenty-five at the most,

American, maybe Asian background. I'm so cold that I'm shaking. I'm also afraid.

"My friends have a room they let out as an Airbnb. Near Japantown. Shall I take you there?"

"Yes, please."

"Got any luggage?"

"No, it's in a locker. Amtrak. Emeryville. I don't want to go there tonight."

I can see him staring at me in the mirror. Then I hear him calling his friends and explaining the situation. It sounds legit, but who knows? Fifteen minutes later, we stop in front of a shabby two-story building.

By this time, I'm truly afraid. The street is eerie, dumpy. I'm holding my cell phone, wondering if I should call 911? But I get out of the cab and stand by the door.

"Hey," he says, sticking out his hand. "My name is John. I'll pick you up tomorrow morning at ten. We'll get your stuff. The trip's on me." But I insist on paying, though I'm careful not to let him see the money in the wallet I had stuffed in my new satchel.

Next thing I know, I'm upstairs in a small, warm apartment, talking to a young woman named Jane Saito. She looks at me quizzically when she finds I have no luggage at all. She brings me a pair of leggings and a T-shirt and tells me to make myself at home as she leads me to a tiny room at the back of the apartment. Japanese style futon on a tatami mat on the floor. Towel and slippers next to a black lacquered stool. A Japanese-style housecoat is folded neatly on the stool.

I gather up the robe and the slippers and make my way to the bathroom I am sharing with Jane and who knows who else. It has a small square bathtub. Japanese style. I've never seen one of these before and am uncertain how to use it, but I lock the door and give it a try, and find that it's perfect, deep, and comfortable despite its odd size. I luxuriate in the hot water that immediately takes away the San Francisco fog chill. When I come out of the bath, feeling silly in the short coat and borrowed clothes, Jane has fixed me a bowl of miso soup and a bowl of rice that she dishes from a white porcelain cooker on the counter. I'm still full from the cioppino, but I drink the soup as additional warming from the cold that has permeated my bones, and nibble at the rice. Jane busies herself in the kitchen. She's short, thin, tidily dressed in loose-fitting white string pants and T-shirt with something written in Japanese on the front. She's wearing glasses with black frames that set off her bright eyes above a smallish nose and mouth.

"You don't have to feed me dinner," I say between bites.

"You're right, I don't. This is a B&B, not a B&D." We laugh together easily.

"What does your shirt say?"

"Ah. You think it's maybe something deep and spiritual?" Jane eyes me with a kindly but reserved and perhaps mildly skeptical look.

"I don't know."

"It's a commercial for a beer company. I work for Asahi."

"That's a Japanese beer?"

"Hai. Yes."

"Kind of like wearing a Nike 'Just Do It' shirt with a swoosh."

"Yes. Exactly." There is a moment of awkward silence between us. "So, what brings you to San Francisco?" Jane asks.

I'm not ready to share my miserable life story with a near-total stranger. "Oh, just getting away for a bit," I say. Jane does not press me on this. She smiles sweetly and leaves the kitchen.

The next morning, John arrives at ten as promised. On the drive we talk a bit. He's working three jobs, drives a cab, does Uber on his own, and works for a software company as a part-time programmer. I wonder out loud if he thinks I could stay with Jane for a while and decide to talk with her to negotiate a month or two. We grab coffee at a café outside the train station and chat some more, nothing flirty, just new friends. Is it possible to make friends, to have a future? John laughs at the amount of stuff I've dragged across the country—the huge suitcase and the backpack—but he laughs in an easy, smooth-edged, laid-back California way that isn't sarcastic. It's more like a sense of joy and wonder at the absurdity of it all. We drive back across the Bay Bridge, the newest skyscrapers south of Market Street gleaming in the clear late fall light off to the left, the rocky prominence of the island of Alcatraz shining in the emerald Bay to

the right, and the Golden Gate Bridge glowing orange-
red in the distance. It's not raining like it often does in
California in the late fall and winter. It's one of those
clear, crisp days with a bit of a breeze, the brilliant
light   simultaneously   revealing   and   shredding
everything. I'm giddy. It's been so long since I've had
any feelings other than deadness and pain. I realize
John has been speaking to me.

"What?"

"I said, are you going to be looking for a job?"

"No. No, I don't think so. I just need to rest." How
can I say that to a man who's just told me he works
three jobs to support himself? But it's true. I would be
useless in a law firm right now. A year has gone by
since the accident, and this trip is the first time that
I'm edging slightly closer to something normal,
whatever that is.

We swerve off the freeway, careening down the exit
ramp out to the Fillmore district. I'm following along on
a street map I'd purchased. Sort of old-fashioned, I
could have used the maps app on my phone, but I like
to hold the map in my hand and look around as I
travel. It's also a way to distract myself. John is a fast
driver. When I drive, I tend to look away from oncoming
traffic, to send my vision to the right side of the road so
as not to see the oncoming cars. Blocking out all
memories of the crash, I can't recall: Was there a
horrible instant with an oncoming truck or did it come
from behind? My memory is twisted and haunted. I
remember calling out, "Dan!" at the last second as if he
could have done something when there was nothing to

be done. After that, I don't remember anything. Being a passenger is worse than driving. Holding the map and closing my eyes helps to avoid helplessness, impending disaster. I was okay in the four days on the train across the country, but here I am in John's car cringing and uttering exclamations at every tap of the brake or swerve of the wheel. John patiently ignores me, for which I'm grateful.

Later, from my room at Jane's place, I call my mother.

"Hey mom, thought I should be in touch."

"Where are you? I have been beside myself with worry. I called your apartment and some girl named Jessie said she was subletting."

"I'm in San Francisco. Found a cute place where I can stay for a few weeks. I just needed to get away. To be somewhere else."

"I can send you money if you need it."

"Yeah, thanks, that would be great. I'm still waiting for the insurance money and all. You can put it in my checking account. I'll keep track. I'll pay you back."

"No worries, honey. I love you. I'll do anything I can to help, until you get over what happened."

"Mom, I'm never going to get over it. I'm just trying to figure out how to go on living with it."

"Sorry. I know. You are my daughter. I love you very much. Keep living." After a long pause, she adds: "For me. Please."

When I hang up, my thoughts are a jumble. Why hadn't I ever told my mother that Dan and I had secretly married? She would have loved Dan Brown and cherished her beautiful granddaughter. I know that she would be shattered if I threw myself off the Golden Gate Bridge, like so many people have done. She raised me. She loves me. I love her. She was going to accept me and Dan and the baby and make amends for all the hard things she and my stepfather had said about Dan. There had been possibilities for a new beginning then.

The next day I walk. Walking is my new salvation. I amble over to California Street and through Presidio Heights. If I only had eight or nine million dollars, I might be able to afford a Queen Anne Victorian. I dip down into the Presidio on winding streets to Crissy Field in the Marina. The weather is still crisp and clear. The bridge looms over all the sail boats and the mesmerizing waters of the Bay. I think: *If I really wanted to kill myself, this would do it.* I read somewhere that people always jump on the side of the bridge facing the city. Saying goodbye to life. I grasp the pendant with Dan and Ella's pictures. *I love you both so much. But I'm not coming to join you, yet,* I find myself thinking. I search for tissues. I always have tissues these days.

Some mornings I leap out of bed with something resembling joy at the idea of exploring another San Francisco neighborhood—eating dim sum in Chinatown or tacos in the Mission. (You can still get those tacos even though I've learned from Jane and by observation that the Mission has become heavily gentrified by the young, hip Silicon Valley crowd, the reverse commuters in private vans who live the urban lifestyle but work in the corporate valley.) Other mornings the blackness weighs down on me so heavily I can't get out of bed. Jane comes and goes, gone all day at her job and some evenings too, attending Asahi marketing events. She doesn't quite know what to make of me. She wants to like me, and I'm slightly more likeable than I was during the worst of my post-accident hostility and reclusiveness, but I'm still not much fun. I cry easily. I mope. I turn down invitations to join her and John at social events. John doesn't come around much; he's too busy working and I think I turned him off with my incessant obsession with the past. I think he wants to tell me to just "Get over it," the man's way of coping with things, but as my therapist Sarah would have told him, that doesn't work for people in my condition. I need to allow, and be allowed, to work my way through all the stages of grief. When I first met Sarah and told her my story, all she said was: "I am so sorry. So very sorry." She told me that it was not my fault and that it was okay to feel the way I was feeling. Sometimes I get impatient with myself, trying to tell myself to hurry up and get on with it. Of course, I'm not the first person who has ever lost two loved ones in a car accident, but I'm the first *me* who has suffered such a soul-crushing loss. I am gradually coming to the realization that I will never be over it. All I can hope for is to stop being just a few wickers short of a total basket case.

An old line from Frost nags at my brain: "Life is too much like a pathless wood." I need a path, a jolt, a sudden wind change, something new and challenging that will gently crack open my shattered heart.

Chapter 4   Meeting the Tribe

Sometimes the surprise is right there in front of you and you don't see it until it's too late. I wasn't going to let that happen to me. But it almost does.

I've been at Jane's for almost a month. It's late December, almost Christmas, and except for walking, I've been staying in my room. One day, after I've been in my room for three days without going out, Jane has finally had enough. She doesn't knock, she just barges in and stands over me. "Please get up. There's an event in Japantown today and I want you to go with me."

I start to protest, but Jane has already turned and left my room. Jane's speech, though couched in politeness, was not a request, it was an order. I get up and dressed, scrub my face, tie my hair into a ponytail. I always describe my hair as black, but compared to Jane's Japanese coloring, it's really dark brown. It looks drab. I pull on a comfortable old purple sweater. Yes, the color makes my hazel eyes green. But what an effort to even try. I frown at my emaciated look and the dark circles under my eyes.

It's high noon, another light-filled sunny day. A day without the customary California winter rains. The short walk to Japantown revives me. We admire the Torii (gate) at the entrance and wander around on the plaza dominated by the five-story Peace Pagoda. Suddenly I'm starving. I had shut out all light and hardly eaten anything for the past few days. It was a fast of sorts except when I had nibbled at rice and Japanese pickles I pilfered from Jane's refrigerator.

"Jane, do we have time to eat? Let me buy you lunch. Please pick a favorite place."

"You definitely owe me. You scrounged at least a lunch's worth of food from me."

Minutes later we slide into a booth at a traditional restaurant. The place is tiny, with a bar along the side and stools. Several booths have low tables where customers sit on cushions with their feet in a kind of well. Divided curtains, with Japanese samurai figures, block off the entry to the kitchen area. I feel like I'm in Japan. I tell Jane to please order anything and everything. I'm so hungry suddenly.

Enjoying my steaming bowl of vegetable udon and the bright, glistening plate of sushi that arrive surprisingly quickly, I ask Jane to tell me about Japantown. She gives me a brief history lesson about Japanese internment during World War II, and the people's subsequent return, most of which I forget immediately as I revel in the tastes. I'd eaten Japanese food in Boston, but it wasn't like this, incredibly simple and tasty morsels, not fancy, almost plain, but delicious. Now I really learn what a California roll should taste like—California!

"So, what are we here for today?" I ask between bites.

"You are out of the apartment, and we are eating delicious food that you are paying for!" Jane says, almost smirking at me. "And, there is a demonstration by a Taiko Drumming group, some Japanese Cultural

Society booths and other Japanese-themed presentations. Nothing like the Cherry Blossom festival that happens in May or the Aki Matsuri, the fall festival. Much smaller and low key so that it can move inside if it rains. I decided it was the perfect way to make sure you didn't die in your little room."

"Jane, thank you. You are so kind." I will tell her more of my story. Soon. I am almost ready.

The Taiko Drummers are set up on a temporary stage in one corner of the plaza. When they start to play, the vibrations, and the fierce, dramatic, athletic performance are turning me inside out. They play a variety of drums from small ones bound in rope to gigantic wooden ones that use unpolished tree stumps as supports. It's not all manic pounding. Some of it is delicate and intricate rhythms, ten or twelve drummers in perfect sync, tapping out complex variations. The music has amazing crescendos and diminuendos and is surprisingly melodic, the sounds varying from deep bass to high notes, with the edges of the drums struck to make the rat-a-tat sounds similar to pizzicatos on a violin. The most dramatic effect comes when all the drummers are flailing away at the largest drums and sending audio shock waves through the audience, and then suddenly the thunderous sounds and wild movements stop. The performers sit quietly as a slight older man in a kimono comes to the front and center of the stage and sits down and begins to play a long, hand-carved flute. "Shakuhachi," Jane whispers in my ear. I am transfixed by the haunting sounds. Jane puts an arm around my shoulders.

Afterwards, Jane explains that at this time of year it's almost always rainy and most of the festival would have been set up indoors. This year, it's continued to be sunny and clear, so the booths have been set up outside. We browse booths where merchants are selling clothing and paper fans, miniature bronze buddhas, and other basic tourist junk, oddly mingled with the occasional magnificent textile or painting. After the Taiko and the Shakuhachi, we keep our eyes and ears open for other interesting performances, but now it's mostly martial arts schools and modern dance groups. Nothing attracts us back to the stage area that has been set up in the plaza. We're almost ready to leave when out of the corner of an eye I catch a glimpse of movement on the raised platform where performers have been showing off their dance moves and their karate kicks. This demonstration is different, and somehow familiar, a kind of sinuous movement that is both wholly un-Japanese in its New Age sensuality and completely Japanese in its expressiveness. The movements are accompanied by a minor key chant I'd heard somewhere before. I turn abruptly toward the stage. Jane follows at my heels. We make our way to the front of the stage, so unlike me to push my way forward like that, but I am compelled. And sure enough, when I get to the front, I see the Japanese man I had met on the Boston Common—I think his name is Sajiro—leading his parishioners, if that's what they are, in their ritualistic entertainment, if that's what you'd call it. The young proselytizer who had stopped me on the Common is also there working the crowd, handing out flyers. I had forgotten how short she was, and how forceful. Her cropped hair is spiked this time and the dark makeup around her eyes sparkles in the sunlight. She's still wearing dangling earrings in the shape of Japanese characters. For such a diminutive person, she creates a huge circle of energy around her. When she sees me, her face lights up. "Hi, you! I remember you from Boston. I am Manami. Remember me? You found us!"

Jane is surprised that I know this person. I don't have time to explain, because Manami is simultaneously introducing herself, handing me a flyer, and inviting me to dinner.

"Stay after the performance, Sajiro Morioka will want to see you."

"Really?" Jane says. I surprise Jane by telling her I'm going to stick around a while. "Okay, thanks for lunch. I'm glad I got you out of the apartment. See you back there." She comes closer to me and whispers: "Then you can tell me how you know these crazy guys."

Manami has wandered off to find others to give out more flyers. I've gone completely across the country to get away from everything and find myself bumping into this weird group, the last people I saw in Boston. Depending on what I want to believe, that's either a simple coincidence. Or no coincidence at all.

Sajiro is on stage, finishing up the demonstration. At the microphone at center stage, he looks down and sees me. He smiles and then he winks, right at me, and it goes to some spot that hasn't been touched in a while. As soon as the performance has ended, Sajiro breaks away from his group, jumps down off the stage, and approaches me.

"Hello again! Nice of you to come visit me."

"I didn't," I start to say, but then I think, maybe I did. "What is that chant?" I ask.

"Shema."

"I beg your pardon?"

"'*Sh'ma Yisrael Adonai Eloheinu Adonai Echad.* Hear, O Israel: the LORD is our God, the LORD is One.' Only in literal translation from Hebrew into Japanese it comes out as: 'Please listen, I pray, you are our bite, it is one thing.'" Sajiro throws me another one of those looks that could be interpreted so many ways. Is he making fun of me? Testing me?

"I don't even know what that means."

He laughs. "Neither do I. It's just goofy machine translation. We recite the Shema, because, as I told you, we are Japanese Jews."

"Oh, yes, I remember, and you are the Jewish-Japanese Messiah. I Googled you."

"So they say." He bows, and with a courteous wave of his hand invites me to an area behind the stage where his group has gathered. Ten or twelve people are taking off the white flowing robes they had worn over their street clothes while they were performing. I don't remember seeing these costumes in Boston. Must be for special performances. The practitioners are mostly in their twenties with just a few older people.

I stand awkwardly. I don't know what I'm doing. Sajiro is answering questions from several people who had been in the audience.

I gravitate towards an older Japanese woman wearing a kimono and standing off to the side, her black hair pulled severely back. She looks to be older, but there is not a strand of grey in her hair. She isn't participating, just overseeing, perhaps even controlling, without doing anything.

"What do you think?" She speaks with a strong Japanese accent.

"I'm not sure. This is only the second time I have run into these, these people. I think I met this group briefly just as I was leaving Boston. It's a strange coincidence to meet again this way."

"Not a coincidence. Come have dinner at our new group house. Sajiro will give you the address. It will be good for you to meet a new group, an interesting one. I think it may help you."

Everyone thinks I need help. In reality, I do. Just days ago, I was contemplating leaping to my death. Or, maybe this group thinks everyone needs help.

"My name is Maya," I offer.

"I am Kumiko. Kumiko Morioka, Sajiro Morioka's mother." She bows formally, but then gives me a gentle, kind smile. I wish I felt more like accepting her kindness. They are too friendly, all of them, overly friendly, to each other, to me. It's not that it isn't sincere. It's too sincere, like they're prying into me, trying to sense my hurt so they can empathize with it. As they take off their costumes and put on their street clothes, they are so comfortable with each other that they touch each other freely, engage in group hugs. I must either go with the flow or get out of here. It all comes from the movements and sounds they make when they are *davening*. I remember from a childhood friend that that's the Hebrew word for what they are doing, since they insist they are Jewish. They are praying.

"Are you a cult?" I blurt out to Kumiko. She doesn't answer, but Sajiro answers me from behind in that half-facetious, half guru-pontificating voice:

"Are we a cult? No, we are not a cult." I turn quickly to face him. "People come, people go. We share our truth and joy to help people free themselves and to free the world. We are not the only answer to healing the world, but we give love and healing freely. In Hebrew—" (I laugh silently at the thought of this Japanese man quoting Hebrew to me) "—it is called Tikkun Olam."

I don't know if I am comforted or further frightened. I wish Jane had stuck around.

"We are seeking the you in us," Sajiro continues. "If we know the you, we can heal the you." I can't tell if his syntax is just broken English, or if there is a deeper meaning there. What did he mean by "the you in us"?

Instead of standing there looking stupid, I ask him: "What do you mean by 'the you in us'?"

"I know you, but there is no you. You know me, but there is no me. All the broken pieces of light gathered up and put back together. No person whatsoever. Just God."

I smile and nod, but I'm looking around. I need to make my escape, even though no one is keeping me there in that open public space with the group. "I've gotta go," I say.

"We will see you again," Sajiro says simply.

"What do you call yourselves?" I ask.

"We are the Tribe of Dan. Check the flyer," he said, not by way of correction but perhaps a hint? The flyer is still in my hand. I glance at it and see the Tribe of Dan logo for the first time beneath the title. It's a Jewish star replacing the red rising sun in a field of red and white stripes emanating from the sun, a weird amalgamation of the Japanese and Israeli flags.

I don't know why, but I don't ask why either. I quickly read that there's a "weekly dinner on Wednesdays, all are invited" and an address somewhere out in "The Avenues" as I've learned to say in my brief stay here.

Instead I say: "One of the Lost Tribes?"

"In deed," he says, saying it as two words, I swear. I've been rude to Kumiko, but she looks on imperturbably and doesn't say anything as I back away in embarrassment.

"Nice to meet you all," I say, scurrying away, clutching the flyer Manami gave me. *Of course they're a cult*, I think. *They believe they emigrated from Israel to Japan several thousand years ago. They believe they are participating in the coming of the new Messiah, originating from an unlikely location to bring scriptural predictions to fruition. What else would you call them?*

Chapter 5 Jane's Story

Back at the apartment, I'm with Jane. We sit on cushions on the floor with our legs under a table. My legs fold comfortably. I fit easily even though I'm more than a head taller than Jane. A dark red flowered quilt covers the table, topped by a tray the size of the tabletop. Saké and edamame, pickles, Japanese crackers, and dried fish that have been broiled, permeating the air with a pungent fish smell. A heater under the table that Jane calls a *kotatsu* warms us— the apartment is rather chilly. I'm wearing a black and white wool shawl that I picked up at the vintage store down the street.

I can tell Jane is upset, but she doesn't show it, except for a puzzling tightness in her radiant smile. "I went to see my cousin and while I was there her dog got hit by a car. Fluffy. A black and white stray that I found in Golden Gate Park years ago. My cousin took her in. I used to take Fluffy for walks on Ocean Beach near my cousin's house." I'm distracted and not all that sympathetic, but I say I'm sorry. It seems a bit over the top for being about a dog.

"I can't get over it," she says. "I can't go on from where I am."

The tone and quality of Jane's voice gets my attention. It has desperation in it. Something I recognize. My gut, my chest, everything tightens.

"So happy and cute. Always jumping up on people. Never biting." Jane pauses. She's finally reaching the thing she wants to tell me. "Fluffy was there when it happened."

"When what happened?" I ask.

It's an odd role reversal. Jane has been the one to offer comfort. I am totally unprepared for the story she tells.

"It was more than a year ago, September." Jane's voice is tremulous, her face pinched into the shape of someone who is crying, but she doesn't cry. "It was a beautiful morning. I took the dog for a long walk on Ocean Beach. No one was around. I thought the beach was a safe place for me. I was walking on the hard sand at the water's edge. This young guy was running toward me and he stopped. At first, we just chatted. He was really cute, with blond curly hair and eyes as blue as the sky. He seemed okay, friendly. He played with the dog. Then he was all over me. He held me down, forced me. I remember the pain, and my shouting and pulling at his hair. I can still see the wisps of white clouds and blue sky through his curls and feel the wet sand against my back. Fluffy jumped and barked and even tried to attack. It lasted only a few minutes. No one came by. I was crying. He just laughed, pulled up his pants and ran off."

"I never told anyone. After that I broke up with Joe, my boyfriend, and moved here to be alone. I only rent to female guests."

"Oh my god." I move over and sit next to Jane and wrap my arms around her and pull her into the warmth of my shawl. She moans softly, the wetness of her tears against my cheek.

"You have to go see someone. Get some therapy. It wasn't your fault." I find myself saying many of the same things that Sarah told me when I was on that red velvet couch in Boston.

"I've been keeping a journal," Jane answers. "But I should do more." We drink the warm saké and chat until finally Jane says:

"Now tell me."

Instead of answering right away, I get up and clear dishes. Jane waits. I sit back down on my side of the kotatsu.

I take off the locket I wear around my neck, the one with Dan and Ella Rosa's pictures. I pass it to Jane who opens it and looks up at me.

"We were on our way to Maine, to meet my mother and step-father. Mom had never seen the baby. Her husband hated the idea that I was with a man who wasn't white. He was controlling and nasty about it. My mother had stood up to him and they were coming around slowly, and he was about to accept the situation. My mother was even talking about a wedding. I hadn't told her that Dan and I were married already, that we'd had a town hall ceremony right after Ella was born. I was happy. We would have a family celebration, acceptance, normality."

I stop, catch my breath.

"A telephone repair truck hit us while we were stopped by the side of the road. No chance," I say between sobs. "Just headlights, and then blackness."

Jane comes around to my side of the kotatsu and wraps her arms around me.

The next morning, we wake up in the living room lying next to each other on the cushions, still fully clothed, with my shawl as a blanket over both of us. Two women bound together by pain and loss, finding comfort in confiding to each other. After a quick hug we get up and clear away last night's dinner.

"I never do this," Jane says.

"What, sleep on the floor with a near-stranger?"

"No, leave the dishes unwashed after dinner." We laugh. Our friendship has deepened overnight. Perhaps we have both been healed, even just a bit, by what we shared. Jane is rushing around the apartment getting ready for work. I'm still the footloose tourist with no plan. When Jane asks me what I'm going to do today, I shrug.

"I might not be home for dinner," I say.

"Oh? Got a date?" Jane is trying to be kind and have a light touch, but she sees me wince and flutters her hands in a silent apology. "I mean—"

"It's okay, Jane. Talking with you last night made me realize that I have to make a change, do something." I don't tell her about the possibility that I might go to the Wednesday night open house at the Tribe of Dan. It's odd in a way, that I am staying with a lovely young Japanese woman who wants nothing to do with these other Japanese people I have met. It puts a distance between the two of us that I wish weren't there. Jane disappears into her room and comes out a minute later ready to go to work. I'm standing at the sink washing the last of the dishes. She waits for me to finish, then takes my hands in her hands. She is giving me something. I don't quite get what she's doing, and almost drop it. I open my palm and examine a gold pendant in the shape of two Japanese characters.

"I thought you could put this on the chain with your locket, I mean, if that's not too much," she says cautiously, a tremor in her voice. She's unsure how I will take this gesture.

"What does it mean?"

"*Ichi-go Ichi-e.*' 'One life, one chance.'" Jane searches my eyes. "It can also mean 'one chance meeting,' like ours." We hug. I take the locket off my neck and unclasp it and pass the chain through a gold loop at the top of the pendant. It hangs unevenly but I adjust it so that the two items make a single pairing. Jane's face is solemn, eyes gleaming as she looks out the window to the street. "I have to find a future, a new chance," she says, "jumpstart my body and my heart and mind. You know, in Japanese *kokoro* means heart and it also means mind. Heart and mind are one. I need jumper cables for my soul."

I almost laugh because the idea of jumper cables is so graphic. I give Jane another quick hug before she hurries down the stairs to the front door.

I rummage around in my room and find the flyer I got in Boston from Manami about the Tribe of Dan. Now I have two flyers from Manami, the one from Boston and the one from yesterday with the invite for the open house dinner. Next to the flyer is the package I got from Sarah before I left Boston. Probably a book titled *Getting Over the Accident, How to Overcome Losing Everything that Gave Your Life Meaning, Hope and a Reason to Live.* I put the package back under the pile without opening it.

Two hours later my feet hurt terribly. I have been walking. The Marina and the quixotic blues of the Bay and the view of the Golden Gate Bridge once again have pulled me to them. I must keep reminding myself that it's winter. California has been in a severe drought for the past two years. It's all anyone talks about. But for me as a newcomer, it's lovely to have blue skies and warm weather. The late afternoon sun is low in the sky behind the bridge by the time I leave, and it is giving the Bay its golden glow, which is really a kind of orange, but still is the reason for the name Golden Gate. I continue to wander until miraculously I find myself in front of a store on Lombard Street called Shoes-n-Feet. I try on a pair of mauve pink and brown walking shoes that my aching feet recognize as a kind of homecoming. They're on sale and I buy them. I toss my old sneakers in the nearest trash can and let these magic shoes take me back to Japantown. By the time I get there, it's dark. I haven't stopped thinking of Jane and what happened to her, a violent and life-destroying invasion, so different from my experience. Finally, I end up in the Kinokuniya bookstore, in the calendar and personal planner section, one of my favorite sections in any bookstore or office supply store. Unlike most people my age, I still like to have a paper planner and calendar. Something to carry with me. Something with extra blank pages for doodles and sketches. I pick up an academic year calendar planner with the title "Living Every Day the Meaningful Way." It has

Japanese flowers on the cover along with a saying in somewhat awkward English that describes how the world is a better place because you are in it. I buy it and head back to the apartment.

Sitting at my low Japanese desk in the purple chair with no legs, I open the planner. On Wednesday, I write in "Dinner, Tribe of Dan."

Chapter 6   Dinner with the Tribe

The Tribe of Dan occupies all three floors of a classic San Francisco Victorian on Fulton at the edge of the park, not far from The Airplane House, my trusty guidebook tells me. It's painted in odd colors, but not those of psychedelia. It's the Tribe of Dan logo writ large, a Jewish star instead of the rising sun, on a field of red and white stripes. Three stories tall. I clamber up the steps to the heavy double front door, which is open. I peek in. The place is abuzz with people talking, drinking (tea, it turns out, not saké), and milling about. It's quite crowded in the narrow Victorian halls, so I make my way to the front room that has a bay window where I can stand with my back to the wall and look out if I'm not speaking to someone. That doesn't happen, because it turns into almost a receiving line with person after person coming up to introduce themselves. Half the Tribe are white people. Half of them are women. Their names and faces are a blur. I remember a Jewish guy named Mark, who joked to me that he should be the only one allowed here. A redhead named Fawn who greets me nervously, but I sense something stronger beneath her anxious exterior. A guy named Brad who has the looks of a ladies' man but gives off the affect of a loner. Several others. I could tell easily who was a member of the Tribe. I'd seen them yesterday, but it's more than that. It's, again, their ease with each other and with strangers.

At one point I notice Sajiro's mother Kumiko observing everything from the other side of the room.

Sajiro must have said something to them about my 'Are you a cult?' question of yesterday, because more than one of the Tribe approaches me with comments like:

"The only people who call us a cult are ones who aren't in the cult."

"We don't call each other cultists. You won't have to drink the Kool Aid with us."

"Do I have to be Japanese?" I ask Mark.

"What? To be Jewish?" says Mark. He laughs.

"No, to be a member of the Tribe. Funny, you don't look Jewish," I say to him. Others have joined our conversation by now. They all laugh at my last comment. I'm a hit. Almost like my old self. Almost.

Dinner is a buffet. Bowls are stacked on the table for the steaming noodle soup that is the main meal. It is surprisingly spicy and full of vegetables. As good as what I had in Japantown. I wonder who the cook is. The idea is to keep using the bowls and after the soup go back for the vegetarian sushi and scoops of fried rice served from large, flat, round wooden bowls.

During the meal, I go back to the bay window seat. The young guy Brad comes over to sit by me. He tucks his bony tall frame awkwardly into the armchair next to where I sit, and like many tall people, he works to make himself appear almost at eye level with me. His face is framed by wavy dark hair that kind of reminds me of my hair. Intense eyes and dark bushy eyebrows and a serious expression make him look older, but I'm guessing he's younger than me. Even though he has come over to sit with me, he doesn't say anything for quite a while. For this group, it's unusual. I'm the one who starts the conversation. It turns out he lives in this house on the top floor in an attic-like room. He is a kind of caretaker for the house and works part-time jobs in landscaping and carpentry. *Are all the guys in this group handsome?* I wonder silently as I appreciate his strong body near mine. I've been by myself for more than a year now.

"I'll show you the house after dinner," he says shyly.

Even though he's such a lanky, handsome fellow, I'm not put off or feeling like he is coming on in any way. He's young and earnest and comes across as kind. I'm surprised there's no formal presentation or meeting. Just the members mixing and chatting, freely giving each other and visitors shoulder massages. When they sit with one another, group members are often snuggling close, with one leg over another person's leg. Intertwined. None of it is sexual. More like a group of puppy dogs all from the same litter.

Brad explains the after-dinner routine. We each take our individual bowls to the kitchen, wash them and put them on the drying rack. There's a place to recycle the few plastic forks and throw away wooden chopsticks. All the members of the Tribe have their own private chopsticks that they wash, dry and store in cubbies, each pair in a special lacquered chopstick container with their name written on the side.

Brad shows me around the old and battered though still grand Victorian.

"One of our members is quite wealthy," he explains. "An old friend of Sajiro's mother Kumiko. You've met her?"

I nod.

"Our benefactor member is away in Japan taking care of his aging parents. It's been a year. We expect him back soon so the group will need to find a new home in the next six months."

"Oh," I say, not sure what to make of any of this information. I follow Brad up the narrow back servants' stairs. I notice he lists to the left when he walks. The steep stairs are a challenge for a person of his height.

The former servants' quarters are up and through a last door and an almost impossibly inclined flight of stairs to a funny attic room just beneath the roof. The walls are lined with bookshelves cut to fit the sloping ceiling. There's one comfortable chair, a futon with a side table and a lamp, a dresser, and a cheap hanging rack with shirts and pants hung from it. That's about it. Except books. More books than fit on the oddly-shaped bookshelves. Books stacked against the wall, books on the dresser top, books on the side table.

"Wow," I say. "Are you a Christian monk or something?"

"Hardly," Brad says. I sit in the only chair. Brad flops onto the futon, all elbows and knees but relaxed. *Like all of them*, I think. I notice he looks at me with a kindly, curious, and a bit challenging expression, as if he wonders just who I am and what's my story, but he doesn't ask.

"What's with all the books? Are you a writer?

"No, a reader," Brad says with a kindly laugh.

"Just you and your books, up here in the attic?"

"Yeah, and twenty roommates on the two floors below."

"You come up here to get away?" Instead of answering me directly, Brad takes up one of the books within easy reach, thumbs through it for a minute, and hands it to me open to a page with a passage yellow-highlighted. I read: "I do, indeed, close my door at times and surrender myself to a book, but only because I can open the door again and see a human face looking at me." I turn the book over to read the cover.

"Martin Buber."

"Solitude is the place of purification." I can tell I have surprised Brad, so I add: "I minored in philosophy in college."

"One of the great Jewish thinkers."

"Yes. I wonder what he would think of the Tribe of Dan."

"Oh, he would approve, he would approve!" Brad nods vigorously. It's the first time Brad has been animated. We have a short but intense discussion about the Tribe, Sajiro, and Brad's presence here in the house.

In a brief lull in our conversation, I say: "I thought there would be some kind of presentation or talk about all of this."

"You should mingle more, meet more of the members downstairs." Brad rises instantly, almost as if he'd been waiting for the opportunity to bring me back downstairs.

"Yes, definitely. Let's go down."

Downstairs, I am immediately accosted by a Japanese woman who introduces herself as Mariko. Unlike Manami, who is bird-like, Mariko is a square woman, attractive, but solidly built and almost my height, maybe in her mid-thirties. Mariko tells me she brings new people in almost every week. She's perturbed that I'm not one of her newly shorn sheep. Turns out Mariko not only brings in people through the force of her personality, she also makes all the flyers and booklets for the group. She works as a graphic designer for a San Francisco advertising company. I learn that Mariko's the one who made the Tribe logo, that startling melding of the Japanese and Israeli flags. She's writing a book about the Dan Tribe. I can tell that she's about ready to tell me the whole book idea. To change the subject and escape her fiery intensity, I comment on the meal:

"That was some tasty Japanese food," I say idly.

"I am so happy you enjoyed." Mariko's face opens and she smiles broadly. "I made it. I love to cook for these Wednesday dinners. Feed the people and open their hearts and minds and souls, all at the same time. We all take turns. You should come when Gloria is cooking." She points to a woman across the room with fire-engine red streaks in her dark hair. "I will introduce you."

I'm like the fly caught in the spider's web. Only there are many spiders, too-friendly spiders. Mariko turns me over to Gloria almost like a choreographed handoff. I catch a whiff of expensive perfume. Gloria's dressier than most of the Tribers—in fact she's wearing a black cocktail dress that wouldn't be out of place at a chic restaurant down on the wharf. The black sets off the bright red streaks in her auburn hair nicely. It looks like she's going to hug me so I take a step back, but that doesn't stop Gloria from coming right up to me, putting her hands on either side of my face and saying, "Bonjour!" followed by, "Buonasera!" loudly.

"Hello."

"So, what do you think of this crowd, eh?" Gloria says with a sharp accent that could be French or Italian, I can't tell. Her expansive hand movements suggest Italian. Is that a cliché or a truism? I want to ask which country she's from, and I want to answer Gloria's question of what I think, but it wasn't a question, it was a broad, encompassing gesture that included everyone. "Here," she says, motioning to the crowd again, "we find people who are expressing themselves, being their, how you say, true selfies?"

"I see," I say. "What do you do here? Besides cooking, I mean."

"Besides cooking? Cooking is everything. There would be no Tribe of Dan without the food. Ha ha!" Gloria is enjoying herself. She nods to a couple people who pass us going down the hallway toward the rear of the Victorian.

"Do you live here too?" I ask, because it's implausible, she doesn't look the type.

"Oh yes. One big happy family. It takes all kinds, yes? I know, I know," Gloria says gaily, "I don't look Jewish." She must have heard me in the living room earlier. "But I am. You know what else?" Now she leans in confidentially, conspiratorially. "I am Japanese. In here." She points to her rather large bust. I giggle. Gloria doesn't notice, or if she does, she doesn't mind.

I decide to take my leave, or maybe it is an escape from the Tribe. Just as I get to the front door, Sajiro suddenly materializes and blocks my way.

"See you Saturday."

"Saturday?"

"Yes, nine in morning. In Bunny Meadow. Near Conservatory of Flowers. Left side across street in the meadow. Yes, come! Open your heart. Open your mind. Move your body. Repair and heal your brokenness."

Sajiro takes my shoulders and brings me close. He whispers in my ear, "Come to be with me, support me, love me." He hugs me close, his hands on the small of my back bringing my hips close to his body. There is no movement and then there is movement. A throb of desire pulses inside me and involuntarily I press even closer to the warmth of his body.

"Come. It will heal you. I will heal you," he whispers as he breaths deeply in my ear.

Next thing I know I'm running along Fulton near the park. The cold foggy air enveloping me. I'm running and crying and shaking all over.

When I get back to the apartment, Jane is in her room and doesn't come out. I grab a towel and a robe and head to the bathroom. Inside, I lean against the door, letting the bath water run, hoping the noise will hide the sounds I am making as I sob, and rub myself, and make myself climax, over and over. Finally, after a long soak in the cramped but comfortable tub, I am calm again. *My body is coming to life again. Will my heart follow?* I wonder.

Chapter 7   Saturday in the Park with Sajiro

The Saturday morning air is cool. My sneakers are damp from wandering around the Conservatory of Flowers in search of the "Bunny Meadow." Finally, I see the group. They've set up a tent-like structure on the grass, with a cloth flag on a stick displaying the Tribe logo: Jewish star, red and white rays.

It's not a tent, just a canopy with a roof but no walls. The only thing in it is a wooden platform, two feet high and about four feet square. Sajiro is standing on the platform with arms raised, his fingers in the Vulcan greeting position I recognize from the old Star Trek TV show and movies. It makes me giggle. I'm thinking, *Am I about to boldly go where no one has gone before?* He recites a blessing: "May the Lord bless you and keep you. May my father, the Lord, make his face to shine upon you and be gracious unto you. May he lift up his countenance upon you and grant you peace."

"I always thought that was an Irish prayer," I whisper to the ever-present Manami who has sidled over and is standing next to me, too close to me.

"Old Testament. Numbers Six, Twenty-four to Twenty-six. It's the blessing Moses got from Yahweh and gave to us, the children of Israel."

I let the "us" slide and turn my attention back to Sajiro.

I am surprised there are so many people, about thirty in the group. Some are wearing the white robes they were wearing at the Japantown presentation. Many, like me, are in street clothes, drawn out of curiosity or because they had been proselytized and lured there by Manami or Mariko. Sajiro sees me and smiles. I look away in embarrassment, remembering how he had whispered in my ear and my extremely sexual reaction alone in the bathroom. Soon all the Tribers are up on their feet chanting. Sajiro calls out words I don't understand. Are they Hebrew? Are they Japanese? Some weird combination? The group repeats them, softly at first, but soon it's almost a shouting match with stomping and jumping. Newcomers like me are jostled as the Tribers circle and weave around us and each other, as if they are trying for a physical unification that would bring us all together. It has the opposite effect on some of the outsiders, who pull away and leave. Many, including me, are caught up in the moment. It ends as Sajiro stretches his arms to the sky and looks up. Everyone copies his movement. It lasts a long time. My arms ache from keeping them over my head, but I allow myself to enter the frenzy. I don't even know what I'm doing. I follow as Sajiro leads and everyone starts to sway back and forth. Sajiro ends the trance-like, dance-like happening by calling out, "Yame" in Japanese and then, "Okay, stop now," in English. Everyone relaxes. "Please sit," he says. "I have a few words." More people take this opportunity to escape, because it's too strange, too uncomfortable. The rest of us flop down on the still dew-wet grass.

"You are cold," Sajiro begins. "Your shoes are soaked. You wonder, who is this madman? But inside, you are hot. You burn with an inner light. I must tell you a story. It is the story of the beginning of the world. When God created light, his first act, he needed a place to put it. He made vessels, clay pots, and put the light in them. The pots could not hold the Divine light, it was too powerful. They broke, and the shards, each containing a spark of the original light, scattered across the newly formed universe."

I look around. The members of the Tribe of Dan are transfixed by Sajiro's words and his telling of the story. It's obvious that they all know it, but it excites them anyway. I hug my knees, caught between listening and wanting to make a run for it.

"We, all of us, not just Jews, not just Japanese, were created to bring those shards back together, heal the world, make it whole again. Tikkun Olam!" he intones.

"Tikkun Olam!" his congregation shouts. It's weird, but I am being pulled in by the strength in their unified response.

"Believe it or not, there are male shards and female shards," Sajiro continues.

Okay, now that's weird, I think.

But Sajiro has a way to make it beautiful. "The Baal Shem Tov said: 'From every human being there rises a light that reaches straight to heaven, and when two souls that are destined to be together find each other, the streams of light flow together and a single brighter light goes forth from that united being.'"

And he looks directly at me. Or at least I think he does. He has that master presenter's trick of making everyone in the audience think he is looking just at them, no matter how large the audience. Then he speaks for another hour! But most of the rest of it I forget. Somehow, even against my will, I sense something is shifting inside me. I don't feel the dead spot that has been at my core. At least not as strongly. Is this a new path for me? One that I consider following? The morning ends with a standing meditation, along with a vocalization. Before we make the sound, Sajiro explains:

"Now we finish with a moment of standing meditation. Not silent. We make an approximation of the sound of the twenty-third letter of the Hebrew alphabet." He pauses. "Some of you must know that there are only twenty-two letters in the Hebrew alphabet." Nervous laughter from the uninitiated, knowing chuckles from the Tribe. "It is said that there were twenty-three letters, but one fell off during the hand-off between Yahweh and Moses. It is also said that if this missing letter could be found, and purely sounded, the world would be healed at once and come into perfect harmony." There is an audible gasp from the audience. "When I said before that we make 'an approximation of the sound,' I meant that we do not truly know what that sound is. We try to imagine it. We try to heal the world in that and many other ways. Please join us. The sound is like this." He assumes a relaxed, natural stance, takes an extremely deep breath, and makes a sound that is some crazy combination of didgeridoo, Tibetan throat singing, and the songs of humpbacked whales. Low, with vibrato, but with occasional high squeaks and clacks. Everyone struggles to make the same sound. My mouth opens and I make coughing, wheezing noises. Next thing I know I'm laughing uncontrollably, my whole body convulsing and tears streaming down my face. When I finally get control of myself, I wonder again at the way my body is awakening again. I say a (silent) prayer, *Please God, let my heart also come alive.*

I avoid the members who try to approach me and run to the bus stop. I want to get back to the apartment as soon as possible. On the bus, I am lightheaded. My mind is relentlessly nattering away: *Are you crazy? You should run from these lunatics.* But I am relaxed. I'm floating underwater looking up at the surface of my mind, my thoughts skittering water spiders on the surface of my world.

At the apartment, Jane is sitting in the kitchen slurping noodle soup. She takes in my wet shoes and the grass stains and wet spots on my pants and raises her eyebrows.

"Gotta change, be right back." I head off to my room and put on my robe and slippers.

In the kitchen, Jane hands me a bowl of soup. We eat in silence. Jane slurping unselfconsciously and me sipping away like the genteel WASP that I am, at least on my mother's side.

"So?" Jane asks.

"You first." I'm not ready to share what I have not even absorbed or processed. Something is up with

Jane. She hasn't been around much the last few days and wasn't home last night.

Jane tells me her old boyfriend Joe called her. She told him why she had gone missing from their relationship. He had cried holding her while she sobbed in his arms. Last night they had sex, the first time in a long time for Jane, and it was okay. Not great but okay. "I think I might be okay too, eventually," Jane says.

We sit in silence. I decide to try slurping myself. Jane and I get the giggles over it and laugh easily together.

"So?"

"I'm trying to eat like a Japanese," I say.

"No, so what's up? You're changed too."

I tell her about Wednesday's dinner but not about my strong physical reaction to it all. I try to explain the Saturday morning service, but find I am almost unable to describe it. Finally, I say: "I'm going back for more. They have a Sunday afternoon practice, a hike up Tennessee Valley in Marin. Who knows how crazy that might be? I have to see if this is going to be a way for me to stop being so dead inside." One hand is at my throat, my fist clutching the locket and the pendant Jane gave me.

"If it helps, you should do these things," Jane says. I'm surprised because I know she was repelled by the Dan Tribe when she first saw them on the Japantown plaza. Jane smiles. "But first do the dishes!"

While I'm cleaning up the kitchen, we chat about the holidays. Christmas and the New Year are right around the corner.

"You should come to my family's on Christmas. You'll meet my family." Jane rolls her eyes and smiles. "My uncle owns this building. It's the reason I can afford to live so close to everything."

I'm relieved to have somewhere to go on Christmas, and I think about what to bring as a house gift. I decide on flowers and find a shop that sells chrysanthemums. The morning at Jane's family house is delightful. Jane's parents are warm and welcoming, and there are aunts and uncles and a brood of nephews and nieces. I've been missing family. I've always heard that Jewish people eat Chinese food on Christmas. Apparently Japanese eat Japanese food. Not a goose, turkey, or ham in sight. We sit at a long table and have miso soup, gyoza dumplings, soba noodles with tofu and greens, and saké in flat saucers decorated with cranes. Everyone is politely curious. I tell them that I'm here to make a new start for myself. No one presses me for details. I like that about Japanese, that reserve, that willingness to allow people their space. When I get back to the apartment, in the late afternoon on Christmas day, I call my mother. I manage to get through the holiday week and spend New Year's Eve just walking the city, listening to horns honking, completely alone.

Chapter 8   The View from the Top of the World

It's not that easy, I discover, to get to Tennessee Valley without a car. I suppose I could have asked one of the Tribers, but I'm still clinging to a loner's independence. I take two buses and a long walk to get to the trailhead, at the upper end of a deep valley that leads to an ocean beach. The vivid air smells of sage and salt. It's easy to find the Tribe of Dan in the area in front of the parking lot by the first gate into the valley, a common meeting point. Their white robes make them stand out from the young couples with baby strollers and the avid hikers in shorts and hiking boots. When I arrive, a California Highway Patrol officer is interrogating Sajiro while the rest of the Tribe stand around looking amused. Manami comes up to me immediately.

"Wonderful," she says. "Glad you came."

"What's going on?" I ask.

"Oh, we get this all the time. He just wants to make sure we're not a terrorist group."

"Are you a terrorist group?" I ask. Manami just laughs. The CHP officer soon leaves, apparently satisfied that Sajiro and his people aren't going to blow up anything or throw themselves off a cliff in a mass suicide. The Tribe starts down the flat, easy trail out to the beach, but after a quarter mile they veer onto a steep path up the side of the hill. I struggle to keep up. Sajiro is a good hundred yards ahead already. I can't tell whether his followers are letting him be ahead or whether he's just in much better shape than everyone else. It takes us a good forty-five minutes to crest the ridge. We walk another quarter mile to where the views are most spectacular up and down the coast and far out to sea. I wonder if we're going to do more chanting and moving, but we don't. All we do is face the ocean in a natural stance. Though he isn't saying or doing anything, Sajiro is leading us. Some people have their eyes closed. Others have them open. I'm looking around, wondering when we will finish, wondering what this is all about and at the same time totally enjoying being here on the continent's edge with amazing views of the Pacific.

After the meditation, Sajiro turns and stands with his back to the ocean, facing us. "This is always here," he says, gesturing to the panorama of sparkling water, golden hills, a cloudless day with a heaven full of different shades of blue, sky and ocean meeting at a soft line in the far distance. "Don't be afraid to come back here, any time. Even if just in your mind." The walk down is somewhat easier. I catch a glimpse of the city of San Francisco, just for a minute between the hills. It shines white and pink like a fairy castle in the air. Then Sajiro is walking by my side.

"Very beautiful and peaceful, isn't it?" he says.

I nod, still somehow embarrassed and strained by being near him. He laughs easily and puts his arm over my shoulder and says how glad he is that I have decided to be open to the beauty around me, and that it reflects the beauty that is inside me. I am surprised at the ease and innocence of his gesture and what he says. I laugh easily also, letting go of the tension and uncertainty.

He leaves me, moves to the head of the group, and leads us back down to the parking lot. I see Brad about to get into his car and I call out and ask for a ride back to the city. He looks at me quizzically. "Don't ask," I say. "Two buses and a long walk not knowing where I was going."

We drive in silence for a while, lost in our own thoughts and holding onto our individual experiences.

Driving over the Golden Gate Bridge, I'm struck again by the stark beauty of California. I'm empty and light.

"Want to come back to the house for dinner?" Brad asks. "It's a way to ease into the new year. Plus, we're going to have a meeting about where to move to next. Some search teams are being put together. You might find it interesting."

Brad is trying to suck me into the group, like pretty much everyone else is doing, but his motivation is different from the others. He recognizes that I need to be part of something. So far, no one has asked me much of anything personal. They're all just there. Open and warm and inviting. Yet I sense also a bit of a wait-and-see attitude in addition to the pressing desire for me to join in and participate. Along with the evangelizing, there's a strange undercurrent, a judging going on, like, 'is this person really right for our group?'

It's a smaller number for dinner, some of the members who live in the house and other members who are there for the meeting. The food once again is incredible. Simple and delicious. Italian. Gloria is beaming and serving. Her hair is pulled up on top of her head so some of the dark red streaks fall around her face.

"Spaghetti Aglio e Olio." She says as she puts some cooked spinach in the bottom of my bowl and heaps the spaghetti on top of it. I take the huge square of parmesan wrapped in cheese cloth and grate a healthy amount on top, realizing I am starving from the hike. At the end of the counter, I fill a wine glass with red wine and take a seat at the large wooden table in the kitchen. One sip of the dark red California Merlot and I start to think, *I could really enjoy these people.*

I look around for Kumiko, Sajiro's mother, and am surprised that she's not there. I'm even more surprised to find that Sajiro is not at the meeting. Besides Gloria and Brad, Manami is there, and Mariko, Mark, Fawn (the redhead) and a new guy I'm introduced to named Chuck Baldwin who is clearly one of the insiders but whom I haven't seen before. As the meeting progresses it's clear that Chuck is in charge. He's a bit older than the others, probably in his late thirties. A strong character but soft-spoken. He reminds me of some of the lawyers I had worked with in Boston. Again, I wonder how the group has attracted so many handsome men. Mariko is sitting next to me. She explains what's going on in whispers. Chuck is a successful financial planner. He's married and has a couple of young children, so he doesn't live at the Tribe house. He brings a practical influence to the group. The discussion goes on and on. Chuck mostly listens

to wild ideas proposed like living in caves in Hawaii or
moving to the Yucatan Peninsula or Costa Rica.
Somehow Chuck manages to bring things back down
to the real world, to what's actual and realistic.

"California's just gotten too expensive," Chuck says,
tugging on the end of a blond goatee. His past-the-
collar bleached and tousled hair gives him a surfer-
dude look, but he's sharp. "I'd say we have three
choices: somewhere in western New England, up the
coast in Oregon or Washington, or out in the desert,
Nevada, Arizona. Somewhere land is cheap and there's
still work to be had and places to meet people."

"New England's too cold and the desert's too hot,"
Mark says.

"And Oregon and Washington are too wet," Fawn
chips in.

"Yeah, yeah," Chuck responds to both of them. "We
know we're leaving paradise here in the Bay Area, but
we have to acknowledge there's just no place we can
afford to live around here, given the growth of our
membership. We should look in all three places." I'm
caught off-guard when Chuck turns to me and says:
"Maya, would you like to be on the Oregon/Washington
search team?"

"Me, ah no, I mean, not yet," I stutter, and by way
of excuse I say: "I just got to California, I'm not ready to
think about leaving just yet." But I agree to put my
name, email, and cell number on a sign-up sheet that's
going around for future communications on the
project. Even that would be quite a commitment for

me. It's the first time I've shared my personal information with the group.

A new person enters the room. He's tall, brown-skinned. I flash back to my Dan, the man I had loved. The man with a beautiful smile, the dead father of my dead child. I let out an audible sob and everyone turns to look at me again. I blush red and wipe tears from my eyes as the new person, who of course is not Dan Brown, takes a seat feet away from me and says quick hellos to a couple of acquaintances, not noticing my reaction to him at all.

"Sorry," I say to no one in particular, and the meeting resumes. *Tribe of Dan. Dan's Tribe,* I think, but that is nonsense, this man isn't Dan, my Dan wasn't Jewish, or Japanese, and the whole thing is just a confused mess in my head. I suffer through the rest of the meeting, which is fortunately almost over, and flee as soon as politeness allows. Brad follows me out the door and calls to me from the top of the stairs. "Hey, Maya, hold on a second."

I stop at the bottom of the stairs but still inside the gate to the Victorian. "I've gotta go, Brad." Truth is I'm close to tears again. I appreciate that he gives me some space, doesn't follow me down to where I stand.

"I hope you come again. Some of these people can be aggressive, but they're a nice bunch, really."

"I know," is all I can say. Brad stares at me deeply. I sense his concern from almost thirty feet.

"You're hurting," he says.

"So everybody tells me. You, Sajiro, my friend Jane."

"Can I give you another quote from one of my books?"

"Sure."

"'Nothing prevents happiness like the memory of happiness.'" Brad nails my misery and the tsunami of emotion that had crashed down on me. It's not that hard to do. I'm pretty obvious, pretty unstrung.

"Who said that?"

"André Gide. A writer nobody reads much anymore."

"Except you."

"Except me. Bye."

"Bye. See you again. Thanks." I walk away hurriedly so that I can let out the louder sob I've been holding in without anyone hearing it. I don't know why I said 'See you again.' But I knew it was true.

I walk all the way back from the Tribe house to Jane's apartment. It's a couple of miles and it takes less than an hour, but after all the hiking and the meeting and my emotional meltdown, I'm exhausted. The lights are out as I come up the stairs from the entry. Jane must be off again for the night. I'm missing her in some way. She's the only person I've talked to other than Sarah, my therapist. Still, I'm happy to be alone. I crash in my room under the covers on my futon on the tatami mat. I sleep. No thoughts. No dreams. Just sleep, healing sleep.

When I wake in the morning, before going out to the kitchen to make my coffee, I sit at my low Japanese desk and pick up the calendar planner with the

Japanese flowers on the cover and open it to January. Nothing is written. I have no plans. There is nothing.

I take out my cell phone and call my mother. I tell her I'm okay and that I've met some nice folks. My mother's voice wraps itself around me, encompasses me in a soft and calming way. We don't talk about anything much, but she's happy and I know that it's because I've called and that I've taken away some of her worry, and she some of mine. On the practical side, she agrees to transfer additional funds into my account. When I hang up, I'm still clueless as to what I'm going to do this day, or any day going forward. What I really want to do is go back out to Tennessee Valley and hike that hill again and luxuriate in the wind and the ocean views and the smell of mustard and lavender and sage that is still in my nostrils. That's totally impractical. It was so hard to get there yesterday, and the thought of having to do both the trip there and the return trip by bus is daunting. My indecision is suddenly solved by a text I receive from a number I don't recognize. The text says:

Lunch? Do you like Mexican food? and it's followed by a torii emoji: ⛩

It's not hard to guess that the text must be from one of the Tribe members, but which one? My legal training tells me not to respond to the text, but my heart overrules my logical mind.

Who is this? I tap out. I wait. The answer is not long in coming.

Sajiro-san. The Japanese leader of a Jewish cult is inviting me to a Mexican lunch. What would Mom think of this new twist in her daughter's life? What do I even think about it? But I find myself texting:

Sure. Where?

Sajiro gives me the name of a restaurant, El Toro, in the Mission, and a time: Noon. Is this just a friendly overture, or a date? I don't know, but I do know that either way, I'm intrigued by the prospect. I'm not talking about the tacos. I've been over to the sunny Mission a couple times and yes, I do like Mexican food if it's not too spicy, but the idea of spending time with just Sajiro intrigues me. If I am honest with myself, it also excites and scares me.

I head out to the kitchen to make my coffee when Jane bursts in. I'm incredibly glad to see her so happy and full of light and relieved to have time to stop thinking about the lunch and whether I should have refused and even about what to wear. It is clear Jane is in love or back in love and is in the process of redeeming her soul and spirit. I have a twinge, a brief spasm of jealousy, expressed as a low-level yet profound wish for myself. We talk about her boyfriend Joe and I ask when I'm going to get to meet him. I drink my coffee and munch a piece of toast and then I tell Jane about the text and the lunch. I'm excited yet scared.

"Go for it, girl," Jane says, and I can't tell if it's just her exuberance about being in love and wanting that for me or if it's real. Then Jane looks at me quizzically and tilts her head in an odd sideways movement. She's squinting as if to see me better.

Then she says, "There's no harm. He's just a man, a pretty crazy one. You could use a man, or just lunch with a man. When's the last time you felt this way? Thinking about someone, wondering about what it all means, being attracted and maybe attractive to a man. Just see what happens."

I smile sheepishly and go over to the sink, wash my cup and plate and stack them to dry.

"But what shall I wear?"

We both laugh at that question. Jane has never once heard me worry or wonder about anything like how I look or what I should wear. I guess it's a sign. Then I go back to my room and start trying on different outfits from the meager pickings in my closet.

Standing in front of the cheap full-length mirror that hangs on the inside the closet door, I have a bit of a wavy fun-house look. The one new top I recently purchased, a dark purple, looks good with my jeans and brings out the green in my hazel-green eyes. My cheeks are pink and I'm tan from all the walking I've been doing and from the hike. I shake out my now too-long hair; it curls around my face and down my back. I wonder should I put it up? Mostly I no longer look like the walking dead. I have color and there's energy behind my eyes; they shine with anticipation. Sajiro is waiting outside for me when I get to the taqueria.

"Konichiwa," he says. I have a vague idea this means "good morning" or maybe "good afternoon" but I'm not sure, so I just say, "Hi."

"Thanks for coming."

"Thanks for inviting me."

"Is there a Lost Tribe of Mexicans too?" I ask as we enter El Toro and take our places in line. Sajiro arches his eyebrows.

"Hmmm. I will have to consult the scriptures." He laughs.

El Toro is a throwback to an earlier time when the Mission was truly an enclave for Mexican and Central American immigrants. We wait in line. I order a burrito and point out the various ingredients that I want and the staff behind the steaming trays scoop out ample helpings that they expertly roll into a huge burrito. Sajiro orders an enchilada plate, and we take our trays and slide into a booth along the side of the restaurant. I've been intimidated by Sajiro and his exalted position as the head of the Tribe of Dan. It surprises me that we fall into an easy banter as we enjoy the delicious and fresh food. I think it surprises Sajiro also.

"I know you have a story to tell," Sajiro says. "I would someday like to hear it and perhaps even help you by doing so. In the meantime, let's just be comrades."

I smile, realizing his English is not quite perfect. I also appreciate that he is alluding but not prodding or digging into my story.

"Yes, let's be comrades."

"I have one other thing, a very serious thing, I would like to say," Sajiro adds leaning forward.

"Please join the Oregon and Washington trip. Your thinking, your opinion would be good for the group. An outside opinion."

"You weren't at the meeting. How do you know?

"How do you think I got your cell number? I checked the sheet. It made me happy to see it. Also, Chuck would not have mentioned this to you unless he thought something special about you. Chuck is a deep-thinking man who can guide us in so many of the practical things we must decide. There is time pressure for our group."

Disappointment floats like a dark cloud across my face. Sajiro is not interested in me, just the group and finding a new place. I am getting way ahead of myself thinking he is interested in me. He reaches forward and takes my hand and adds: "And, it would be so happy for me, so wonderful to wake up every day and see your smile as we travel."

"Okay, count me in, comrade," I say. After lunch we walk around the Mission, enter the adobe original church next to the cathedral, admire the famously colorful zig-zag painted ceiling and the simple wooden pews. We sit in the cool silence.

"This is a beautiful place. Too bad they hate us so much," Sajiro says.

"Who? Catholics? I doubt if many of the Mexican American parishioners who come here still hold a grudge against Jewish people. That's so, so medieval."

"You think not," Sajiro says. "I have wondered about this. You don't think that they still think we killed Jesus?"

"No, I don't think so. There are plenty of other people who hate Jewish people," I say, marveling at the depth of Sajiro's faith and his full-hearted identification with the reputed faith of his ancestors.

"I don't wish to be a martyr," Sajiro says, so plainly and sincerely that I have to laugh.

"Do you really think you're a candidate for martyrdom, Sajiro?"

"Perhaps you are not familiar with the persecution of Christians in Japan? For many hundreds of years, the faith was banned and there were so-called 'hidden Christians' practicing their religion at home in villages in the countryside. If they were found out they were hanged, or worse."

"But Jewish people?" I ask.

"No, we were mostly left alone. Until now. My popularity has brought with it a certain—how you say—notoriety," he struggles over the word that brings with it the possibility of martyrdom. He says it matter-of-factly, but there is a hint in his voice that this is a real concern.

"So, stay in America," I say, realizing at once how foolish that must sound in this era of renewed antisemitism in America and elsewhere.

"I would, but there are familial duties I have to attend to in Japan. I'm going there this spring. Perhaps you will come with me," he says, and smiles that killer smile again that melts my heart.

"Let's see how Oregon and Washington go before we make any big plans," I say light-heartedly. We leave the Mission church and walk up to Dolores Park. We watch a pickup basketball game. The outdoor court is in terrible shape, with holes in the fencing around it, weeds growing in cracks in the asphalt. The players are an intriguing mix of black, Hispanic, Native American, and white men, looking like the Mission that used to be, but I know it's an illusion. The yuppie millennials or whatever you call them have co-opted most of the real estate in the district, and these hoopsters are the last of a dying breed. Sajiro looks like he wants to go out on the court and play.

"Basketball junkie," he says to me. I laugh and he says, "May I take you home now?"

First, we go up to the top of Dolores Park where we sit and look at the views of San Francisco. After talking about everything yet nothing important, we walk for a long time in silence. Finally, we are outside the entrance to Jane's apartment.

"Hey thanks for inviting me to lunch," I say.

"Thanks for coming today and also for joining the trip to research places with us," Sajiro says and smiles. He leans in and kisses me on the cheek and looks into my eyes.

"Such beautiful eyes. So green. And you are such a lovely tallness. No need to bend down to look into your soul."

I smile and turn to enter the building. Neither of us is ready for anything more at this moment.

Chapter 9   Oregon, Washington, Change

Things are strewn around the floor and on my futon bed. I'm packing for the trip to Oregon and Washington. My new backpack is propped against the low chair. I've been on a mini-shopping spree: new walking shoes, a pair of short rain boots, a navy lightweight packable down jacket, a rain poncho. It's winter and I've heard stories about the rain in Oregon.

The Tribe owns an old school bus painted with the same Jewish star/red-and-white-rays logo. They use it to transport larger numbers of people to events, but in this case it's a smaller group that's headed north in two cars. It's me, Sajiro, and Manami in one car, Chuck, Mariko, and Mark Singer in a second car. We don't caravan, but we plan to meet up at stops along the way, the first one for breakfast in Fort Bragg up the coast, because we'd agreed to start out early. If we had taken Route 5, we would have been in Oregon in a few hours, and if we had taken Route 101, we'd have been there later, but we're going the slow way, all the way up Route 1, because Sajiro wants to see everything. The coast here is almost as spectacular as Big Sur. I wonder aloud in the car why the group doesn't just look for a place around here.

"Too far from a population center," Manami says. Always the recruiter, she explains that in Oregon they could be on the coast but just an hour from Portland, and in Washington they could be near Seattle. Later, we meet up with the other car for breakfast in a funky

1950s diner that looks like it has spiraled down out of the sky and landed like Dorothy's house on the edge of a cliff overlooking Fort Bragg. A neon rocket ship flies around a globe dotted with twinkling lights, atop a low flat-roofed building with awnings jutting like tailfins on the corners. Except on the inside, the plush red booths of the fifties are long gone, replaced by a rustic look— pictures of loggers standing on huge dead redwoods and circular saw blades mounted on the walls. Sajiro orders the "Lumberjack Breakfast." You can imagine. I have homemade granola and fruit with yoghurt from goats on the steep hill across from the diner. When Sajiro hears what I order he turns to me with a friendly look and says, "Hard to be a vegetarian in Japan. We put fish flakes on everything." Manami and Mariko laugh dutifully.

"That burrito I had in the Mission wasn't vegetarian. Anyway, I just can't eat a big meal first thing in the day." How can I explain to him and the others that I am just getting my appetite back after a whole year when food meant nothing to me?

Over breakfast at the rough-hewn table that isn't much more than a picnic table brought indoors, Chuck explains that real estate values are significantly lower in the Northwest than in California, even along the Mendocino coast where we are now. Manami's idea is also important, he confirms, because the group must keep growing. I speculate to myself about why, but fortunately the moment to ask slides past me. I'm traveling with the group but am not yet of the group. The religious part totally eludes me. The group is somewhat silent, in anticipation of what's coming. Chuck has arranged to see a half-dozen places, three in Oregon, three in Washington state. There's a quiet excitement to the venture and I find myself getting caught up in the adventure of the trip.

We go out to the cars. Chuck has a slightly fancy but sensible Japanese SUV with all-wheel drive and room for seven. I wonder briefly why we didn't all go in one car. The car that Sajiro and Mariko and I are in (Manami and Mariko switched cars at the break) is a thirty-year-old Saab 900 Turbo with a manual shift and no power windows. It's a real antique! I hadn't paid much attention when I first got in back in San Francisco, but the car is a relic, probably not safe on windy Route 1 with its many hairpin turns with no guard rails and steep drop-offs. One good thing is that going north we are on the inside right-hand lane, extra precious feet from the frequent roadside cliff edges.

Sajiro notices me looking at the manual shift, which has a custom knob with the yin-yang symbol on its top.

"I paid extra for that," he says, and he laughs.

Toward the end of long harrowing day of driving along the coast we meet up for a late lunch at a truck stop in Crescent City. By this time, I'm really hungry. My dainty granola, fruit, and yoghurt breakfast hours ago did nothing to sustain me. This time we're in a roadside trucker's restaurant that serves plain good food and lots of it. I happily tuck into a burger, fries and a salad, and even though I know I shouldn't, I drink tea. I just wonder how many times I can ask to stop. The group is restless, disconnected, just wanting to get there. I sense that some people aren't happy about the long drive that could have been avoided had we taken the Interstate. A trip that should have taken a long eleven hours is now going to take at least fifteen hours. We have a reservation for two rooms in Seaside, Oregon, our first destination. At the rate we're going, it's going to require late check-in. Manami calls ahead to arrange that.

After lunch in Crescent City, we leave the coast. Back in the car, I sleep for an hour through the Pacific Coast Range mountains. It's another four hours north on Route 5 to Portland and then an hour west to the coast, which is going to make for a long day. Despite the fact we started out early, we won't get to Seaside before eleven p.m. If I don't help with the driving, I should help by talking. Mariko is sleeping in the back now.

"Hey there," Sajiro says, noticing that I'm awake.

"Sorry for sleeping while you are doing all the driving."

"No problem. I like to drive, especially on those tricky roads where I need to focus and be careful every moment. It makes me feel the way I am when I'm leading. I can't let go. It's easier now on the Interstate. I just have to watch out for all these trucks," he says, as another of an endless stream of semis passes us on the left.

"So, how did you learn to lead a group like this?" I ask. "Did your father teach you?"

"You mean my real father or my Heavenly Father?" Sajiro responds. I can't tell if he's joking or not. "You have to understand, it's, how you say, it's the family business. I have no choice. We have been preserving the legacy of the Lost Tribe for hundreds of years. It's only changing now because some people think I'm an avatar."

"Are you?"

"I don't know. Ask my mother."

"Yes, I can see that Kumiko is a force to be reckoned with. What about your father?"

I notice that Sajiro takes a quick look over his shoulder at Mariko asleep in the back. Maybe he's uncomfortable talking about his father, or maybe there's something else going on. I can't tell.

"My father left the Tribe when he was young, soon after he and my mother had me." I'm shocked but say nothing. "He didn't receive the calling, and the weight of responsibility was too much for him. I never see him. Fortunately, Kumiko more than makes up for his absence." Is he being ironic? I don't know. I do know he's sharing things with me that are on the edge of what he's okay with sharing with anyone.

We drive for a long while in silence.

People have always liked to tell me their stories. They would often cry as they did so. I would joke that I should be a therapist, though I had never actually been to a therapist before the accident. I would always add that my advice would simply be, just get over it. Of course, now that I have experienced my own unsurmountable, impossible-to-get-over, life-altering disaster, and been to a therapist, things have changed. I would never give such unfeeling advice now. I wonder what my new advice would be? Try to learn to live? Seek some happy moments? That is my real challenge, living. Why should I be alive? Do I want to be alive? Do I even have the right to be alive?

I lean my head back on the old-fashioned head rest. A tear runs down my cheek. Sajiro reaches over and wipes it away. Then he takes my hand and holds it loosely until the winding road and the gear shift absorb his concentration again.

By the time we reach Seaside everything is closed. We check in to a musty motel that smells of sand and sea, the three women in one room, the three men in the other room, and go to bed without dinner.

We're all up early in the morning. We meet in the parking lot and all agree that none of us wants to stay a second or third night in the motel. We check out and throw our stuff in the cars. Manami leads us to the Ocean Bakery Café. It's in a Best Western Hotel right on the beach. The waitresses are young, bouncy, and charmingly friendly. They bring coffee, and much to my surprise it's steaming hot, strong, and good. I order a three-egg omelet with feta and spinach and a side of toast. I add a side of bacon to the order and contentedly sip my coffee. Nobody talks. The only communication is a lifted eyebrow from Sajiro with a smile when he hears my order.

By the end of breakfast, we've decided that we'll make the Best Western our staging place for the next two days. It's not all that far from the places Chuck has lined up for us. It's not fancy but it has unobstructed views of the Pacific, and it doesn't smell of age and wear.

When Chuck goes off to make the reservations, I catch up with him at the front desk. "Hey, would it be okay if I get my own room for the next two nights? I am happy to pay my way. I just need down time and some privacy. I can book it on my own."

"Sure." Chuck chuckles. "I totally understand. Go for it."

I plunk down on one of the comfy grey couches in the lobby area and do the booking on an app on my cell phone. There's a notion nagging in the corner of my mind that this decision has to do with privacy and with Sajiro, but I dismiss that thought.

We drive out of Seaside and up into the coastal hills. The first place we visit is a former community college that's gone bankrupt. It consists of one enormous rectangular brick and glass building with white columns out front—someone's demented Ivy League-inspired West Coast vision of what a higher education facility should look like—plus a couple dorm houses and a gym. All the classrooms, the student union, administrative offices, and everything else except living quarters and sports are in this one edifice that perches on a hillside facing a view of hills on the other side of a steep valley. It's magnificent, and completely unrealistic, too large and too expensive for the Tribe of Dan. If we, I mean if they, were a larger group, it might make sense. We wander around, giggling at the grandeur of it all, while the commercial real estate agent, an aggressive young man with a buzz cut and an ill-fitting sports jacket who's on his cell phone half the time he's with us, shows us around and insists on taking us into every classroom even after it's clear that the former Saddle Mountain Community College is not right for the Tribe. Chuck is patient and pleasant even after the rest of us, except Sajiro who is unfailingly polite, are long ready to abandon ship. Finally, the unnecessarily long tour is over, and the agent roars off in his racing red sportscar with flame-striped detail. We assemble again in the parking lot. There's some grumbling about the waste of time, but Chuck is ever the businessman.

"Look," he says to the five of us as we are getting ready to leave, "that guy has a business to run. It behooves us to let him do his thing. Plus, our next appointment isn't for another hour and a half." As Chuck starts to open the door to his SUV, Sajiro raises a hand. Everyone freezes, even Chuck. *They really are followers*, I think to myself.

"Since we are here, and since we have the time, let's bless this place for the next group that makes use of it," Sajiro says. Like a magician, he has pulled out from somewhere a bottle of saké, a container of salt, and a sage smudge stick. He proceeds to lead us back over all the ground we had just covered with the real estate agent. The buildings are locked now, so we just do the outsides. Sajiro sprinkles saké and salt in every corner. Mariko waves the smudge stick that she has lit with matches Sajiro has supplied. Manami, Mark, Chuck, and Mariko are chanting something I can't quite make out. I just follow and listen. It's all incredibly strange and subtly powerful.

When it's over, I ask Mark: "Was that some Jewish ritual? Kabbalah, maybe?"

"That was straight Japanese, honey," Mark says with a smirk.

"What was he doing?"

"Chasing out the bad demons, inviting in the good ones. Purification, plain and simple."

"And what were you guys chanting?"

"I have no idea," says Mark. "Something in Japanese. I just know the sounds. Sajiro has a business in San Francisco, as a kind of Jewish Shinto priest, blessing houses when people move into them. He's quite popular, just from word of mouth."

I nod, but this news takes me by surprise. *There are layers to him*, I think, with a thrill in my heart.

The next place we go is as deep in the valley and as dark and depressing as the Saddle Mountain college was high and shining on the hill. We descend by a series of switchbacks into a rain forest of ferns and mossy trees, everything exceedingly lush. We arrive at an old hunting camp along the Lewis and Clark River that makes our rank first night's motel smell daisy fresh by comparison. Mold is growing everywhere, and there's a water line three feet up the outside wall that shows where a recent flood had crested. The real estate agent hasn't arrived yet. I tcam up with Mark as we start to walk around and ask him, "Why do you think we're looking at this place?"

"Well, it's not 'location, location, location,' the real estate mantra," he says. "It must be price." Chuck has overheard us and says to the group by way of explanation:

"This one is almost a teardown, but it's well within our budget. With some sweat equity, this could be a nice place again, right here along the river." Sajiro has already turned away from the camp house and gravitated to the river's edge. We all follow him. There's a sandy beach, and up and down the river the murmur of the water and the deep shade are extremely soothing. It's obvious to everyone that this is not the place for the Tribe, but Sajiro leads another meditation, and we all follow him, swaying to the gentle rhythms of the river and the wind.

By late afternoon we have seen two more places farther from Seaside and closer in to the Portland area. The first is an old farm-style house. Run down, with lots of references to the "P" word: "potential." Some land, no charm and no magic. The last place sounds magical in the information the real estate agent has sent the Tribe. A sixteen-room, white, late 1800s Queen Anne abutting a bird sanctuary and conversation area. Built as a private home, then used as a boarding house from the mid-1900s on, it had more recently been boarded up and semi-abandoned but, according to the brochure, "lovingly maintained." It has a huge room over the garage that would be ideal both for a sanctuary, and as a place for the physical movement in the prayer gatherings Sajiro likes to lead. As we drive up, we are astounded. It's glorious. It even has a widow's walk. How could this exquisite structure possibly be in the price range for the Tribe of Dan? When we get inside, we learn why. We run through the place, past doors with gold room numbers from the hotel/boarding house days, briefly look into the huge formerly well-equipped kitchen and then run gasping for air onto the back porch. Uncontrolled laughter erupts and we breath in as deeply as humanly possible. The current owner has turned the entire place into a kennel for breeding standard poodles. Every inch of the first floor reeks of urine. There are still dogs in cages in some of the rooms. The kitchen is the absolute worst of the foulness.

Standing next to Sajiro, I ask him if he has any of the purification tools left over. Even Sajiro can't stop laughing.

"Some things are beyond my powers and the collective power of my Jewish and Japanese ancestors. Let's go back to the sea and walk on the beach. We need to clear our minds."

"And our lungs," I add.

"And our noses," Mark says.

The only single room available at the hotel is a corner room on the fifth floor on the ocean view side. I'm completely tickled with myself. I need to get away from the Tribe, to think. What am I even doing with this group? I had freely given my opinions during the day and enjoyed it all, but now it's just incredibly perfect to be alone. Any earlier thoughts I had about Sajiro are gone. I take a long hot shower. Both are necessary after visiting that beautiful, foul-smelling dog house. It's nearly ten and I'm nodding off, when I hear a soft, timid knock. My stomach flips. I had convinced myself that I wasn't waiting for a special knock. It was completely nothing to me. Now I find anticipation and excitement washing over me.

At the door, I peek through the peephole to check and open the door slowly. "Can I stay with you, please?" Manami says, pushing her way into the room. "Mariko is snoring so loudly I just can't stand it. You have two beds. That's wonderful!"

The concept of privacy is different on an island nation like Japan. I know that. Manami assumes that I won't refuse her. But I've paid good money for this evening of aloneness, and I intend to have it.

"I'm sorry," I say, as I'm striding purposefully over to my suitcase. "I think I'm coming down with something from all the dampness and mold up here." I retrieve a package and hand it to Manami. "These might help." I fold her fingers around the ear plugs. Then I walk to the door, leaving no question that I expect her to leave. Manami gives me a cold look but says thank you. I say nothing as she goes out into the hall and I softly close the door behind her. I hope she can hear me adding the additional safety latch. It takes me two hours to get to sleep.

At breakfast, Manami doesn't speak to me. Mariko is distant also. I wonder if it's for the same reason, or a different one. Did Manami say something to Mariko about the rude *gaijin* (foreign) woman? There's also the possibility that one or the other of them is jealous of my relationship with Sajiro, such as it is. I mean, nothing's happened. Plus, I suspect they've seen this play before. It's just a sense that I get, that no one is taking Sajiro's obvious flirting with me seriously. Or maybe they're all waiting to see what happens. So am I.

Today we're going to look at three more places, stay the night in Seaside, our third, and then tomorrow we're going to drive back all in one day, the same way we drove up. Sajiro likes these marathon drives. At least that was the plan, but right after breakfast Chuck tells us that one of the three places has canceled. He's busy juggling today's schedule and says we won't be going anywhere until noon. I'm delighted, and plan to go back to my room for more alone time, when Sajiro comes up to me and asks me if I would like to take a walk on the beach with him.

"Sure," I say. "How about in an hour?"

"Ten minutes?" he says. It's a challenge. Just what kind of follower am I? I guess we'll find out.

"Okay," I say. I rush off to change.

The beach at Seaside is wide and flat, bordered on the south end by a rugged promontory and a state park with hiking trails. To the north, the mouth of the Columbia River is up the coast. The beach stretches out, windy and largely deserted on a weekday morning.

We walk north, pushing into a suddenly strong wind that almost always blows from north to south along the coast. The tide is coming in and waves are building to frothy rollers. The beach that yesterday was calm and soothing now stirs up my insides and frightens me like it used to when I was a child on family vacations on the coast of Maine. My mother would hang towels on the line to dry, and the violent flapping in the wind would push a panic button deep in my gut. I would run back inside to the safety and warmth of the house. Now there's no safe place.

"It'll be easier going back," Sajiro says, but he doesn't turn around yet. He takes my hand. I lean into him, so our shoulders are touching. He puts an arm around my shoulders, and we bend almost as one into the wind. I fit comfortably in his embrace, but panic is starting to wash over me. My hair is whipping back from my face. We haven't gone much farther when it starts to rain. A cold Oregon-coast rain. Sajiro raises his hands up to his shoulders in a shrug. As we turn away from the wind, he stops me and puts his hands around my face to keep my hair away and he gently kisses me, first on the forehead and then softly on the lips.

"You must tell me. If not now, soon," he says.

I try to speak but I am sobbing, and harsh heaving sounds I can hardly recognize are coming from my mouth and my body. I fall to my knees, shaking uncontrollably.

Sajiro lifts me up. I think he is going to try to carry me but I shake my head and stand on my own. He strides back toward the hotel, holding me tightly around the waist so that I won't fall again.

The next thing I know I'm in my room with Sajiro. I enter the bathroom and heave and heave into the toilet. Emptying, emptying. Still shaking, still cold, as if emptying myself of everything, driving away all that has been inside me, becoming void, making room for something new. What? I know I'm hoping for warmth and human comfort, but I don't deserve it. I don't deserve the happy carefreeness of these traveling days. I don't deserve to be with a man. I don't deserve to be.

Sajiro lifts me again, his body against mine. He takes off my smelly clothes and piles them in a corner and still fully clothed himself he brings me into the shower. I rinse my mouth out in the rushing water. Sajiro soaps me all over, rinses me, washes my hair with shampoo. It reminds me of when I was a child and my father would wash me forcefully. I start to sob again, but softly, moaning against Sajiro's body.

Finally, Sajiro wraps me in a white bath towel and guides me over to the bed. He puts another towel around my head and hair and covers me up with the blankets, adding more covers. He changes quickly out of his sopping clothes into a white robe supplied by the hotel. Instead of getting into bed with me, he draws up a chair and sits for a long while, holding one of my hands in one of his hands. It's incredibly tender and soothing. "Sleep," he says. I have no shame at knowing that he has seen me naked and put his hands on me to wash me. He has made no sexual advances. He has taken care of me. It's what I need most in the world. I fall asleep.

When I wake up, I'm alone. There's a one-word note on the side table that says: "Downstairs." Four hours have passed. It's mid-afternoon. *I must have missed the caravan to look at properties*, I think. *Sajiro will be gone too.* I don't hurry as I dress and get myself ready, but when I descend from the second floor of the hotel, I see

Sajiro waiting for me in the lobby, uncharacteristically reading the local newspaper.

I rush over to him, apologizing. "Are they gone?" He nods. "I'm so sorry. Can we catch up to them?"

"Why would we want to do that?" he says with a smile. "We're alone. We're free!"

I tilt my head and give him a look. He can see I am not understanding. "Even Jesus took a break sometimes. He went into the desert. Where shall we go?" I see that he is truly happy not to be the leader, the guru, the avatar, at least for a few hours. We sit in the lobby and make plans. A stroll through town, not on the beach, and then dinner in a Japanese restaurant Sajiro has discovered from reading the paper. The restaurant turns out to be delightfully authentic. It's a hole in the wall. "This is just like in Japan," he says.

The owners are a middle-aged Japanese couple, the husband the waiter and the wife the cook. Sajiro converses with them easily and orders in Japanese.

"They are going to make us a special dinner, things not on the menu, I hope you don't mind."

"Lovely," I say. My mind is going back to my meltdown on the beach. "You must think I'm a complete mess," I say.

"I've seen worse," he says. "I've done worse. One time me and my brother ate chili dogs before we ran a half-marathon and at the finish line, we both puked like you wouldn't believe."

I laugh. "Chili dogs? Really?"

"And beer. Someone told us that's the way to prep for a long run. What did we know?" The waiter, a short, square fellow with a stubbly grey crewcut and amused eyes, brings us the first course, which turns out to be six shallow bowls, each one filled with a different kind of mushroom in a different kind of sauce. The food is sensationally delicious, a veritable feast with a profusion of tastes. One of the sauces is a curry. One is predominated by chili oil. One has bits of spiced pork. We pass the bowls back and forth, sharing freely.

"Save room. This is only the first of many courses," Sajiro tells me. His 'taking care of' has not ended yet.

"You have been incredible today. I can't tell you how much it means to me right now. Thank you."

"You have to understand," he says. "I take care of the group in so many ways. I teach them. I give them direction. I make them feel important. They are supposed to take care of me. They try, but they don't really get it. In Japan, it's different."

"How?"

"People understand that to get the most out of a teacher, they have to take care of the teacher. There's a practice called 'sensei care,' making sure the teacher's needs are met. The student knows the teacher will be able to give their best. It's a subtle Japanese thing that takes a long time to learn. Even though they don't do a good job, poor things, I'm so much more comfortable and relaxed here in America where it's all less formal.

For an instant I see Sajiro clearly across the compact square table in the corner where we sit eating Japanese food and enjoying ourselves. He's vulnerable, like me. He's even scared like me, but he can't show it to the world because of who he is, and it bothers him.

"I'm going to say something to you now," he says. "You think of yourself as weak, but I sense that inside you are strong. Stronger than me."

"Stronger than you?" I say, thinking of how helpless I was just hours ago.

"Yes. Without my mother to push me along, I'd probably be an ordinary salaryman with an office job in Tokyo. She's the one who told me I had to come to America, grow the Tribe here."

Yes, Kumiko, the ultimate helicopter parent. I can see it, I think, but to Sajiro I say only, "I'm glad you are here. Thank you."

The waiter comes by and unobtrusively removes the now empty mushroom bowls. Sajiro orders saké. The man nods and withdraws. He's back again soon with miso soup, incredibly simple, just a milky broth with miniature cubes of tofu and flecks of green scallion floating in it. I follow Sajiro's lead, forgo the spoon and sip the miso straight from the bowl. I notice the bowl. It's homely, homemade, rough around the edges, totally lacking in ornamentation, no designs, no patterns, just a piece of crude monochromatic black pottery. "It's supposed to be that way. *Wabi sabi*," Sajiro says. "It means imperfect simplicity; everything is empty and impermanent."

"It sure is." I laugh at the seriousness of what Sajiro has been saying and add: "Works for me."

Sajiro laughs sheepishly, realizing he's been in total teacher mode. He says: "You are better. That's good."

By the time we get back to the hotel, it's evening. The others are nowhere to be seen. Either back late from their travels or out somewhere for dinner.

Sajiro escorts me up to my room. We stand outside the door. It reminds me of the time after the first dinner when I had crazy stirrings of passion. I lean forward and let my face and hair brush along the side of his face and then slowly, bring my lips up to meet his. I turn toward the door, while somehow still leaning back so that I am in contact with him as I fumble in my purse for the key card. My body is making an open invitation to his body and we walk almost as one to the bed.

Everything happens slowly and gently at first. Perhaps this is what we talked around at dinner but never said directly, the need we both have for another to see our scared and vulnerable parts. The need to have someone make us feel safe, complete. Still standing, we take turns undressing one another and gently exploring, touching, caressing, kissing.

As I sit on the edge of the bed and wrap my arms around Sajiro's waist, his erection between my breasts. I open myself to him. We come together powerfully, our movements slow, then rapid, strong then soft, overwhelming and almost violent. I am crying out and moaning and can't stop myself. Afterwards, we lie next to one another and stay as close as possible as we fall into sleep.

The next morning, I wake early. Sajiro is asleep. He's beautiful. I smile as I see the peaceful, satisfied look on his face. I put on the white robe, the one Sajiro

used when he sat by my side yesterday afternoon, and
go out onto the deck. It's cold. The sun is just starting
to reflect off the ocean. There's no wind, no rain. I look
down over the railing at the beach and I wonder what's
happening to me. Is this a good thing I'm doing? Is it
healing or just animal desire? I lean my head on the
railing, the cold metal on my forehead. Then Sajiro is
behind me, his warm hands cupping my breasts. He's
entering me again, slowly and gently from behind. No
one can see us, but we have the view of the long beach
before us, the waves endlessly rolling in. *Yes, this is
animal desire*, I think, and I give myself to it
completely. Afterward we shower together. *Was it only
yesterday that he had showered and cleaned me when I
was sick?* When I suggest room service for breakfast,
Sajiro suddenly becomes slightly remote.

"I have to check in with the group," he says while
pulling on his pants. "They might think I've abandoned
them."

*This is the way it's going to be. I will never have
Sajiro entirely to myself.* "Of course," I say. "Why don't
you go ahead? I'll be down in a few minutes."

Visibly relieved, Sajiro kisses me gently on the
forehead, the mouth, gives me a long hug, and is gone.
I will have to share him knowing that I can't be
exclusive with him. Even though I am tremendously
needy, I can't be clingy or expect to have him to myself.
My decision to send him on ahead works perfectly.
When I join the group at the Ocean Bakery Café,
Sajiro's at a table with Mariko and Mark. I sit down at
a different table with Manami and Chuck. Everybody's

already finished breakfast, and they're just sitting around; obviously they've been waiting for Sajiro. I signal the waitress and order the Timberbeast breakfast, three eggs, ham, two pancakes, and coffee. My large appetite doesn't go unnoticed.

"This ocean air gives one a good appetite, doesn't it?" Chuck says.

"I was sick yesterday. Sorry I missed the trip. Puked my guts out."

"How unpleasant," Manami says. There something cold in her comment that makes me glance at her, but she's not looking at me or Chuck, she's staring out the window at the beach. I shrug mentally. *Jealousy? Judgment?* I wonder. I let it pass.

"How were the places you saw yesterday?" I ask Chuck. He gives me a thumbs-down. "Both needed too much fixing up. This part of the country is struggling economically, and the places for sale reflect that state. Still, we had to look."

"What's on for today? Are we driving back?"

"Too late to make the trip in one day now," Manami says. Sajiro and I have thrown off the group's rhythm, not just for yesterday, but for Sajiro's plan to make the long drive in a single day. I'm pretty sure the group is happy to make a quicker trip back. I know I am. I wasn't looking forward to another winding drive on the outside lane careening around corners with rocky steep drop-offs to the Pacific Ocean. Chuck, the organizer of the trip, adds: "I've arranged for us to look at a place near Shasta on the way down today. Then we'll stay in Redding and finish the trip tomorrow."

"Is Redding a large enough city to be near for recruiting purposes?" I ask.

"Not really," Manami says. She's still staring out the window and looking away from the table. Chuck starts to give more detail.

"Redding itself is not all that great, but Mount Shasta is a power spot. Lots of alternative types live near Shasta, for the vibe. I think we can draw on them, because what we have is authentic and that's what people are looking for."

I know I'm not a true follower as I track my own thoughts: *Japanese Jews from a lost tribe. It's alternative enough, to be sure, but is it authentic, or is it just crazy-making and weird?*

We pack up, check out of the hotel, and stand in the parking lot as we have done before, sorting out who is going to ride in which car. Sajiro asks if he and I can ride with Chuck on this leg. It's not a request. Whatever Sajiro says, goes. Mark, Manami and Mariko go in Sajiro's car. Sajiro and I go with Chuck. It's seven hours, most of it straight down I-5, to the town of Mount Shasta. Since it's ten in the morning already, we won't see the place until around five in the evening, and then it's another fifty miles to Redding. I think it's my fault, but I hear Sajiro in the front seat making an apology to Chuck.

"Sorry, we lost track of time," he says, which is a slightly vague and elusive way to broach the subject.

"No worries," Chuck says again. He glances in the rear-view mirror at me but doesn't ask Sajiro or me anything about what might have happened between us while the group was off looking at properties. I decide it's Sajiro's place to make an announcement, if any is going to be forthcoming. Today, at least for the moment, everything is new and bright and full of promise.

Mount Shasta rises out of the flatness, towering above everything, a majestic, fairly symmetrical volcanic mountain with a well-formed cone at its summit. On the way up we'd been along the coast and hadn't seen it. Shasta floats over the landscape in the deep blue sky like an alien spaceship. No wonder people are attracted to it. We travel toward it forever, the mountain gradually filling the horizon as we approach. Then, wonder of wonders, the place Chuck has arranged for us to see is perfect. It's a two-house compound with views of the mountain out every front window. It's got a "great room" that would be ideal for meetings. There's a fruit and vegetable garden, a flat field for outdoor meetings, and a large gazebo at one end. It's owned by an old rock-and-roller who's downsizing, so it's also got a recording studio in an outbuilding, and the gazebo is open in the front and set up as a stage with rows of benches for concerts; it could serve equally well as a temple for the Tribe of Dan. We're all a bit shocked and surprised. Even the price is reasonable—the old rocker needs the money now, the real estate agent tells Chuck, and is willing to take less to get it sold. The group is excited, but I notice that Sajiro is unusually quiet. We spend two hours at the place, leaving just at sunset, the magic hour, when photographs are most dramatic in the early evening light.

"What are your reservations?" Chuck asks Sajiro.

"It's the timing. I go to Japan soon. My cousin is getting married in April and there are other family matters I must attend to. It won't work because of this."

Chuck and Sajiro talk for a long while about how to handle the property. Chuck thinks it can work. It could take two or three months for inspections and financing approval. Sajiro says he'll think on it and that the group should meet when they get back to San Francisco.

"Chuck, tonight I would like a room for myself, and if Maya agrees, she will stay with me." He looks over the back seat at me and smiles. I nod in agreement. "We have things to discuss."

So that is how this announcement is going to be made, I think. *Very direct.*

When we get to the hotel, arrangements are adjusted accordingly and when everyone is ready to go off to a group dinner, Sajiro asks me to go to the room with him. He asks Chuck to bring back some takeout dinners for the two of us.

Suddenly we are awkward with one another. Not finding anything to say. Not touching or being close in any way. We sit at a table in an alcove in the room.

"I want you to come to Japan with me."

"I would love to," I say, "but can I think about that one?" I'm secretly thrilled by his offer. I'm also frightened. Am I really coming back to life and something approaching normal or is this an easy patch, a walk along a comfortable trail, with the same precipice looming ahead? The same black hole. I shudder and close my eyes.

"Of course. I want you to tell me."

He doesn't say what, but we both know. I knew this was coming, but I'm still not prepared. I shake myself out of my thoughts of the looming black hole of pain. I don't want to go back there. At least not yet. How do I explain everything to Sajiro? Do I even want to? Do I simply show him the locket with Dan and Ella's pictures, the way I did with Jane? I want to tell him. After all my hysterics, I owe Sajiro an explanation.

"A little more than a year ago, I was in an accident. My baby daughter, Ella Rosa, and my husband Dan Brown, her father, were killed. I survived. I wasn't even seriously hurt." Then, just because it is so much easier than words, I take off the locket, open it, and show the pictures to Sajiro. He looks at the images for a long time. He closes the locket and brings it to his lips and kisses it. Tears stream down his cheeks. We sit in silence. Sajiro closes the locket. He fingers the pendant Jane gave me with the Japanese words *Ichi-go Ichi-e*. Finally, Sajiro gets up and comes to me. He puts the chain back around my neck. He stands behind me with his hands on my shoulders, power and energy emanating from his hands.

I'm amazed that I haven't cried in the telling. How can that be? I must have expressed all my fiery pain to him, all my anguish, on the beach and after. The hole at the bottom of my being is still there. I'm soothed by his hands on me.

"About Japan, can we talk about that back in San Francisco?" I ask.

"Of course."

"And, I need to say something practical."

"Yes?" Sajiro's eyes are on me now. He's moved back to his chair.

"We can't make love until I get birth control. It was crazy to do what we did."

Sajiro gives me a rueful smile. "I wouldn't have risked that with you, but you don't have to worry. I can't get you pregnant. I can't father children. Doctors say it's because of an infection I had as a child. It makes me a free spirit, even if I don't always want to be one." Once again, I'm surprised by Sajiro. Have I been so absorbed in my own sorrow and loss that I'm insensitive to everyone else? It is almost too much to think about. I'm saved by a knock at the door. Sajiro goes to the door, thanks Chuck for the food and says good night. He brings Styrofoam containers over to the table. We take out plastic forks and spoons, twist the tops off two Pacifico beers that Chuck thoughtfully included, and sit quietly as we eat the delicious Mexican take out. We hardly talk at all. It's easy, comfortable between us as we get ready for bed. We don't make love. We hold one another and fall asleep.

Chapter 10 Japan

Back in San Francisco, I'm happy to be at Jane's, away from the Tribe, away from Sajiro for a while, on my own so that I can sort things out. I take long walks through Presidio Heights past all the colorful grand homes and down through the Presidio itself to the Marina. It's unseasonably warm and there's no rain as I sit on the Marina Green, viewing the Bay and the Golden Gate Bridge. I think about Sajiro and how he had brought out my passion and my pain, touching me and bringing me back to myself. It's confusing, his position in the Tribe and all that it entails, and the fact that he can't have children. I laugh at myself. *What? As soon as I have sex, I start to wonder what our kids will look like?* Now that's not an option, and I ask myself: *How important is that to me?* I have no answer.

I call my mother. In the last years, since she remarried and while I was with Dan, she hadn't been someone I could turn to for advice. Her new husband, Frank, was a right-winger and a bigot, so different from my dad. I could barely be in his presence. Yet he had softened toward me and Dan at the end. There must have been reasons she married him. She didn't need his money. I need to talk with her the way I did when I was younger, when my real dad was alive.

"Hi Mom," I say as she picks up the phone. "Is this a good time to talk?"

"Anytime is a good time to talk with you, honey. How are you? I haven't heard from you for so long. I wanted to call, but then I didn't. Not sure why."

I'm surprised that I tell her about Sajiro right away. I tell her about the wacky group I'm involved with, about having slept with Sajiro. I even tell her that he wants me to go to Japan with him. To a wedding! And then I wait.

"Maya, you do pick some interesting fellows." She laughs. "But seriously, anything that makes you happy, makes me happy. Maybe it'll turn into some great part of your life. Maybe it'll be just a break, a way to put one more bit of distance between your time of sadness and now."

I cry and tell her I love and appreciate her and that I'll send her a postcard from Japan because I think I'm going there soon. I guess I've made up my mind. I'm going.

Soon it's time to plan for the trip. I'm upset when I learn that it is only me and Sajiro who are going to Japan. It's family business, not Tribe business. I'm surprised by this decision, and it's clear that others in the group are also taken aback by this news, especially Manami, who is visibly shaken when she hears of it. I've become accustomed to seeing Sajiro with an entourage of people following him and taking care of him. I wonder what it'll be like on this trip with just the two of us. I wonder how it'll be for me to spend so much time in a foreign country. How well do I really know Sajiro? It's been such a short time. If I'm honest with myself, so much of it has been in my body and the experience of the physical part of being with him. Brad pulls me aside one night at the Tribe house. We go up to his garret room. He flops on the bed. I remain standing rather than take my usual spot in his one chair.

"Have you ever been to Japan?" he asks.

"Nope."

"It's not like other places. It's not like a foreign country, more like, I don't know, another planet."

"You're exaggerating, Brad," I tease him.

"Maybe. But I've seen what happens to some people when they go there."

"What are you talking about?"

"It's so different, some people, uh, kind of lose themselves."

"I'm lost already," I say honestly.

"That's what I'm worried about."

"Brad, look, I appreciate your concern, but I'm a big girl, an adult. I can take care of myself."

"I know you can. Just be aware that it can be disorienting for visitors in Japan. You're a gaijin, an outside person. You'll see."

"I guess I will."

To lighten things up I add: "Any quotes for me today?" Brad looks up, ponders my question, and rummages through his chaotic stacks of books until he finds the one he's looking for.

"Yeah. Please take this to heart: '*I have found out that there ain't no surer way to find out whether you like people or hate them than to travel with them.*' Mark Twain."

"Do you think I'm going to come back hating Sajiro?"

"I think you might find out a whole lot about him, and yourself, on this trip. That's all."

We go downstairs. Chuck is giving the larger group a summary of the Oregon scouting trip, with the Shasta property as an open question, to be decided by Sajiro while in Japan if the property is still available. Mariko, always visual, has made a DVD of the trip that strung together videos to some dreamy music. She projects it for everyone onto a meeting screen through her laptop. The video draws laughs at us running outside for air at the "dog house," and ooohs and ahhhs at the sunset lighting up in pink the snow-capped peak of Mount Shasta from the front porch of the rocker's fantasy house.

Mark Singer comes up to me after the meeting ends. We chat about his work. He's an assistant editor at a music magazine, I can't remember which one. I like him because he's stubborn and challenging and doesn't accept everything with blind allegiance.

I sense he wants to say something more, so I just nod and leave some space for him to continue. After a pause he says, "Don't worry about the Tribe back here when you go to Japan."

"I won't," I say, surprised by his words.

"The Tribe runs along just fine without its figurehead. Sometimes better."

"I see," I say, though I don't see at all.

"What I mean is, he's the flagship of the brand, but he's not the engine that drives the brand. Still, it should be an interesting trip for you. I've never been to Japan and none of us have met any other of the family. Being Jewish, I have wondered whether the bloodline really does go back to Israel. Anyway, it'll all be new and different for you."

"I'm excited and nervous," I say.

I have just enough time to get my passport renewed because it would have expired while I am overseas. Sajiro's planning a two-month trip. When I broach the subject with Jane, she says that as long as I put my stuff in a closet so that she can rent the room to short-term guests while I'm away, she'll save a place for me when I get back. I'm certain Jane doesn't think this trip is a good idea, but she doesn't say so.

The weeks have flown by. At the end of March, I'm pretty much ready to go. I head over to the Tribe house. I don't text Sajiro, but I'm hoping he'll be there and that we can talk about things, about the trip. Instead, when I get there, I find his mother, Kumiko, in the large entry room, about to put her jacket on. She looks up and sees me. "Good, just the girl I want to see. Come, take a walk with me. Unless you have an appointment with a certain young man?"

"No, no." I'm awkward around Kumiko, not sure what she thinks of me or the fact that Sajiro is involved with me. We head out the door in the direction of Golden Gate Park.

We enjoy the unusually warm weather and clear sky, me not saying much, mostly nodding as Kumiko comments on the flowers and trees. As we enter the park, Kumiko glides toward a bench and we sit down.

"Please don't worry about this trip or your involvement with Sajiro. You should just enjoy. Have fun. Watch and study and see what happens."

"Yes, that's my life right now," I say. Then I ask, "Did Sajiro tell you about what happened to me?"

Kumiko nods and takes my hand, a strong gesture coming from her.

"Japan will be strange and foreign, but it's a great experience for foreigners, especially the first-time visit. Enjoy and explore. Talk to people, even if you need someone to translate for you. It's the people, not the mountains and cherry blossoms and temples, that make Japan a special place. Have fun with Sajiro. He's more relaxed when he's with you. It's quite beautiful. He's my son and I'm happy for that. For you, I must say one more thing." She's still holding my hand. "Protect your heart."

I hear echoes of my mother's advice in Kumiko's words. I'm not quite sure what she means, but I don't ask, and I don't say anything back. I just smile and nod. We leave the bench and walk again. We don't visit the Japanese Tea Garden, it's too far away, but we spend some time in the immense white greenhouse of the Conservatory of Flowers. For March, it's strangely hot and humid, not normal weather for this time of year in San Francisco. We stroll through the place, Kumiko pointing out flowers and shrubs from different parts of Asia.

Kumiko notices that I'm sweating, and she smiles: "You're lucky you are going at this time of year, and to a mountain region. In summer in Japan, and even in

September in the flat lands like Tokyo, it is much hotter than this, and more humid too. This will be a beautiful time. There will be cherry blossoms. It is possible it will be warm so bring light clothes. Maybe buy some Japanese outfits while you're there." We leave the conservatory. Kumiko leads me toward the sound of music coming from somewhere close by. A lone saxophonist is standing at the edge of the tunnel leading under the JFK Drive through the park. He's a black man, muscular, tattooed, bearded, blind, wearing a colorful dashiki print. Kumiko calls out to the player and he smiles broadly and nods in her direction—they know each other! She deposits a dollar in the open case at his feet, and I do the same. He starts to play, a long jazz solo, somewhere between bebop and Coltrane-style hard jazz, with lots of emotive squeaking and shrieking from the sax. The sound reverberates through the tunnel and back, creating a layered echo effect that adds to the performance. Kumiko rocks gently to the beat. When the saxophonist ends his piece, the group that's gathered applauds, and Kumiko goes up to the man and starts speaking to him in some language that's not Japanese or English. It takes me a few seconds to understand that it's French. I look at Kumiko, amazed, and I begin to understand: I've underestimated her. She's not the "old auntie" of cultural cliché, she's a complex woman with a personal history as mysterious as that of the Tribe. I wait to the side while she and the musician have a short but intense, friendly exchange, and then hug each other.

On the way back to the Tribe house I ask Kumiko where she learned French.

"In France, of course. I lived for a year there on my own after college." I hadn't known that Kumiko even went to college. "That fellow," she says, nodding her head back toward the park, "was famous in France in a certain period. Now in America he can't find any work as a musician except playing for donations. In Japan he would be a National Treasure, like a *chado* tea ceremony master or a calligrapher. Your country doesn't value its most important assets." I vow never to misjudge Kumiko again.

Finally, it's the last week of March and time to pack for the trip. Chuck volunteers to take me and Sajiro to the airport for the flight, which leaves on a Monday, the first of April, in the late afternoon. I spend a last evening with Jane. I'm wishing for something that has disappeared for us, at least for now. Is it just because we aren't focused on our pain and instead are focused on our relationships? I was hoping for the warmth and intimacy that marked our first few weeks together. It's just what happens when women are bound up in the business of sex and being with a man; my involvement with Sajiro, and her own renewed affair with her boyfriend Joe are changing the dynamic between the two of us. We joke about "those men" but there's a truth in it that prevents us from going much deeper than simply acknowledging the situation. I sleep poorly and wake up unrefreshed and dreading the eleven-hour flight to Tokyo, almost twice as long as any plane ride I've ever taken.

We're flying on Japan Airlines. I'm enchanted by the politeness of the flight attendants and the cleanliness of the plane. Even though I had been determined to travel lightly, I hadn't been able to resist a trip to Kinokuniya, the Japantown bookstore. I have three smallish books, one that includes audio phrases I've downloaded onto my phone.

Sajiro smiles as he sees the books in my lap. The *Japan Travel Guide* includes tips on what the author wishes she'd known before going to Japan along with some travel phrases. A book of children's stories has Japanese on one side and English on the other side and language lessons at the end of each story. He picks up the third book, one about the Japanese Mind, and says, "This one makes me nervous. If you understand the Japanese mind, then I may be in trouble."

Before we are an hour into the trip, Sajiro has fallen asleep. He's put on an eye-mask, ear plugs, inflated a travel pillow, and looks to be out for the duration of the trip. I cozy up next to him. I enjoy the Japanese way everything is done. The flight attendant hands out hot cloth towels before the meal, a not-bad bowl of soba noodles and vegetables. I order some saké and am even more delighted when another hot towel arrives after the meal. I read a bit in each book and listen to the audio learning words like *arigato gozaimasu* for thank you and *onegaishimasu* for please. I'm pretty sure I'll need *wakarimasen* for I don't understand, frequently.

About three hours into the flight, I look over at Sajiro, sleeping peacefully. He's no fun at all even if he's doing all the right things—not eating or drinking, blocking everything out and sleeping. I'm starting to fidget and fuss and turn endlessly in my seat. The air in the cabin tastes stale. I resign myself to being up all night. I know I'll be completely fried by the time we arrive in Tokyo. My excitement has given way to a gnawing sense of alarm and dread. Whatever am I doing entering the world of the Japanese mind, a strange, foreign place?

The scene at the airport, once we've arrived, heightens my agitated state. Sajiro is excited about returning to his home country. Narita Airport is an assault on my senses. Most of the signs are in English so I'm not terribly lost and besides I'm with Sajiro. As we wait for our luggage, Sajiro puts an arm around me. "Don't worry," he says. "Soon everything won't be so strange. You'll get your feet on the ground of Nihon."

I lean into him, wanting to be protected by him. We collect our bags and pass through Customs uneventfully. On the other side of the exit gate a mass of people hold signs and shout greetings. Sajiro isn't expecting to be picked up by anyone, and he's surprised when a voice calls out his name. A middle-aged man and woman rush up to him but stop short of hugs and bow instead. A rapid-fire exchange in Japanese ensues, while I stand off to one side. The Japanese couple don't think I'm connected to Sajiro at all, and the woman registers a subtle uncomfortableness that I'm standing so close to their family reunion. Sajiro immediately draws me in. "Maya, this is my Oba-san, my aunt, Yukiko, and my Oji, uncle, Kazuki. This is my special friend Maya, who is part of the Tribe in America."

I am terribly awkward, not knowing whether to bow, curtsey, or stick out my hand for a handshake. I smile and do nothing. I'm dazed and tired in my bones. Neither Sajiro's aunt nor uncle speak much English and Sajiro has been rapidly translating bits of the conversation. Yukiko is short, stout, and round-faced, with a severe expression. Kazuki is smaller than his wife, balding, with a more open and friendly face marked by a nose that looks like it has been smashed in more than once. Sajiro is moving us forward, speaking simultaneously to his uncle and to me. He learns, and tells me, that someone from the States, probably Chuck, has called ahead. The notion of my accompanying Sajiro was lost in translation.

Maybe it's because they're family, but neither Yukiko nor Kazuki are in awe of Sajiro like his followers are in America. Even without understanding their conversation, I can see that they treat him like the nephew from America, not as the avatar of an esoteric religion. I do notice a Star of David pendant on Yukiko's neck. I tag along determinedly as we navigate a maze of walkways to a parking garage, even though I have an incredible urge to simply lie down right where I am and sleep. We pile our luggage into the trunk and get in the car, Sajiro and his uncle in the front, me and the aunt in the back. At five-foot-eight and 140 pounds, I tower over Yukiko. She has me beat in the girth department and I'm uncomfortably close to her in the back seat. Yukiko attempts some welcoming words in English, but soon gives up. We ride together in silence. I don't mind. The less I have to interact right now the better, at least until I get some sleep. As we drive, Sajiro points out landmarks. Though I strive to watch and listen, I can't help myself, and soon I'm dozing. I wake with a start, embarrassed and hoping I haven't been snoring. We're headed to Nagano prefecture, about two and a half hours by car from the airport. From what little Sajiro has told me, the Tribe is loosely connected with the Shinto shrine Suwa Taisha there. His family, the Moriokas, live on the slopes of Mount Moriya. They are the hereditary wardens responsible for a yearly ritual called *Ontohsai* that is held at the shrine and clearly mimics the episode in Genesis when Abraham is called upon to sacrifice his son Isaac. I'd heard of this event in one of Sajiro's sermons back in California. It's one of the strongest pieces of evidence that the "Lost Tribe" story is based in reality. Now I'm going to see it in person. The planning for the festival will begin after the wedding. Apparently Sajiro has some part to play in the preparations and the festival.

We arrive at the family home, which is a compound of several houses perched above terraced rice fields on the lower reaches of Mount Moriya. All the structures are built in the old Japanese style, with thatched roof tops. Young people run out to help with the bags and stop still when they see me. They bow uncomfortably and continue their chore. One girl, maybe six or seven, too young to be involved with the luggage, stands in front of me, staring up at me, as if she has never been this close to a Westerner before. Inside, I walk through an inner courtyard and notice the walkways and gardens. I walk down a hallway. The rooms all have rice-paper interior walls and sliding doors. One of the young women who had helped with the luggage welcomes me. She introduces herself as Momoko, a member of the Morioka family, second cousin to Sajiro. Her English is good. She explains that she will take me to my room.

"You must sleep some hours to get rid of the jet lag. I will bring you dinner. There are many here tonight. Just relax and I will show you everything."

Once in the room, I smile. Even in my jet-lagged state, I notice all the things that have been done to make me comfortable: the washcloth and towel on the low dresser next to my futon bed, the single white flower, some kind of orchid, in a thin porcelain vase, the bottle of water and the snack of gummy mochi cubes on a delicate, shallow plate with a pattern of blue leaves circling its edge. I lay down on the futon on the floor and unconsciously sense the comfort of the room around me, the softness of the bed. Within seconds I'm far down into the deepest sleep.

What must be hours later, I hear a tapping on the sliding door and hear it slide open. The cute girl who had stared up at me peeks around the corner. Momoko is at her side.

"This is Aki," Momoko introduces the girl. "Her name means 'to sparkle.' She's a cousin to Sajiro also." Aki is following what is being said and she laughs and opens her hands next to her sweet round face, trying her best to sparkle.

Momoko is carrying a tray with food. I'm starved. She places the tray on the table near the door.

"Please enjoy this food and we will come back soon."

"*Ofuro?*" Aki says in her sweet high voice. She lays a kimono style cotton robe on the stool next to the table and dangles some wooden sandals, the kind with elevated wooden slats on the bottom. I don't know what she's referring to and wonder especially about the wooden sandals. I decide to just let the unfamiliar wash over me and wait and see.

I've been smelling the food all the while, and my stomach lurches as I kneel before the table. Something stops me from digging in. I admire the dishes, the delicate arrangement of the food and breathe in the aromas. I eat slowly. When I'm done, the door slides open again, and Aki sticks her head inside.

"Come. *Ofuro.* Come." She must have been just outside the door waiting impatiently. She points to the robe and slippers and beckons me to follow her.

Momoko greets me in a changing room. She is wearing a robe and she apologizes for not letting me have privacy as she says she will explain and show me what to do. We hang our robes on wooden pegs and take seats on wooden stools, each stool in front of a faucet. Momoko fills a plastic bowl with warm water and begins to wash. She smiles at me, inviting me to copy her. We both scrub and wash and rinse our bodies and shampoo our hair. I have never felt so clean.

"Now we are clean, we can relax." Momoko slides open the door and says simply "*Ofuro,*" revealing a large natural pool dug into the earth and lined with smooth rocks. It's filled with steaming water. We ease into the water, saying nothing, relaxing and soaking. On the way back to my room, Momoko shows me the toilet room and the sink for brushing teeth. The bedding on my futon has been smoothed and the cover pulled back. I sink back into sleep. When I wake again, I've completely lost track of time. I don't know if it's night or day, and if daytime, what day. I search around for my cell phone knowing it will have updated the time zone, automatically, and am surprised to find it's two in the afternoon. I've slept through the night and half-way into the next day! I have no idea if this is normal or odd behavior. All I know is, I needed it. As far as I know Sajiro has not come by to check on me. I wonder about that. I wonder whether I should go out into the house and explore or simply wait until someone comes for me.

I take a minute to pull out my Japanese calendar booklet so that I can fix myself in time. That may help because I can't yet fix myself in physical space. I'm pretty much lost in space. I flip back over the past weeks, noticing my notes in the extra space on the left side of the calendar. The calendar is a kind of despair barometer measuring my anxiety and misery. Until recently, most were about Dan and Ella. I haven't been writing about them since the start of my involvement

with Sajiro. Am I simply forgetting my past by having
fun and adventure? Do I deserve to be having fun, a
life? When I told my mother about Sajiro and this trip,
she said it might be a major part of my life or it might
just be an adventure, and something about putting
distance between what she had called my "time of
sadness" and the present. Remembering her words
gives me a lift, a kind of permission to stow my guilt
and sadness in the hold of my personal ship and leave
it there for a while. I smile a bit to myself and think
Titanic. Still, for the moment I will not go down in
grand defeat.

A beautiful chest of drawers sits in the corner of the
room by the window that looks out over the courtyard.
It's ancient, with dark wood and finely wrought metal
hinges and drawers of various sizes. With renewed
energy from all the sleep I've had, I decide to unpack
and put things away. I guess I'm going to be settling in
at this family compound and may as well get used to
that idea. On top of the dresser, I line up the three
travel books, my calendar, and a travel jewelry box.

I change into fresh jeans and my favorite deep
purple top, the one Sajiro admired when he talked
about looking into my green eyes. *Where is that man?* I
wonder and as I hear a soft knock on the door, I think,
at last.

When I get to the door and gently slide it open, Aki
is smiling up at me. She gestures an ask to come in. I
smile down at her. Once inside, she looks all around. I
remember the children's book and am happy to have a
way to communicate. We sit on the futon, our backs

against the wall. I have the book on my lap. First, I try to ask how old she is. I am using an app on my phone and counting with my fingers. She smiles again and I realize how apt her name is. She's seven, but somehow makes me understand she'll soon be eight. We start in on the first story, "The Moon Maiden." I read the Japanese that is written phonetically under the Japanese characters and notice Aki is following along. *Is she reading Japanese kanji already?* I wonder. Then I read the English side to myself. It's an ancient and sad story about a bamboo-cutter and his wife, who desperately wants a child. He climbs to the top of Mount Fuji where his wife has seen a vision of a child and finds a moonchild cradled in bamboo stalks. For many years Princess Moonbeam lives with the couple, bringing them great joy. A butterfly explains to the couple that the Moon Princess must go back to where she is from. The story ends with a magical scene where a radiant Moon Lady descends from the mountain in the moonlight. She wraps her silvery moon-body around Princess Moonbeam and ascends the mountain. The bamboo-cutter, his wife, and people from their village watch in silent awe. The wife is sad, and the Princess weeps as she leaves. She will miss her earth family. Her tears send a message of love and comfort to the bamboo-cutter and his wife.

By the time I've finished the story, tears are streaming down my cheeks. I let the book fall to the side. I'm hugging my knees struggling to keep it together. I don't want to have a full-blown meltdown in front of Aki. She kneels at my side and puts her arms around my shoulders. We stay that way for a long time. What would my Ella have been like at seven going on eight?

After Aki leaves, I find the bathroom down the hall from my room and freshen up and even put on a bit of blush and eye makeup. Back in my room I open my jewelry box, take out the locket and pendant I haven't worn on this trip and put them around my neck. I take a deep breath and head to the door.

Just as I slide the door open, there he is. I step back into the room and Sajiro stands in the opening, not entering. There's something slightly different about him. He's dressed in a loose-fitting shirt and pressed slacks. I would never imagine him wearing these clothes in California. But it's not that; it's something else, the way he carries himself. It's like he's shrunk slightly. Perhaps a little stooped, shoulders rounded and forward, something humble and, well, repressed. Is he constrained by the family setting or the fact that he's not center stage? Or is it simply being in Japan? I put these thoughts aside. I'm happy he has finally come to get me.

"I don't have to ask if you slept well," he says, his charming smile filling my heart.

"*Ohayōgozaimasu*," I say, proud of having remembered something from my language study book.

"Hmmm. Good. That's for 'Good morning.' For mid-afternoon we would say '*Konichiwa*.'"

"Darn. I have been studying up." I think he's criticizing me. His gentle smile shows me he's just teasing me over having slept so long.

"*Konichiwa*," I say. "The bath and the futon bed were wonderful."

"I'm glad." He still hasn't entered my room. I gesture for him to come in, but he remains in the doorway, half in, half out.

"Perhaps it was a mistake to come here right away. I should have given you a chance to acclimate," he says.

"I'm okay," I say. I understand that he's talking to himself and that he needs time to settle himself as well.

"I think we should go to a *ryokan* and have time to ourselves. Then we can come back."

"Oh Sajiro," I make a tired face and think, *How can he even suggest travel right now?* "I have just unpacked and put my things in that beautiful dresser."

"*Tansu*," Sajiro says. "Yes, that's an ancient family heirloom. There's no need to unpack. Just take enough for a couple of nights. We're only going part way up and around the mountain. Maybe forty-five minutes." I can see that he's made up his mind already, and getting away from his aunt and uncle and the closeness of the house has great appeal. I understand he needs to get away from it all to get his bearings.

"Okay. What's a *ryokan*?" It isn't a word I've come across yet in my reading.

"Special treat," he says. "Japanese hot spring retreat. Like your *ofuro*, but a whole place devoted to relaxation."

"Sounds great. Won't your family mind you are leaving so soon?"

"They'll understand. We'll be back soon. Just give you a chance to, what is the expression? 'Get your feet on the ground?'"

We stay one more night with the family while Sajiro makes a reservation for the next two nights at the local *ryokan*. I realize everyone is trying to make me welcome, but I'm self-conscious and uncomfortable. Sajiro is right. My feet aren't on the ground. I'm discombobulated, a word that always made me laugh in grade school but now is highly descriptive of my state of mind. Why am I here? What is going to happen to me? I try to focus on the food, which is simple but delicious country fare. The only way for me to relax is to pay attention to Aki. She delights in teaching me the names of things and after our reading together and her genuine ability to comfort me, I am totally open to her. She does not point, but when I take a piece of potato from a dish that's been placed before me, she says: "*Yama imo.*" She giggles when I drop the potato, fortunately right onto my plate, but I can use chopsticks better than that, and when I pick up the piece and put it in my mouth, she claps. My relations with the rest of the family continue to be awkward, less easy. Even if we understood each other, which we don't, I'm not sure we would have anything to say to each other.

After dinner, Sajiro walks me back to my room. He explains that we will share a room at the *ryokan*. I can tell he wants to be sure I'm okay with that. I smile. I am more than okay. I have been missing him physically and can't imagine how anyone has any intimacy or love-making in this old house with paper walls.

"But we take hot springs separately," Sajiro adds, with another of his dazzling smiles.

"Oh? Why?" I ask.

"Custom. Like *mikvah*," he says.

"I've never been to a hot spring," I confess.

"There's lots of things in Japan you haven't seen or done. It's going to be fun."

Sajiro slides the paper door shut behind him and stands close to me, gazing into my eyes. I recognize how sensitive and beautiful he is. We put our arms around each other and hold one another. Passion and longing are coming back into my body. It's what has saved me these past months, overpowering the deadness that has been there for so long. I know Sajiro is also looking for a way to find his center.

When I'm alone in my room, I look up the word *mikvah*, on my phone. It's a term I know only vaguely, but enough to know that it's Hebrew and has to do with a Jewish woman bathing after her menstrual cycle. Fortunately, I had my period a good week before the start of the trip. I had felt relief. I was content to know I didn't need to worry about getting pregnant, but I did worry. It's natural for women to worry. A seed of mistrust sprouts at the back of my mind. Could I trust what Sajiro told me at the hotel near Mount Shasta, about not being able to father children? My last period had brought maximum discomfort, much more than usual. I was annoyed, had headaches and cramps, and was about as grumpy as I could be. Once again, it's clear being a woman is not all that easy. I had trusted Dan so implicitly, never doubting him. I smile remembering him. Perhaps I could get to a place where I remember my love for Dan and still leave myself open to the idea of being with another man.

Breakfast the next morning is like dinner: miso soup, a piece of fried mackerel, and rice. No lumberjack breakfast here, and no coffee either. I sure hope there will be coffee sometime soon.

Driving the forty-five minutes to the *ryokan* is terrifying. I must have been too tired to recognize we were driving on the other side of the road when we came from the airport. Now, on the mountain road, I'm keenly aware of it. The PTSD from the accident is fully activated. I look out the window at the countryside, recite poems that I memorized early in my life and finally just close my eyes and breathe deeply.

Suddenly, the car is stopping. We're in a town at a coffee shop! I kiss Sajiro on the lips when we are out of the car and tell him how his getting me coffee is making me happier than I have been in my whole life. He holds himself awkwardly away from me. Again, there is discomfort. We're not in San Francisco. He can't express his affections or receive my touch easily. I think that when I'm back at the family compound I need to read the book about the Japanese mind. Something is different being in Japan. Sajiro has snapped back into his Japanese body and self and it constrains him and keeps me at a distance.

In the village and during the rest of the drive, I begin to comprehend how disoriented I am by my surroundings. I can't read much of anything. I've never felt so much an outsider—not able to understand what's written over the tops of stores or on the road signs. I tell Sajiro how I'm feeling. "You know the word for foreigner in Japanese," he says, "is *gaijin*. A more formal word is *gaikokujin*. It's three *kanji* that together mean 'outside-country-person.' It's for everyone, not just white people, everyone who is not Japanese. We're an island culture that has always resisted outsiders. I have a double dose of this at times because in many ways it's the same for Jews, though Jews are not an island people. As Jews, we use the word 'gentile' to describe all who are not Jews. Some use the Yiddish word 'goy' or 'goyim.'"

This is the old Sajiro, teaching and explaining. As I listen, I relax, forgetting about the scary turns of the drive, and warm to the comfort of our car-world with just the two of us together. I assume we're going to climb up the mountain, but toward the end of the drive we begin to descend into a steep and narrow valley, following the course of a rushing stream. I glance over at Sajiro questioningly, but he's focused on negotiating a swift series of hairpin turns. Down and down we go, the walls of the canyon closing in on us. The road dead-ends at a cul de sac with space for just a dozen or so cars to park along its curving turnaround. Before we are even out of the car a young man approaches, bows to Sajiro, casts a quick inquiring glance at me, and speaks to Sajiro briefly in a low voice, then takes our light bags and indicates we should follow him. We

enter a place that is pure Japan. Everything simple.
Everything low. Bare wood beams and posts in the long
hallways. Tatami everywhere. The lighting muted. We
fall into silence that fits the place. We are handed
exquisitely folded blue and white checked *yukatas*
(unlined cotton bathrobes) with cotton belts. When we
reach our room, our guide simply slides open the thin
sliding door and then leaves. There is no need for him
to be there. Everything is perfect. Two futon beds laid
out on the tatami floor. A bottle of saké resting in a
warmer, as if it was taking a *ryokan* bath. Salty
snacks, *edamame* and rice crackers, awaiting our
pleasure. I follow Sajiro's lead. We change into the
yukatas immediately, sit cross-legged on plump
cushions across from each other. Sajiro pours saké for
me, and then indicates I should do the same for him.
Another Japanese custom I would not have known
about.

"It's considered rude and bad luck to pour your
own saké," he says. "But the real reason to pour for
each other is as a way to make friends. So, friend," he
says, as I lean over to pour him a cup in a shallow fired
ceramic dish that can hardly be called a cup, but
whose glaze shines with a peculiar glint that is so
suggestive of warmth that it's almost an emotion,
"here's to your Japanese adventure." He kisses me. We
raise our saké dishes to toast, and I say, "*Kanpai!*"

"Very good! Do you know what it means?"

"Ah, no," I say, with a sheepish smile.

"Empty cup!"

"Lovely!" We spend time doing nothing, which is just what I need. The room has a balcony that looks over the stream. I notice a couple of places where the stream has been diverted and surrounded by bamboo fencing for privacy.

"Do we take the hot springs right in the stream?" I ask, excited by the idea.

"We can. The indoor pools are easier to get in and out of. We might start with them."

I remember his telling me that there are separate areas for men and for women, and I assume this means the ones in the stream also. After a half-bottle of saké I'm ready for a nap, but Sajiro suggests a bath. It makes sense, it's why we came here rather than, say, a hotel in Tokyo.

"Sure," I say.

I enter the women's bath and I'm glad that Momoko had given me a lesson in the basics. I don't embarrass myself by entering the water with soap on my body. I do a long and careful washing and rinsing as Momoko had shown me, before stepping down into the bath, and I don't dunk my head. There's a view out to the tumbling stream and a lush forest growing on the steep bank on the other side. The designers of the *ryokan* had taken every advantage of the rustic setting. It is fabulously beautiful! I stay in for what I think is a reasonable amount of time, but I still find that I wait quite a while for Sajiro in the outer room. When he comes out of the men's bath, he is surprised to see me.

"Next time go to the room," he says in a flat voice. I can't tell if he's angry with me or just surprised that I waited for him. I'm so relaxed from the deeply soothing effects of the bath that his curtness doesn't bother me.

"I could live here," I say.

We fall into an easy intimacy. I know it's only a brief respite from the duties of a son and nephew on an important visit, but Sajiro is much more relaxed, like me. The brief time at the family compound was tense in so many ways.

We take off our *yukata* and lie naked in front of a real wood fire that is burning a wood with a strong scent, maybe cedar. We drink the rest of the saké, which has been mysteriously replenished and reheated.

I slip under the covers of my futon bed. I know it must be jet lag, because the pull of sleep aided by the warmth from the bath and the saké is a force impossible to resist. Sajiro lies next to me and we wrap our arms and legs around one another and sleep.

When I open my eyes, Sajiro is awake, his head resting on his right hand. He's smiling down at me. All the warmth, from the bath, the saké, and the fire, is inside me. If I move, it may overwhelm me. I'm just aware enough to know that I don't want to moan and cry out the way I have before with Sajiro. I smile back, breathing deeply, while at the same time panting, staying still, waiting. Sajiro gently kisses me and moves down to caress and kiss my breasts and continues down my body. I'm completely open to him until finally, he enters me. Everything is slow and gentle. I remain silent, but soon am arching and tightening myself around him as we move together so quietly. Keeping all the sounds inside and being constrained by my surroundings makes everything build as we move together. Quiet, repeated explosions take place inside me and I'm alive as I have never been before. After another short sleep, we both get up, and put our robes on again.

"That was beautiful," Sajiro says with a smile. "But aren't you hungry?"

I am hungry! We've hardly eaten since we arrived, except for snacks in the room.

"Come, let's go to the dining room and see if we can catch the last of the mealtime." Sajiro is sitting on a stool near the window beside the deck that looks over the stream. The light behind him causes a glow around him. He looks beautiful and ethereal. I sit on his lap, straddling him. I'm surprised when he rises up to me and I lift myself and then lower myself catching him inside me. I hang onto the windowsill and throw my head back. He gently kisses my breasts and again we are still together hardly moving. Slowly I start, rhythmically, until we come quickly and wildly, but still silently, together. Finally, I rest my head against his chest and say, "Yes, let's go find some food!"

The dining room is empty. Most visitors take their meals in their rooms, I discover, and for the rest of our stay we do the same, but this night we sit in the quiet space and enjoy a meal that echoes the one I was served at Sajiro's family home—not fancy, just simple, delicious, composed of ingredients that could be found on or near the mountain. Here are some of those *yama imo* Aki named for me, which I had looked up and learned meant "mountain potato." At Sajiro's they'd been peeled, but here they are in their skins, which are covered with a prickly fuzz that takes some skill to remove. The main course is a whole mountain trout, caught that day from the stream that passes by the *onsen.*

"Don't they get cooked in the water?" I ask. Sajiro finds that funny and laughs out loud.

"Fish like the baths too," he says. "But they know where to go and how long to stay in the hot water." We pick at the fish with our chopsticks, sharing the plate. The intimacy of this act warms my heart. A simple salad of daikon and other pickled vegetables rounds out the meal. Rice, of course. Rice at every meal. Rice even with potatoes. Dessert is simply green tea ice cream.

After dinner, I'm surprised when Sajiro again suggests the baths. We head over and I clean myself in the washing area and soak for a short time. This time I head back to the room, remembering how Sajiro took a long while the first time and that he wasn't all that pleased when I waited for him. Over the next days, I come to understand Sajiro is a hot springs fanatic! He'll go back more than a half-dozen times, and each time he stays for long sessions. When I ask how he can stay for so long in the hot water, he describes how he drapes a white cloth over his close-cut hair and tells me to try the technique for cooling off while remaining in the bath. He also tells me to pour wooden buckets of cold water over my head. I'm taking all my cues from what the women are doing. They're much more demure and more discreet than Sajiro. I have yet to see any woman doing either of these things.

Back in the room, I doze for a while, read, and take some notes in my calendar. I really do need to sort things out. I think about Sarah, my therapist, and how I haven't been in touch. I wish I could talk with her. Being in Japan is stirring up more questions than answers.

On a blank page, I write 'Dear Sarah,' but then I just put down notes to myself.

- *Not falling in love with Japan. Home = my feet on the ground.*
- *Sajiro is so beautiful and wonderful. What would a life with him be like?*
- *I am not a member of the Tribe, not Jewish, not Japanese.*
- *Sex? Would it have gotten this wild and crazy with Dan if he had lived? Okay? Selfish to feel alive?*
- *Pain, sadness, wanting to die transformed = sex?*
- *Set aside time for a call to Sarah. A letter is too hard. Email first?*

I hear the door to the room sliding open and close the calendar. Sajiro enters, walking backwards and carrying something that he's not letting me see yet. He turns around to show me. He's brought me flowers, not a stuffy bouquet like one might bring someone in America, but a single long stalk of intensely fuchsia azaleas in a slim crystal vase.

"Thank you!" I cry. "Where did you get these? And where is your bathrobe?" I ask, because I see that he is dressed. He points to his *yukata*, neatly folded on a low side table on his side of the bed. He must have come in while I slept.

"I took a walk. Would you like to see where I found them?"

"Oh, yes!"

"Too dark now. We'll go in the morning."

For the rest of our stay, including breakfast early the next morning, a young woman brings our meals and leaves them outside our door with a quiet knock. More fish, another mackerel. More rice. I start to long for a breakfast burrito or an omelet. But it's all so good, I can't complain. The lovemaking and the mountain air have given me a robust appetite!

Fortunately, I'd thrown in my sneakers when we packed for this trip, so I'm prepared for walking. Just after sunrise we set out, immediately climbing a steep trail. After a mile or so the path levels out and we pass through a dense grove of bamboo, much bigger than any I had seen in gardens in the States, thirty feet tall and as thick as birch. Walking up a ridge, we are still in forest and have no views. I can hear the cries of some animal, but I don't know what it is. I ask Sajiro.

"Monkeys," he says. "We might see them, but probably not." And then, unaccountably, in a clearing in the woods we come upon a solid granite obelisk, ten feet tall, weathered and rough, with *kanji* carved into it. Sajiro stops, bows, and touches the stele lightly with one hand, closes his eyes, and stands quietly in deep meditation for several minutes. When he finally drops his arm and looks up, I ask, "What is it? Why is it here in the middle of nowhere?"

"This monument commemorates the sacrifice of Abraham. Here," he says, taking one of my hands and tracing the faded *kanji* with it. "This says *'Abraham took the ram and offered it as a burnt offering instead of his son.'* It's from Genesis, the first book of the Torah."

I'm speechless. Sajiro is trying to show me that his life, the legacy of the Morioka family, is not just a myth but something real, historic. We have a drink of water. Sajiro prays silently. I close my eyes to see if I can understand the meaning and gravitas of the place. Nature is all around me, the sweet perfumes of the flowers and trees. But a gulf is growing between my true heart and Sajiro. All the things that I am not, that I wrote down the night before, flash again through my heart and my mind. *Later. I will think about this later.*

When we walk again, and just as I'm beginning to wonder if we'll ever get any views from this high up the mountain, we turn a corner on the trail, the vista opens up before us, and there, distant but magnificent, is the almost perfectly conical shape of Mount Fuji, still glowing pink in the morning light! We've had two nights at the *onsen*. I'm hedonistically relaxed and at the same time aware that this is for the moment. For now, I'll let the all-consuming sex and the deep experience of Japanese culture overwhelm my senses. At the same time, there's another truth, a deeper part of me that is being held in reserve. *I'll enjoy these days, then think more deeply, later, when we're back at the family compound.*

On the final morning, Sajiro wakes me at dawn, the sun barely lighting the sky. He whispers, "Let's hike to the sacrifice monument one more time." I'm sleepy, but I go along. The hike is easier this time. I stand silently as Sajiro prays. Again, I close my eyes to meditate. The spirit of the place, if not the meaning of the monument, pervades my consciousness. The coolness of the morning is splendid. The sounds of the trees, the far-away sounds of the monkeys. Something is awakening inside me. It's not just that my own troubles and sadness are at bay. Sajiro is teaching me something. His deep prayer and meditation reflect the meaningfulness of his chosen path. What is my way forward? Do I need to be here? Do I need to do something differently? Is there a way to discover a life power inside myself? *Later,* I tell myself again. *I will think about this later.*

As we hike back, Sajiro asks if I want to try a dip near where the hot spring water enters the descending stream. I'm delighted. It's something I've wanted to experience. We head down a steep narrow trail. I hold onto tree branches to support myself on the way down. Soon we come to a clearing where the water is pooling along the edge of the stream.

"We have to be careful," Sajiro says. "The hot spring water can be unpredictable and is sometimes too hot."

Soon we're both naked, sitting on a rock dangling our feet into the pool of hot water. It's hot, but no more so than in the baths. We sink into the water. The stream is lazy here and we go from the hot pool into the cold water of the stream and back again easily.

"Let's rest and dry off in the air," Sajiro says.

We stand by a hardy gingko tree with low branches and put our arms around one another, tears on my cheeks. Sajiro wipes them off. I notice tears on his cheeks. Something is changing inside both of us. For now, how beautiful to be in nature, naked, like Adam and Eve. We hold each other and then instead of getting dressed as planned, take a final soak in the hot pool and finish by swimming in the cold water of the stream. This time we get out and put our clothes on even though we're wet.

We arrive, crumpled and disheveled back at the room just as breakfast is being delivered.

"Sajiro, I need coffee and a regular kind of breakfast. I don't think I can handle fish and rice right now."

Sajiro laughs and goes off to check us out while I pack up my things. Soon we're on the road and heading toward the nearby town, to a coffee shop run by a fellow who lived in France for many years. It's not a breakfast burrito or a lumberjack style breakfast, but when I have a café au lait in front of me and a plate with an *omelette française*, a croissant and a side of crispy bacon, I know that, at least for the moment, I'm where I want to be.

We arrive at the family compound in mid-afternoon. No one is around. When we have our luggage in hand, Sajiro leans over toward me. I can't say if he wants to kiss me or make a formal bow. We're back in his family's constrained world. I smile and laugh. He bows, smiles his sweet smile, and says, "It was a wonderful two days. Now I must meet with family and get ready for the family wedding and other events. I will send Momoko to you to let you know what is happening. The schedule."

Back in my room, I gather my things and make a pile of clothes that all need washing. I'll ask Momoko what I need to do about that. I look at the books on my dresser and pick up the one about the Japanese mind and realize that I don't want or need to read it. I really don't need to understand the Japanese mind. I need to understand my own mind. My road back, if there is one.

The next two days are filled with visits from Momoko, washing of clothes and delightful visits from Aki, reading more of the children's stories in Japanese and in English. At the end of the afternoon on the second day, Momoko invites me to her room. She has a surprise for me. When I get there, Aki is there and two teenage girls, Sajiro's cousins, giggling and covering their mouths. They want to dress me up in a brocaded silk kimono that hangs with a horizontal stick through the arms like a scarecrow. Momoko explains to me that the family crest is woven into the pattern. She points out the Jewish star, elaborately filigreed and integrated into the overall design, but unmistakable. I'm extremely uncomfortable and sure that I don't want to be a doll for these young girls to play with, but it's impossible to refuse them. They have a force about them, a kind of quiet insistence and I end up letting them have their way. The process is surprisingly complicated. It's not just the outer layer of the kimono. Beneath there's a white slip, an inner belt, an outer belt, and a final, formal, brocaded belt. Finally, white *tabi* socks. The girls flutter around me. Momoko, who has been providing me with Japanese words for the clothing, tells me the girls are impressed that I have a reasonably firm body. Apparently, they have the impression that American women are soft and fat. When they laugh and point at my feet, Momoko explains that they think my feet are strangely skinny and narrow. Finally, I have it all on and I can hardly bend over. The kimono has no pockets. It really is like being a doll. They parade me over to a mirror. I take one look and am about to burst into tears when I glance at Aki's proud, expectant face and from somewhere within me a childlike laugh comes out instead. I'm losing my identity, my mind. That makes me want to flee, to cry, to escape. But Aki is a kind of grounding rod. I also know this really is just for the moment. My feet will land on the ground, but not here, not in Japan.

Sajiro walks in, raises an eyebrow, smiles, walks out again without saying anything. The girls want me to walk all around the porch that lines the inner courtyard. I want to resist, but Aki takes me by a hand and leads me out of Momoko's room as the teenage girls titter and almost shriek at the sight of my pigeon-toed walk in the tight kimono. They take cell phone pictures of me, and selfies with me in them. I have completely surrendered, if just for Aki. I smile and let them enjoy themselves. Aki especially is proud that I am wearing the costume of her ancestors, though I notice she's in jeans, sneakers, and a T-shirt with a logo from a children's anime film. We don't make as much of an impression as the girls might have hoped. All the adults, excluding me, are busy with preparations for the impending wedding. Neither the wedding nor the reception will be held at the family compound, but this is the staging ground and more and more people are arriving. More people, all Japanese, each one doing that subtle double-take when they see me and then immediately hiding their surprise behind emotionless faces or tight smiles.

Finally, the girls take me back to Momoko's room. It had taken a long time to get into the kimono, but in minutes I'm standing in the comfortable white slip. I could be happy just in the slip as a dress. I put on my own clothes and when I look in the mirror realize I'm totally under dressed. I rush off to my room to get suitably dressed to meet more of the Japanese guests who have arrived. I put on a simple, cobalt blue dress, a pair of lapis lazuli and gold stud earrings and the one pair of flat but elegant black shoes that I brought with me. Now, when I look in the mirror, I look like myself.

Back in the courtyard, I try to mingle. I'm introduced to many people whose names I never learn. I learn from Momoko that there are so many people the dinner evening is going to be held outside on tables set up in the interior courtyard garden. Everything is awkward. I notice that the Japanese maneuver easily in the increasingly crowded courtyard. The narrow walkways left after the tables are set up are no problem for the family, only for me. I can't move without bumping into someone or something. At dinner I sit with Momoko and Aki and a couple of strangers. Sajiro is at the head table with his aunt and uncle, his brother Taro and Taro's fiancée Yua, who have only arrived a couple hours before the dinner and to whom I haven't yet been introduced. There's toasting, not with saké but with high quality champagne. I ask Momoko about the saké and she tells me the saké is reserved for the *san san ku do*, a ritual three cups drunk during the wedding ceremony. I make a point to not drink much even though I'm so on edge I would like a tall double vodka tonic or some southern bourbon. I can't relax and am afraid I will make some terrible *faux pas* if I get tipsy.

The meal isn't as elaborate as I might have thought, perhaps because of the number of people in attendance; it's miso soup, then sushi, sashimi, grilled meats and of course, rice. Ah, but what sushi! What sashimi! We're in Nagano, sixty-five miles from the Sea of Japan to the east, but the fish in the sushi and sashimi glistens with freshness. Platters are passed around. On one I see that a headless shrimp is still alive and wriggling. I almost lose it! I take items that I think I might recognize—a slab of tuna and what looks like it might even be a California roll or some variation if it. Aki tugs at my dress. She points to her plate and makes clopping sounds as her hands prance on the table. It takes me a second to get it—horse sashimi! I blanche and must have turned whiter than usual, because Aki's happy face is replaced by one of concern, and she quickly gets up and takes her plate away and comes back with a new one.

Sajiro ignores me for the entire meal. I'm okay with that. After dinner the men start drinking expensive Japanese whiskey while the women clean up. Momoko must have been given the night off. She and Aki take me for a walk past the other house in the compound. The fronts of all three houses are decorated with twisted rope hangings whose purpose I can't discern. I ask Momoko if they're connected to the wedding.

"Sort of," Momoko says. "They're *shimenawa*, for purification. They can ward off evil spirits."

"Oh," I say. "Like saké and salt," thinking of Sajiro at the school in Oregon that we didn't buy.

"Yes, exactly! Hmm. You know," Momoko says approvingly. Aki giggles.

"You little rascal, trying to feed me a horse," I tease her. Aki turns red, but she understands I'm just joking. We walk happily along, out of the compound and up the road before turning back. Even this brief respite helps me restore some semblance of balance.

The wedding is scheduled to take place the next day in late afternoon at the Suwa Taisha shrine, just miles from the family compound. Momoko walks with me back to my room. She asks me what I'm planning to wear to the wedding. I take out a floral dress that I had picked out especially for the wedding. It seemed perfect for the late spring weather along with white dress sandals. Momoko makes a sound like a hum of indecision. I've been around Sajiro long enough to know that this indicates disapproval.

"Momoko, isn't this appropriate?"

She shakes her head slowly and explains that it is a traditional wedding, old style. A guest, especially one connected to a member of the family, should wear black. I'm at a loss, but then remember I packed one basic, sleeveless black dress. While Momoko runs off to her room, I put on the black dress, put on my pearl and gold earrings and a lovely necklace of white pearls. I stand frowning in front of the mirror. Am I underdressed? Momoko comes back with a black lace jacket. It fits! I receive her gentle smile of approval.

The Suwa Taisha shrine is a place like nothing I have ever seen before, a long low brown wooden building, aged and weathered so that it has taken on the qualities of the earth it stands on. As we approach the main entrance in a loose procession led by a priest in Shinto garb and carrying a fan, the first things I notice—I can hardly help but be struck by them—are the huge, immense, what did Momoko call them, *shimenawa*, several times the size of the ones hanging on the houses at the compound, adorning the entrance way to the shrine: thick plaited straw made into thick coils with bristling ends hanging down like bells. We'd walked from the parking lot to the broad courtyard, where we stand around while final preparations are being made inside. Sajiro unexpectedly takes me by an arm and leads me up to his brother Taro and his fiancée Yua and introduces me as his "special friend" from California. It's an odd time for introductions, but Yua is friendly and relaxed, not at all like I would have expected from a bride-to-be. Taro, on the other hand is like Sajiro at his most reserved. He nods to me but doesn't offer to shake my hand or, god forbid, hug me. Sajiro is making a statement by taking this opportunity, in front of everyone gathered for the wedding, to make plain his relationship to me. *Why?* I wonder. I don't think it has all that much to do with me and our actual relationship.

A waiting period ensues, while the bride and groom go off to prepare for the ceremony. Two long lines of tables face each other with an aisle down the middle. We sit at chairs along the groom side. A Shinto *tokonoma* altar is at one end, cluttered with an odd assortment of items including several dolls wrapped in plastic. I have no idea what that's about. I'll ask Sajiro or Momoko about it later. A white tent-like structure held up by four poles stands in front of the *tokonoma*. A *chuppah?* The groom's family is on the left side, with the bride and her family along the right side. Sajiro, the oldest male other than his brother sits at the head of the table with his uncle and his aunt. I'm way down near the end of the table sitting with Momoko and Aki. Momoko has explained that if Sajiro and I were married, I would have been right next to him, but because I'm a guest, and new to the family and everyone else, that was not considered proper. *By whom?* I wonder.

We are all arranged and sitting when the bride and groom appear. I almost gasp when they enter, walking slowly. They have been transformed. Taro wears a black kimono with just a hint of white showing at the lapel. Yua is in a magnificent brocaded white kimono that makes what I had put on the day before look like a simple robe. Her head is covered by a large white hood. Both Yua and Taro are wearing white *tabi* socks and white slippers. They walk slowly down the aisle until they are facing the altar. Taro bows formally to Yua and an attendant removes the white hood to reveal her hair. It's a wig formed into great arching shiny oiled waves and decorated with colorful ornaments. I notice Yua's face is whiter than normal and her lips are ruby red.

The ceremony goes by in a blur. Momoko told me it would have a bit of Shintoism and some Jewish parts. Apart from the *chuppah*, the only thing that is vaguely recognizable to me from Jewish weddings I've attended is when Taro steps on a glass wrapped in a cloth to break it. And there's the *san-san-ku-do* ceremony that Momoko had told me about, the bride and groom drinking three cups of saké. Thankfully it's not a long ceremony.

After the ceremony we move to a place at the side of the hall where bleachers are set up for the formal photographs. Everything is being done at the height of Japanese efficiency. The picture-taking process goes quickly and smoothly. I'm not included in any of the family pictures, but Sajiro makes a point of having our picture taken separately by the photographer, a moment that attracts disapproving looks from many of the older family members.

When photography is over, we are again shepherded along to a side reception room set up with tables for dinner. The newly married couple sit at a side table on a platform in their formal wear. Guests greet them, handing over envelopes that the bride puts in the sleeves of her kimono. After a while, the bride and groom make an exit and the guests find their seats at the tables. I'm delighted to once again not be at center stage. I'm with the young cousins, and Momoko and Aki are by my side. They've been my saving grace, keeping me informed, entertained, and involved while at the same time preventing me from making any terrible social errors, at least thus far. An open bar is set up to one side and many of the guests are leaving their seats to mingle around the bar. I go and order a large gin and tonic. I put up two fingers to suggest that it be a strong one. The bartender, a Filipino worker, smiles at me. I have a hunch he knows what I'm going through.

I'm standing by a large column sipping my drink and watching the interactions around me, about as much of an outsider as one can possibly be, when I feel a hand on my elbow.

"Are you okay?" Sajiro asks, standing straight and apart from me even though he has just gently touched my elbow.

"Was it hard to be a complete outsider when you first went to San Francisco?" I ask.

"No. There I have the Tribe, and my mother. California, at least San Francisco, is a crazy welcoming place. Not like Japan that doesn't welcome strangers except on the surface. I miss San Francisco."

"Why did you bring me here, to this?" I wave my drink towards the crowd. Sajiro looks unsure of how to answer. I add: "I think you want to prove something to your family. I'm here to help you do that."

Before Sajiro can answer, soft rock music starts to play as the bride and groom reenter the room. Yua is wearing a full-length western-style wedding dress, designed like an elegant white evening gown. The wig is gone, and her own hair is tied back with colorful silk ribbons leaving long tendrils to frame her face. She looks incredibly beautiful and chic. Taro is wearing a dark blue tuxedo.

Sajiro bends toward me and whispers in my ear, "Let's talk tomorrow. Meet me by the fountain in the garden at two o'clock. Let's go for a walk. I know a nice short trail."

I nod. We drift away from one another, as everyone is heading towards their seats for the lavish dinner. I make two more trips to the open bar. When dinner is over, I'm more than ready to go back to my room to sleep it off.

As we're leaving, Momoko guides me along, keeping me safe. The bride and groom appear one more time, in jeans and T-shirts, ready to drive off for their honeymoon.

The next afternoon, I'm seated in the garden by the fountain waiting for Sajiro. I have my planner with me and am making notes. It's clear to me that I won't be able to stay for any other Jewish-Japanese events. It's all too weird, too far outside my world. There have been wonderful moments being in Japan with Sajiro, especially at the *onsen*. Watching him connect to his religion has inspired me. But it's painful watching him struggle having me here. And it's clear there's nothing for me here. I must leave.

When Sajiro appears, looking sweet and handsome in blue jeans and a black T-shirt, we head off down a path that takes us away from the compound. After we've walked a while in silence, we come to a log that has fallen across the path. We sit straddling the log, facing one another. Sajiro speaks first: "I brought you here for my own personal reasons. I needed a strong way to say 'no' to my family. I apologize. I'm sorry I did that. I needed to show them that I can't come back to Japan. I can't marry as my brother Taro has done. I need my freedom. I'll stay for the next ceremony, *Ontohsai, the sacrifice of Isaac.* That's the big one. After that I go back to San Francisco. I am going to email Chuck to see if the Shasta property is moving ahead. That will be a wonderful power spot for our group. I think I also helped you. Making love the way we have has brought you back into the world, at least part way. It is something I will always cherish."

The tears come before I can reply. *Yes,* I think. *Sajiro helped me by being kind, by inviting me into his life. Other parts I must heal myself.*

"I'm leaving," I say. Sajiro jumps up so quickly he almost falls over. His eyes are wide with surprise. "I'm going to say my goodbyes to Momoko and Aki, and then I'd like you to help me make arrangements to leave. I've loved being with you," I say. "But I have to go."

"Will I see you in San Francisco?" Sajiro asks.

I don't say anything, but I'm thinking *probably not.*

Sajiro is silent. I can tell that I've hurt him, but I had to say what was in my heart. He sits back down and takes my hands in his hands. I don't resist, but there's no warmth in my gesture either. We sit on the log for a time, occasionally looking into each other's eyes but more often looking away, into the underbrush, no views here. Having made my decision, I'm conflicted. Relief and panic are engaged in a tug-of-war inside me. I need to go, as soon as possible, so that I don't suffer a complete meltdown here at Sajiro's family home.

When I say my goodbyes, Momoko and Aki are sad to see me go, but not Sajiro's aunt and uncle, though they are unfailingly polite. I'm a disruption to the harmony, a strange and vulnerable *gaijin* whose emotions are too close to the surface for the reserved Japanese family. I'm also an unspoken challenge.

Sajiro makes it easy for me. That night he takes me away to Tokyo. We stay a night in a fancy high-rise hotel in the center of the city, the kind of place Bill Murray and Scarlett Johansson frequented in *Lost in Translation*. It's not just expensive, it's ridiculously expensive, but Sajiro tells me not to worry about it. He books me a first-class ticket to San Francisco by changing my return flight and upgrading using miles he has accumulated from many trips back and forth. We eat dinner at a trendy *robatayaki* place where you have to know somebody to get a reservation. Sajiro does know people. He's not just a weird Jewish-Japanese man. He's a highly respected figure from an ancient family. Is he trying to dazzle me at the last

moment with the hotel, the restaurant, the flight? I
don't know. I try to be cheerful and intimate with him,
but in my mind I'm halfway home already, and I just
want to be gone.

Back at the hotel, we make love quietly, enjoying
each other's bodies for what I know in my heart is the
last time, in the massive king-size bed with its satin
sheets and samurai-themed wall hangings—a fantasy
hotel room for the rich.

I wonder what's wrong with me. I wish I could
accept this gentle, intelligent man. I've enjoyed myself
with Sajiro and some of what I've experienced in
Japan. At the same time, it's clear that I can't be the
wife or mate of this man. Sajiro, the Lost Tribe, are not
my future. I'm not worried about Sajiro. He's had other
women, other followers before, and will have them
again. I know this. It's part of why I can't stay with
him. Mostly it's because I need to find my own path,
my own true self. The death of Dan and baby Ella is a
low-level stream of pain that I'll likely swim in for the
rest of my life.

The next morning, we order room service, western
style breakfast—granola with yoghurt and fruit, steak
and eggs(!), and excellent coffee. We sit at a table with
a view of Tokyo.

"It's been wonderful being with you. Thank you for
coming to Japan with me. It made things clear for me
also," Sajiro tells me. "I'll take you to the airport."

I smile. I want to be kind to Sajiro, but I want a
break now. I can't face a goodbye scene at the airport.

"Sajiro, let's say goodbye here. I'll order a cab at the desk. It'll be better. The airport is so crazy."

He smiles, takes a deep breath, and nods agreement. He packs his things quickly. We hold each other one last time and after a gentle kiss between us, he is gone. I sit staring blankly at the crazy business of Tokyo stretched out below the window. Next thing I know, I've dialed my mother's phone. She answers.

"Hi Mom, sorry if I am calling too late."

"No, honey, I am always glad to hear your voice."

"I'm going back to San Francisco by myself. This was a completely absurd wrong turn for me. I'm so stupid, such a fool."

"You are no such thing. You are my incredible and amazing daughter. You are doing just what you need to do. I wish you could be here with me for a bit. Why not schedule a trip when you get back to the States? I could meet you in Boston. Perhaps you can make an appointment to see Sarah to rebalance yourself?"

"I don't know, Mom," I say weakly. Talking to her is triggering memories and emotions.

"Honey, I have some news," my mother says. "Frank and I are going our separate ways."

"Oh Mom, I'm so sorry." Wow, I'm not the only one going through turmoil. I always think my troubles surpass everyone else's. "I feel terrible Mom. I'll call you when I get back. Let's talk. Perhaps we should meet up. I'll call. Gotta go catch a cab to the airport."

"Okay, call me soon. Love you." We hang up.

BOOK II   THE BON VIVANTS

Chapter 11 The Bon Vivants

I call Jane from the Narita airport in Tokyo to give her some advance warning that I'm coming back early. I'm looking forward to being back in the apartment, to talking with Jane about what has happened with Sajiro. She has been my only real friend in San Francisco. I sense an air of reserve in her voice when I ask how she is doing, and she tells me that her boyfriend Joe is moving in. I know I should be happy for her, but I'm not.

"Hey, that's great," I say, my stomach knotting up. I force a happy tone to my voice.

"Look, let's talk when you get here. I do want to hear about the trip and why you're coming back so soon. You can stay here for, uh, a while. I'll have to talk to Joe." Her voice trails off and I realize it will have to be a short while.

"Hey, thanks for taking me in even though it might be inconvenient. I really appreciate that. See you soon."

After I board the plane, I take a couple sleeping pills and pass the entire flight in a stupor. *What am I going to do?* The question circles and repeats itself over and over in my unconscious brain. Toward morning, I drink some coffee and try to think. Leaving Japan was the right thing to do. I know that. But instead of being liberated, I'm in a panic. My mother's suggestions to come home, be with her, see my therapist, have great appeal; they might keep me from slipping back into a world of despair. But I can't do the easy thing even if it

might be the right thing. Being with Sajiro taught me
something. It opened my eyes to the fact that I need to
find my own path, or I'll slip and slide into total
darkness again. I must make a go of it on my own.

When I arrive at Jane's apartment, it's awkward
from the start. I enjoyed the room I had and the
comfort of the Japanese style of things, but now that
Joe is around, things are tight. Sharing a bathroom
most of the time is not fun.

"I'll get a place in the next week or so if I can," I tell
Jane at breakfast. She is sympathetic and kind, but
when Joe is around, they're naturally extremely
involved with one another and remote. I sleep through
a day because of the jet lag and then start my housing
search. I buy the paper, register for some online
apartment sites and search in earnest. I realize how
lucky I had been to land at Jane's. San Francisco is
preposterously expensive. The hi-tech millennials have
taken over everything. The old, relatively cheap
neighborhoods of the city, where the workers who built
downtown had put up their Craftsman cottages, in
places like the Outer Mission and Noe Valley, are no
longer even remotely affordable. I still haven't received
my insurance settlement. My lawyer tells me it'll be
another few months. I'm scraping by on the last of my
savings and help from my mother. I expand my search
and start looking in the East Bay, where prices are still
incredibly high, but within the realm of possibility. In
two days, I look at a dozen places, taking Uber rides
between them. They're all dreadful. Too much money
for what they offer or are in borderline or outright

dangerous neighborhoods. I check Airbnb, but they're also expensive and for the most part just offer a short-term solution at hotel rates. On the third morning, I'm anxiously scanning the ads in the East Bay paper when I notice an ad, not for an apartment, but for a part-time job as assistant property manager in a multi-unit building. It comes with a "private room," whatever that means. I look up the address on my phone map. It's down along the flats near the freeway in an industrial part of Oakland, but at this point the idea of finding a place to live and making money at the same time is appealing, regardless of the location. I make an appointment with somebody named Max who claims to be the apartment manager, and take BART, what the locals call the Bay Area Rapid Transit system. I'm pleased to be getting familiar with the lingo and with how to get around. I take the train and then a bus just to see how difficult it would be to live in the zone of warehouses and the spaghetti coil of highway offramps down by the water near the foot of the Bay Bridge. The address is in a neighborhood called Jingletown, south of Jack London Square and just off the Alameda. When the bus drops me off, I can't believe this is the place. There don't appear to be residential units anywhere, just warehouses, a cement plant, and boarded-up abandoned buildings with razor wire guarding them. I locate the address and stand outside in disbelief. I can still read the words "Industrial Laundry" in faded stencil along the front wall. It's so depressing I decide I'll skip it and just cross the street and wait for the bus back to downtown Oakland.

I'm about to do that when a satyr with black curly hair and wild eyes opens the heavy door to the building and peers out at me like he hasn't seen the sun in many days. "Are you Maya?" he asks. I nod. "Well, come in, come in. I'm Max. We talked."

"What is this place?" I ask. Part of me, the sensible side, tells me I should just turn around and walk away, but there's something sweet, genuine, and almost innocent about the guy that makes me follow him in. As the door closes behind me and my eyes adjust to the filtered interior light, everything changes. The entire center of the building is a gigantic atrium, filled with plants and trees, some thirty feet tall, around the edge of the opening to the sky, the center area cleared out as a performance space. Vines hang down and entwine the railings in elegant sweeps of green. A walkway runs around the second floor, with apartment doors every few yards on both the ground and upper story. There's a strange echo to what I am seeing. It reminds me of an urban, blue-collar version of Sajiro's family home, a verdant inner space that in this case belies and contradicts the harsh industrial exterior world. The trees offer shade, and the space is open to the sky.

I can see the delight on Max's face. He must be used to this incredulous reaction when people first enter.

"It's my home," says Max, his eyes twinkle but then there is a raucous laugh that follows. "And the home of the Bon Vivants." I cringe and stop following Max where he is leading me, toward the stairs to the second floor in the corner of the building.

"You're not some kind of group or religious cult, are you?" I ask. It would be just my bad luck for that to happen again.

Max's laugh is more like a howl. "Hell no!" he says. "This is the place where everyone does their own thing. We party together, we appreciate each other's work, but other than that, it's every man and woman for his or herself!" I've trailed behind him as he didn't stop when I stopped, and when I catch up to him, he's twisting the doorknob on one of the apartments. "Check it out!" he says grandly and throws open the door.

A bewildering array of twisted metal pieces meets my eyes. They're sculptures, many of them done in rusted iron, all of them abstracts, none resembling creatures or humans or anything else recognizable. "This is where I live and work. We have writers, artists, musicians, a couple bands, all living together. It's grand! Wild!" He stops for a moment, "Are you okay with wild?" he asks.

I don't know what to say. I've heard about terrible fires in funky communal spaces. "As long as it's safe," I say.

Max's face turns serious for a moment. "Yes, safe. We do everything to code here."

"I need a place to stay, so I'm not picky. The ad mentioned a part-time job?"

"Yeah, yeah, shuah! And keeping us safe, property management, that'll be part of your job, if you take it."

I catch a whiff of a Boston or New England accent in his speech. "Come on, I'll show you your digs, if you want them. All ya have to do is help me with a little janitorial and management, collecting the rents. That's not as hard as it sounds. We're artists, but we're not starving artists. Some of us are getting to be successful. Like, I'm having a show at the Breit Gallery next month. Heard of it?" I had to admit I hadn't. "Well, never mind. You'll go, I mean, if you want to." Max has left his place with the door wide open and jog-walked down to the end of the corridor. As I follow along, I peer down into the atrium. It's surprisingly beautiful, plants in bloom, sunlight filtering through the leaves of the larger trees. I note a couple large marijuana plants in one corner. Rhododendrons as big as those in Golden Gate Park! Max pushes open the last door in the row. "This one is too small to rent as an apartment, but it might suit someone like you. It's got its own john, and it's got nice light. If you like light," he says, and again comes that wild mischievous laugh. The bathroom is the tiniest bathroom I have ever seen, but it has all the basics. Tub, miniscule sink, toilet. Industrial style rectangular windows high on the wall line up in a long row across the back of the studio. A countertop with a bar sink next to an apartment size refrigerator. *I could live here*, I think.

"Sign me up," I say. "Do you want to see my resume or references?"

Max just looks at me. At one point he closes his eyes and just stands there. Then he says, "Let's have a beer in my place and you can tell me about yourself."

Back in his apartment, Max sets out a couple of glasses, two bottles of Anchor Steam beer and a plate with crackers, cheese, and some delicate pastries. "I made these myself," Max says as he offers me a taste.

The taste is delicate and spicy at the same time. Max can see I am surprised, and he smiles happily. We talk for an hour. I learn that Max inherited family money that enabled him to buy the building in partnership with another fellow, a restaurateur named Jacques Cardinal. Max works exclusively as a metal sculptor. He's surrounded himself with a lively group of characters: musicians, writers, dancers. He calls himself and these tenants "the Bon Vivants" and is proud to enable a creative chaos, along with a sometimes-raucous party atmosphere. He hates the details of running the place and Jacques is too busy with the restaurant. Max needs administrative support.

I tell Max that I worked in a law firm after college for three years. That I was even considering going to law school, but then my life took a bad turn. I am shocked at myself when I blurt out my story, the accident, finally leaving Boston, the past months with Sajiro and a weird Jewish-Japanese cult. My dash back to San Francisco and losing my place at Jane's. I'm trying to hold it together but soon tears are running down my cheeks. I grab a napkin and take a deep breath. Instead of being put off, Max makes a surprising gesture. He raises his beer glass to me.

"That's what we like here, we Bon Vivants. Real life, with all its joys and sorrows. I toast your future happiness," he says with such gravitas and sincerity that a laugh breaks through my quiet sobbing.

"If this is a job interview," I say, "it is the strangest job interview I could ever imagine."

Max just sits there for a minute, takes a sip of his beer, a bite of a pastry and says: "When can you move in?"

"How much does it pay?" I ask.

"I don't know. I hadn't even thought about that part. How about free rent and $1,500 a month to start? For managing the rental income and light janitorial, just sweeping and swabbing. If anything breaks, we call the plumber.

"I could move in on the weekend," I say.

"Great. I'll bring over the paperwork I need you to handle, and you can start right away."

Max drops me off at the BART station, so I don't have to take a bus. On the train, I think about what I have just agreed to. My story elicited a great kindness from the wild-looking sculptor. It's unclear how much work "light janitorial" constitutes and exactly how extreme or derelict the place may get. In fact, as I think about it, everything is about as unclear as it could possibly be. I know nothing about the place, the people, or the situation. I don't care. I need to leave Jane and Joe. I need to keep moving forward. I'll meet the tenants, see what it's like to live in an industrial neighborhood, and go from there.

Back at Jane's I'm delighted to find no one is there. As I start to pack up my stuff and clean up my room, a strange sadness takes hold of me. Am I missing Sajiro?

I look at myself in the mirror. I see myself. I see loneliness. I smile at myself and shake out my hair. I look pretty, almost like myself.

I sit down on the low purple chair at the desk to make a list of what I need to do:

1. *Shop for some absolute basics for the apartment*
2. *Call Sarah?*
3. *Call Mom*

Before Jane and Joe show up, I take a last Japanese-style bath, luxuriating in the tub, thinking back to the wonderful Japanese baths and hot springs of my trip to Japan. It's so odd. The Japanese culture is appealing to me with its almost dainty charm, its emphasis on simplicity. I liked Sajiro's body and how we were in bed. I made good friends in the Tribe. I don't miss him. Or the Tribe. Something empty at the core of our relationship keeps me from any thought of rushing back to him when he returns. I'd have to say it was him, his bland acceptance of his role as leader. Though he gave me his full attention when I was with him, it could just as easily have been someone else, as there undoubtedly had been and would be again. I am not meant to play the role of the king's consort of the moment. For Dan Brown, my beloved Dan, I was the only one, and that made all the difference.

I don't have to rent a truck to move. I make a couple BART/bus trips over the next couple of days. Max had given me keys at our first meeting, and I am free to come and go.

Sunday morning is my last at Jane's apartment. Jane, Joe, and I have a cup of strong coffee and some croissants. They are a beautiful and unlikely couple. Joe's the *gaijin*, the blond white guy who towers over Jane. I can see the love in his clear blue eyes when he looks at Jane and now that I have a place to go and am relaxed about leaving, I'm happy for Jane. I'm sure they are happy to see me go.

"Boy did I miss my morning coffee in Japan. Just rice and fish and fish and rice, at every meal." Joe and Jane laugh and reach out to hold hands with one another.

"I have something to tell you," Jane says. She looks uncomfortable and I wonder if I have done something to upset her. Perhaps I have really been there too long, completely overstaying my welcome. What she says next catches me completely off-guard.

"You pretty much brought me back to my life," she begins. "Got me on track. I've been wanting to tell you that. You were the right person at the right time. In some subconscious way, I knew you would understand, and I was able to tell you what happened to me. You said all the right things and told me of your unimaginable-to-me sorrow. I really want to thank you."

I'm stunned. Tears well up and I smile through them.

"You certainly saved our relationship," Joe adds. He's still holding Jane's hand and he reaches out to hold mine across the table. I'm happy for them and for myself. Somehow even in all my pain, I helped them.

Over the next days, I spend time fixing up my studio. There's a loft space where I put the blow-up bed

I've purchased along with some crate boxes for end-tables that I found in the storage room. To get up to the loft, there's a ladder, but I'm comforted by the railing around the edges of the loft. There's just enough room for a table and chair, also pilfered from the storage room. I can sit and look up at the blue California sky without seeing any of the industrial buildings.

Over the next days, I wander out and am surprised to discover that the neighborhood I thought was just an industrial wasteland harbors hidden gems—a fantastic café run by African Americans that serves only Ethiopian coffee and food. An old-fashioned hardware store where I find many things I need to fix up my new digs. And, wonder of wonders, a used clothing store with all kinds of colorful items from the global mélange culture that inhabits this corner of Oakland. I think I may have stumbled on one of the last corners of the Bay Area that has kept its character alive. Even this place is on the verge of gentrification—rents going up, people of color moving out.

On Friday night, I bring in some food for an early dinner. I'm tired from all the walking and schlepping of furniture. I sit in the tub and use a shower attachment to wash my hair. Cleaning oneself before bathing reminds me of Japan. I get all squeaky clean and then sit and fill the tub with hot water. Finally, I get in my PJs for a quiet night, when a party breaks out in the atrium below. I peek out over the railing. Max has brought two enormous grills into the parking lot and there's a culinary competition going on to see who can make the most smoke and flame as they cook. A band has set up in the center of the atrium. My anticipated quiet evening of sleep is shattered. It's like being inside a bass speaker. Despite a couple loud knocks on my door during the evening, I keep to myself. I'm not ready to meet the Bon Vivants *en masse*. I put on my Bose headset and play meditative music, but that too is overwhelmed by the sounds that rise from below. The next morning I'm surprised to find that the atrium is not a littered mess. Black plastic bags are stuffed full and placed in a corner. The ground beneath the trees needs raking. That's about it. I see Max only briefly because he's busy moving some of his sculptures to the gallery for his upcoming show.

"That was quite the party last night," I say in passing.

"Oh, no, that was just our Friday night get-together. Wait till we have a real blow-out."

After doing minimal sweeping and clean-up of the main area I go back up to my room. I get out a tote bag that I hadn't opened when I was at Jane's. I hang the few items of clothing on the industrial rack in one corner of the room. It's black steel with a bar across the top and three shelves about a foot and half high at the bottom—the perfect closet for a post-industrial laundry apartment. At the bottom of the sack is the package from Sarah in the Trident Bookstore wrapping paper. I send Sarah a quick text asking when would be a good time to chat. Just as I'm unwrapping the book, the phone rings.

"Hi Maya," Sarah says. "I am so glad to hear from you. How are you?"

"I'm just unwrapping the book you gave me. Oh, it's a blank. Like me. How lovely. Thank you."

"Yes, it's empty, but you can fill it up. Just like you." I envision Sarah's professional, noncommittal smile as she says this. I tell Sarah that I've been keeping a bit of a journal in my daybook and that's been helpful, and that now I want to start writing more. We chat and I ask if I can set up phone sessions with her, not right away, maybe in a few weeks or months. I thank her again for the journal, and we leave it at that.

Next, I text my mother. She calls me right back also. We chat for a while. At least just for this moment, I'm the one checking on her and wanting to be sure she's okay. We agree on a weekly time to check in: Sunday afternoon or evening.

After the calls, I'm claustrophobic. I can't stay in the studio any longer. I go down to the atrium and sit in one of the chairs near the marijuana plants in the corner. My feet are up on some weird foot stool, or is it a sculpture? The air is clean and fresh from the oxygen the trees and hanging vines supply.

My phone pings and I see a text from Max: "Dinner tonight. My place. Just Jacques and Taisha. Eight o'clock."

"I'll be there," I type and I'm glad for the contact and the chance to meet some of the players of this wild space. "What can I bring?"

"Got you covered," Max answers. I walk out to a local liquor store and buy a bottle of decent California red anyway so as not to arrive empty-handed. Something is changing. New pathways are opening in front of me, here in this odd industrial setting. I'm almost enjoying myself. Max's place is just doors down from mine on the second floor, but we haven't been crossing paths much yet. He hasn't asked me to do anything more than a little sweeping. Around the appointed time I knock on his door, but no one answers. I wait around, knock again, and—nothing. I'm just about to leave when I see Max plowing through the front door downstairs with two bags of groceries. He lurches up the stairs and sets everything down triumphantly. "Running late," is all he says. He opens the door to his place, which I had forgotten but am instantly reminded is a mass of twisted metal sculptures, and shepherds me in.

"What about Jacques and Taisha?" I ask.

"They're late too," Max says. He's already in motion, washing tomatoes, chopping onions, setting the table, all at once. He reminds me of one of his sculptures, all twists and turns and manic energy. I offer to help, and he sets me to peeling potatoes, while at the same time taking my bottle from my hands, opening it, and pouring us each a hearty glass in mason jars that double as wine glasses.

"Don't we want to save some for your guests?" I ask, wishing I'd brought more than one bottle of wine.

"Oh, no," Max says. "What is this? Old Vine Zin from Lodi, nice, but I'm afraid Jacques would disapprove. He'll bring the wine, and his own wine glasses."

"Oh," I say, having never heard of anyone bringing their own wine glasses to dinner. What do I know? I soon learn that Jacques Cardinal is 30 years old, that he's from Quebec, but according to Max has pretensions of Frenchness, and that he runs a bistro called "Le Mistral." "You must eat there some time soon," Max says. "It's not far from here. Jacques believes that his cooking is on the same level with Picasso's art and Satie's music. I think having artist types around him inspires him and it makes him more creative."

"I see," I say. Even though I really don't. "And what about Taisha?"

"Ah, Taisha. There are no words. When you meet her, you'll see. She's the inspiration for this place."

I learn more about Taisha as Max swirls around the kitchen. At one point he sets me to stirring a simmering pot of spicy sausages in a fresh tomato and basil red sauce. He works fast and talks fast as he goes.

"Taisha is the heart of the matter, the why of the space. She's a professor of Black Women's Literature at Mills College and a writer. It was her vision to have a salon-type place and that's what we have created in this space."

Max stops for a minute and waves the knife he is using to cut up fresh parsley in an inclusive gesture that takes in all his surroundings.

"It's this fantastic living and working space that we all share. The Laundry!"

I understand by the way Max talks about Taisha that she is the force and inspiration and that he and Jacques are following her lead. It resonates with me. Might be damn good to be in a woman-inspired place for a while.

"Are Jacques and Taisha married?" I ask.

Max laughs his high-pitched raucous laugh and says, "They're the First Couple of the Bon Vivants. I never asked if they were married. This was their idea. I came up with the name, but they're the ones who want this place to be a salon. I'm just one of the lucky few."

A knock on the door, and in sweep the First Couple, arm-in-arm, laughing. Jacques is short, a bit hunched over, large aquiline nose, every inch the Francophile that Max said he was. Taisha is statuesque, with a hefty Afro, liquid brown eyes, perfect teeth, and a no-nonsense expression.

"Max, my man!" Jacques says and gives Max a hug. Taisha does the same, but silently.

"Jacques, Taisha, this is our new assistant apartment manager and resident of The Laundry, Maya Marinovich."

"Hello," I say, hands at my sides. Taisha sticks out her smooth ebony arm with bright red-colored nails at the ends of her fingers. I shake hands with her firm grip. Jacques is inspecting the food prep already, rolling up his sleeves, he nods in my direction, but doesn't bother with formal introductions.

"You have an alliterative name," Taisha says. Later on, I understand why she says that, but at the time it makes no sense at all.

We open the wines, unpack some dramatically balloon-like wine glasses that we line up along a shelf and settle in to chat and drink while the men cook together noisily, with much laughter.

"Sometimes I think Max should go work in the restaurant as well as being a sculptor. He brings such crazy energy and laughter to all his creations," Taisha says. We sit quietly for a minute and she turns and looks at me, focusing on me with her brown eyes like pools encompassing all. I am not uncomfortable, but there is an intensity in her that makes me alert and I wonder what to expect.

"Everyone has something to offer at The Laundry," Taisha says. "Max has his sculptures, and Jacques has his cuisine. What do you offer, Maya?" Taisha asks me.

Don't ask me why, but at that moment I remember that Taisha is part of the name of the Shinto shrine Suwa Taisha where Sajiro's older brother got married. How weird is that?

"I offer my sadness," I say, without tearing up at all. I don't have to. I'm pretty sure that Max has told her some of my story and besides, I'm transparent.

"That's beautiful," Taisha says. "You'll write about it someday."

"How do you know?" I ask, as surprised as if Taisha had glimpsed into my blank journal.

"Oh, I had you pegged for a writer right away. Takes one to know one."

"I haven't written anything yet," I say apologetically.
"Doesn't matter. You will." I'm simultaneously
pleased and taken aback by Taisha's presumption.

I'm enjoying just listening as she tells me about the
classes she's teaching at the college, what it's like, the
students, and how few are motivated and talented. I
ask if there are mostly African Americans in her
classes or if white students are also drawn to them as
well. She raises an eyebrow at the question, giving me
a smirk, but doesn't answer directly. I'm betting she
must be an inspiring professor. I tell her more about
my academic background, college, what I had been
thinking of doing when I was working at the law firm.

"You're a writer, not a lawyer," Taisha says.
"Although I do know some pretty good lawyers who
gave it all up to become writers."

I tell her how my therapist had encouraged me to
write a journal and almost choke up.

The frenetic cooking goes on for a long time, but
when dinner is served it's a relaxed affair. We sit
around the heavy wood table and Jacques and Max
take turns at bringing out course after course, each
one more subtle and delicious than the one before.
Each one on its own plate. Three kinds of pasta. A rich
and heavy Potatoes Anna. Multiple salads. A cheese
plate with artisanal cheeses from up north.

After dinner we sit in the one area of Max's art-
crowded apartment that has a couch and couple of
well-used stuffed chairs. The coffee table in the middle
is another crazy sculpture. Taisha brings in two
bottles, a Cognac and an Armagnac along with some

fancy crystal glasses and a dish of dark chocolates. The men sit with us a while, but soon are back in the kitchen talking and laughing again. Taisha and I sit on the couch, our shoulders touching lightly. It reminds me of the ease the members of the Tribe had in being physical with one another and how I was never quite comfortable with that casual physicality. I'm surprised how easy I am with Taisha. It could be the countless number of glasses of wine I have had and the apéritifs that are topping everything off rather nicely.

Taisha starts to tell me about her ideas for meetings at The Laundry. Poetry readings, book parties, music, dance. It's all starting to happen. She gets out her phone and shows me pictures of past events.

"Now you show me some pictures," Taisha says.

"I can't. I haven't looked at any pictures for such a long time. I don't think I can."

"No just some recent ones. Not going way back."

I'm okay with recent photos. I fumble for my phone, open it and hit the photo icon. We flip through photos of me with Sajiro in Japan.

"Handsome," Taisha smiles. "Very."

A picture of Dan, Ella, and me pops up. Suddenly I'm holding a napkin to my face. Taisha puts her arms around me and holds me to her breast. I rest against her. We hear crashing of dishes coming from the kitchen. Max and Jacques are cleaning up. After a bit Taisha releases me and stands up. She isn't drunk at all, even though she's had at least as much wine and liqueur as me. "I have something for you. Wait here."

Tall and elegant, she strides out of the apartment. She's gone for only a minute or so and returns with a book that she hands me without ceremony.

"Read this." I read the cover: *Monkey*, by Wu Ch'êng-ên. Translated by Arthur Waley.

"What's it about?" I ask. I'm not in great shape for a literary discussion, and this is an odd book to give me as I sit on the couch crying. Instead of answering my question, Taisha says:

"Hey, Let's have coffee tomorrow morning. Late. I'm taking the day off. I'd like to talk with you more about the book and your life." Taisha squeezes my hand. Max and Jacques come in from the kitchen and the spell between us is broken. I'm not used to partying this hardy and find myself almost dozing off. When I start to excuse myself for the end of the evening, Taisha walks me out the door and keeps an arm around me as we walk to the back of the building to my place.

"This is my place," Taisha says, pointing to a door we pass that has a poster of what I guess is a Chinese goddess on it. Even in my drunken state I sense the peaceful power emanating from the picture.

When we get to my door, Taisha says: "Pilgrim Maya, welcome to The Laundry. See you tomorrow morning around eleven."

I wake up the next morning surprisingly early, shocked that I don't have even a trace of a headache. I remember that I'm going to be having coffee with Taisha later in the morning, but I need to get out, to walk. I put on an old pair of jeans and my walking shoes, sling my bag over my shoulder. I stop and look at the book for a minute and then throw it in my bag.

On the walkway, I pass Taisha's door and take a long look at the poster. The goddess figure is seated on a red cushion, or is it a lotus blossom? She's beautiful and serene. Green water swirls around her. In the atrium I take out my phone and order an Uber ride to Mills College where Taisha is teaching. I walk around the peaceful campus. It's an oasis tucked into the bustle and density of Oakland. I find a coffee shop outside of the college and sit and read, not *Monkey* but the morning paper. I'm back at The Laundry by ten. I sit in my tub and clean myself completely. Fill my tub and soak and relax. *What a strange book*, I think. I've only glanced at the preface. Why would Taisha want me to read it? What is she seeing in me?

At eleven I find myself again in front of the poster and knocking on Taisha's door. When she answers, I enter a space as elegant as she is. All the art, the wall hangings reflect her African-Americanness—a Masai warrior, a poster of Jimi Hendrix. Many, many books, with shelves lining the walls wherever art isn't taking up the space. The whole vibe is strongly feminine, and powerfully black. There isn't anything of Jacques in the place.

"Doesn't Jacques live here?" I ask. I learn that they each have separate loft spaces, side-by-side. You have to go outside to the walkway and knock to enter each space.

Taisha brings out a pot of coffee, fruit, whole grain pastries and a frittata, still warm in a cast-iron pan.

We're awkward together after our booze-enabled closeness of the night before. Taisha makes me a plate of food and pours us both coffees.

"I got up really early and walked around your college. Lovely."

"Did you start *Monkey*?" Taisha asks. I knew she would ask me. She's direct that way.

"I brought it with me, but, no, I didn't start it yet. I can tell it's a strange book, though. What's it about?"

"It's the famous story of the journey that the monk Tripitaka makes from China to India to bring Buddhist scriptures back to China. The story shows up in many plays, movies, even TV shows."

"What's Monkey got to do with it?"

"Monkey's a rascally character who is assigned by the Bodhisattva-Kuan-yin, that's her on my door, to accompany the monk on his journey along with a couple of other weird sidekicks—Pigsy-the-pig and Sandy-the-horse. The Monkey is also known as the 'Great Sage, Equal to Heaven.'"

I hardly know what to say. "Kuan-yin?"

"The goddess of mercy and compassion. She makes Monkey act as Tripitaka's bodyguard."

Since I can't get away from the strange monkey business, I finally ask, "Why give this book to me?"

"Maya, you're also on a powerful and strange voyage. You've become a pilgrim like Tripitaka, without wanting or intending to be one. You'll find your way back. You're a Seeker, like the Chinese monk." I just sit and listen. What Taisha is saying reverberates with what my therapist Sarah told me back in Boston.

Taisha continues: "I'm around young people and older folks who want to tell their stories. They need to express themselves. Many of them don't start out with much in the way of talent. Most of them don't have the fortitude to keep trying and to work to develop the talent. Most of them never finish a book. Teaching over these years has given me a sense of when someone will benefit from the writing path and do the work that's required. Because it's hard work." I recall Sarah telling me the same thing about therapy, that it's hard work but rewarding. I don't say anything. I'm just sitting, sipping my coffee, listening, and being drawn in. "You have a story to tell. You're a writer. I have no doubt about it."

"I'm a poet and I don't know it?" I joke.

"Exactly. It's not too much of a spoiler to tell you that the monk Tripitaka meets the Buddha. If you follow your path, I predict that you will also meet the Buddha."

"What?! I'm not a Buddhist," I protest. "I don't have any religious leanings. I went to Sunday school, got confirmed, and pretty much never went to church once I left my parents' home." Suddenly it feels like I'm in a therapy session with Sarah, and I'm uncomfortable. It took me a long time to trust Sarah, and here I am telling this English professor I hardly know things about myself. Taisha notices my unease and breaks the intensity by asking me if I'd like another piece of frittata.

"Yes, please. Delicious."

As she's cutting me another slice of the warm egg dish, she says, "It won't happen here, though."

"What do you mean, 'here'?"

"The Laundry. This isn't a place for the inward turning that Buddhism and writing require. It's a place for outwardness. Expression. You could use some of that too," Taisha says, laughing at the contradiction, but I understand what she means. I'm coming out of myself, slowly, and to become a nun-like person isn't where I need to go right now. Silently I resolve to put *Monkey* away and read it only when it makes sense for me to do so. As if she could read my thoughts, Taisha says, "Anyway, there's no hurry."

"So, how does this jibe with you being a professor of Black Women's Literature?"

"Now, don't put me in a box, white girl," Taisha answers, and I think that I'm to Taisha like Aki was to me: enthralled by the newness. "Don't make me all Toni Morrison and Maya Angelou. I've got my own thing going. As my man Jimi said"—and here she nods at the poster of the guitarist in fringe and headband, guitar draped around his neck, both hands raised toward the sky in a way that reminds me of one of the Tribe's movements—"*I'm the one that's gonna die when it's time for me to die, so just let me live my life the way I want to.*"

"Sorry, I didn't mean to put you in a box," I say.

"Look, you were the mother of a beautiful black baby. You may not have even understood what that was going to be about. You loved and opened yourself."

I laugh self-consciously. "I was living in Cambridge. Working in Boston. The liberal center of the universe, or at least one of them."

"I know. I know." Taisha says. I can tell she is starting to work up to what might turn into a lecture.

"You know what I try to do, here at The Laundry and everywhere in my life? I try to expand the boundaries. The world's a beautiful, bountiful place. I pray to Kuan-yin. I'm living with, or at least next door to, a Canadian chef who wants to be a Frenchman. I'm hosting parties with people whose music might not be my first choice, but it's different, it's sounds I've never heard before, and that's good for my ears, you see? My friends are sculptors like Max. I want to get the most out of life. Then I want to teach Morrison and Angelou to people who've never heard the caged bird sing."

I get the reference, thank goodness. "Maya Angelou," I repeat. Taisha smiles.

We laugh, drink our coffee, nibble on the pastries, talk about literature.

The next morning I'm up early to escape my room. I'm sitting in the atrium with my planner, trying to think what it is I should be doing with myself. I am restless, I need to move. Walking had been my salvation, first in Boston where I would just keep on going for hours to escape the blackness, and then in San Francisco where I often ended up in the Marina, looking out over the Bay and the Golden Gate Bridge. As beautiful as The Laundry is inside, from the outside it's the height of industrial ugliness.

Suddenly Max comes bursting out of his place with a bicycle.

"Hey," I say. "Where are you off to? Are there places to bike around here?"

"Sure. I take a ride most mornings. I go over the Park Street bridge to Alameda. They've made a kind of highway for bike riders. Alameda has lots of shops and restaurants. That's where Jacque's restaurant is. I'm going there now. Walk with me and I'll show you the way. It takes about ten minutes on the bike, longer if we walk."

"Sorry to slow you down."

"No problem. Good to have a chance to talk."

"I'm buying a bike," I say impulsively. "I was just thinking how much I miss walking, but around here walking isn't so inviting. A car isn't in my budget right now, but a bike could be just the thing."

"Especially in summer when it just doesn't rain much," Max agrees.

"Having a party this Friday. A new band is playing. I could use your help for it," Max says. "I'll take you to Alameda Bicycle. That's where I got this beauty. They call it a commute and pavement bike. Perfect for the city."

"Thanks, Max." We head out and into Alameda on Park Street. On the other side of the bridge, we're immediately in the popular commercial district of restaurants and shops, including the bike store. Without much thought or effort, I buy a new hybrid, a helmet, gloves, a lock, and a neon yellow safety vest that Max insists I get for urban riding. He guides me through the purchase and raises his eyebrows and makes a low whistle when he sees the total I'm spending. Many of our millennial friends, especially my new creative ones, are on a tight budget.

"Cheaper than a car," I say as I put it all on a credit card. *Yes*, I think. *It is expensive and I will have money soon.* Inside my head I turn away from the path that will lead me to all the reasons I will soon have money. Definitely not going there right now.

We pedal over to Le Mistral. Jacques doesn't care that Max is late. He greets me warmly and hands me a steaming café au lait in one of those ridiculously oversized cups that look like a giant's teacup. Max, on the other hand, makes himself a jet-black espresso in an absurdly small cup. Jacques shows me around. Le Mistral is an intimate place, fewer than a dozen tables. A chalkboard replaces menus. Jacques explains that the menu changes daily, depending on what he can find in the markets. I notice there are no salt and pepper shakers on the table, and comment on it.

"My food does not need additional seasoning," Jacques sniffs. "That's *my* job, in the kitchen."

"Whatever you do, don't ask for ketchup for your *steak poivre*," Max whispers to me wickedly. Kitchen prep is underway already for the lunch crowd, and soon I'm just going to be in the way. I say my goodbyes.

"Can you find your way back?" Max asks.

"Sure. GPS." My bike is equipped with a mount on the handlebars for a phone.

"Okay, safe ride," Max says. He's starting to be like the big brother I never had. Jacques has disappeared into the kitchen in the back. I tell Max to say goodbye for me and pedal off. Instead of going straight back to The Laundry, I decide to ride around the Alameda. For an urban setting, it's surprisingly green. There's a bunch of parks, and bike paths everywhere, even a state beach. I take a nice ride along Shore Line Drive, where I can watch the planes taking off from Oakland Airport every couple of minutes. I'll be able to ride over to Alameda, lock up the bike and do some walking in the early mornings.

By the time I make my way back over the Park Street Bridge, my legs are aching. I have the key to the storeroom in the back on the first floor as part of my official duties. I put the bike there, locking it to a pole in the center of the space. Back in my room I jump into the bath to soak my tired body.

Chapter 12 The First Party

For the next few days, I get up early every morning, jump on the bike and go over to Alameda. Sometimes I lock the bike up and walk around the parks and the residential streets for hours. I meet with Max a couple of times. He hands me a bunch of paperwork and some files that need to be put in order for a meeting with the accountant. Asks if I will go with him to that meeting later in the month. It's all about rents and expenses, things Max wants me to handle on a monthly basis. Turns out Max is incredibly sharp and business savvy. I'll learn by doing some of this drudge work so he can focus on his art.

For the party on Friday, Max asks me for help with the setup and buying food. We set a time to meet Friday morning for the food run. Turns out the party is going to be part rock and roll, part dance, and part performance art.

"The rock and roll part's easy," Max says. "Peter Hansen sets up and runs the P.A. system, and the bands bring their own equipment. You'll get to see Ariana and Hannah in action Friday afternoon, planning and coordinating so it can all be free form in the end. Ariana's an artist. She's bringing her whole art class. Hannah's a dancer and dance teacher. She'll either dance solo or bring her students into the mix. Sometimes we all join in. Make sure to wear something wild and comfortable." I have no idea what this means. I briefly consider my skimpy wardrobe and acknowledge to myself that there's nothing "wild" in it. There's always the local thrift store I found. "I haven't met Peter yet. I've met Ariana and Hannah but just in passing," I say. I don't say what I'm really thinking, that those brief meetings were enough for me to experience the strong wind of their forceful, stormy personalities. All the women at The Laundry are forces of nature. When I encountered Ariana a couple days ago my first thought was "banshee." She has a mane of pure white hair, piercing dark eyes, and a formidable handshake. We've only exchanged casual greetings, but right away I have the impression she's searching me, like Taisha but different. Hannah dances her way by me and Max while we're talking in the hallway one afternoon, planting a wet kiss on Max's lips, smiling and nodding in my direction, and zooming by. "My part-time girlfriend," Max says with a sheepish grin. I laugh at the casual yet intimate interaction. Hannah has the classic dancer's body, lean, lithe, fit, attractive, but with a slightly hard face, perhaps because she's just past her prime as a dancer and now spends most of her time training younger, more beautiful women with even finer bodies. She shakes loose her pile of fiery red hair as she continues her glide to the door.

On Friday morning I sneak out to the second-hand store early to find something "wild" to wear to the party. I find a black sleeveless dress with scarlet red roses all over it and try it on over my shorts and T-shirt. The skirt comes to my mid-calf and has layers of material. I twirl and stomp around in an amateur imitation of a Spanish dancer. Right next to the dress, perhaps paired with it, is a large triangular shawl, with long red fringes. Even if I can't dance, I'll look like a dancer of some sort. The store also has jewelry and accessories. I buy a pair of dangly earrings with black shiny red and black beads. I pick up a black and red silk scarf I can use around my neck or in my hair. To top off my good luck, I find a pair of black slip-on lacy shoes, so comfortable it's like being barefoot.

When I get back, Max is ready to shop for food. We don't go to specialty stores but instead to an ordinary local supermarket. There's a food kitty to which all the tenants of The Laundry contribute, "from each according to their ability," Max says. We buy tons of hamburger meat, hot dogs, sausages, veggie burgers and tofu pups, enough potatoes to make a salad for an army, jugs of wine but not the cheapest stuff, cases of microbrew beer, and an array of chips and salsas. This isn't one of Jacques culinary gatherings; this is a down and dirty summer barbeque.

When we get back in the early afternoon, Ariana is there with her art class students, hanging immense rolls of blank paper from the second-floor balcony, using two rickety stepladders that have appeared from somewhere. The paper is to remain blank until the party starts, Ariana announces in a strict teacher voice, heading off students who want to fill it up right away. Hannah dances in, a whirlwind of energy, nods approvingly at the hanging paper and makes a sudden movement as if she's going to hurl herself at it. Ariana doesn't flinch, but I see a smile creep across her face. The two women hug and call me over.

"Hi again," Arianna charges ahead. "We'd like some help with the timing and set up." I nod in response.

Hannah doesn't say anything. It's her turn to look me over. It's not exactly that all these women are judging me, but it's like they are looking at me to see what I have in me, what I bring to the table, what I might have as an inner creative spark. It's a kind of appraisal.

When Hannah finally speaks up, she simply says: "Have you danced?

When I shake my head in the negative, she simply laughs and says:

"Well, you have a great body for it. You're tall and kind of dramatic looking. I think you would look good as a dancer. Tonight, you will dance!"

"And paint," Arianna adds.

They both laugh and suddenly Hannah reaches out and gives me a dramatic bear hug. Arianna joins in for a minute and they both take me by the hand over to a table where supplies and papers are laid out.

"Let's plan the show!" Arianna says. "Everybody gets to play tonight." I don't know what this means, except that Max had hinted that *sometimes we all join in.*

Later in the afternoon Peter Hansen arrives, lugging in a tangled mass of wires and a box that's the amp for the P.A. I've got the overall picture, from both Ariana and Hannah, so I have a vague idea of in what order things will be happening. I take Peter's entrance as a chance to make an escape. I go over and introduce myself.

"Peter? Hi, I'm Maya. Can I help?"

"Sure, sure. Nice to meet you. Come on, I have a half-dozen mikes and stands to bring in from my truck." I like Peter right away. There's something calming about his personality amid The Laundry chaos. We chit-chat and I quickly learn that he's a carpenter, he works as a handyman and is the drummer in the band that's playing tonight. I always think of drummers as nervous energetic types, but Peter isn't like that, maybe because he's older, in his forties I'm guessing. He's handsome, with a weathered face like he's spent time surfing and working in the sun. His brown hair is tied back in a ponytail. He has a full beard and is solidly built.

I know from talking with Max that Peter is divorced and has a couple of kids, so I ask, "Will your kids come to the party?"

"Yeah, Sean will be here. He's a guitarist. I'm guessing tonight he will sit in with us. He's fifteen and can shred it better than most people twice his age, or, in my case, three times his age. My older boy has a hot first date and I don't think this is the place to take a girl first time out. Maybe later."

"What's the name of your band?" I say as we cart in another two boxes of electronics.

"It changes, depending on the venue. Tonight, we're The Grateful Dadas, because we're going to do a Dead set when the—you know—gets going."

I don't know, but I don't say I don't know.

More band members arrive. Peter introduces me to his fifteen-year-old son, Sean, who is a striking young fellow, tall and lanky and handsome like his dad. Max has come down again and we're setting up in the atrium, with tables for food, drink, plates, and all.

At six-thirty, Jacques and Taisha make their grand entrance. They lug in several coolers and bottles of wine and wine glasses and set it all up near the front entrance.

When I go over, Jacques says, "This stuff is just for us, so we can have something a little more, shall I say, reasonable, and good wine before it all starts to go downhill." He says it with a kind of sly smile, and I understand it's his way of contributing to the giddy atmosphere by providing what he values most.

"Everyone!" Taisha shouts. "Take a break! Come down and over here."

Before we start Taisha has us all stand in a circle and hold hands. I notice a couple of the older band members are kind of awkward and almost rolling their eyes, but they join in. After a minute of silence, Taisha says:

"May this evening be blessed."

"With the wonder of life expression," Ariana adds.

"With the beauty of life movement!" Hannah says.

"With some kick-ass Dead-head music!" Peter adds.

"May my sous-chef be able to handle the crowd tonight because otherwise I'm on call," Jacques says.

Everyone laughs and the circle breaks up to enjoy the fine appetizers and wine.

Taisha comes over and gives me a hug. "I like to do something beforehand to kind of bless the space and these creatives. Keep it all safe and inspired."

I simply nod. The whole way these people operate is a joy to be a part of and a wonder to me. I certainly wonder what the evening has in store.

Around eight in the evening, people start arriving and I go up to my room to change. At the last minute, the dress is too much. I'm already self-conscious around these folks, and I need to see everyone in action before making some big statement. The irony of my self-limiting thoughts is not lost on me. Part of my self-judging self is thinking the Bon Vivants don't give a flying fart what I wear or don't wear, and I shouldn't care. Still, I put on a pair of black leggings and a black sleeveless top. The lace shoes are perfect. I simply wrap the large black shawl with the red fringe around my shoulders. Later I can tie it around my waist if I want to dance. I put on the dangling black and red earrings and tie the scarf around a section of my hair. I look in the mirror and approve of what I see. It still surprises me. Well, for tonight, let the good times roll!

I open the door to a full-on rock and roll party. The band has started playing—exceptionally loud music that I was already hearing in my room, I just wasn't paying attention to it. Ariana's art students have arrived, and the crowd is starting to build. The students help serve the cooked burgers and sausages. Warming trays hold the hot food and piles of ice surround food that needs to be kept cool. Everyone is eating, mingling, drinks in hand.

I go over to Max who is standing on the sidelines, smiling and appraising the situation. "The cooking, part one, is done. I'll fire up a second round later."

"So, when does the crazy part start?" I ask.

"What do you mean?"

"You know, the dancing, the painting, the performance art part."

"That's up to you," Max answers.

"Me?!"

"Yes, you. Didn't Hannah and Ariana tell you?"

"Uh, no."

"Yeah, you're the belle of the ball tonight. Whatever you do, goes."

I think about making a mad dash for my room right at that instant. I've gone from being a helper to being the star of the show, in one second, without even knowing it.

"No, Max. No. That can't be right." I'm about to protest further when Ariana appears in front of me, holding two outrageously over-sized paintbrushes, each coming to a point like an artist's implement, not a housepainter's wide, flat tool. I mean, these things are as tall as I am, with thick wads of foot-long bristles. They don't have any paint on them, yet. She hands me one.

"Come on, honey, it's time to play!" she yells over the pounding music. Ariana drags me over to a corner where several buckets of paint in different colors are waiting, dips her brush in electric blue, gestures for me to copy her. I go for neon orange, and we face off in front of the band, who pick up on the energy and play even louder and faster, if that's possible. Ariana thrusts, I parry, halfheartedly at first and then with growing excitement, and all of a sudden, I surprise

Ariana and myself by taking off my shawl and whirling it around over my head violently. A screech in my ear makes me look around for the source of the sound until I realize, it's me! I run at Ariana, miss her, and plow right into one of the hanging paper sheets, which doesn't rip but absorbs a good bit of orange in a blotchy streak. Hannah joins the fray, attacking me from behind. I turn to face her and get a chest-full of angry purple down my thrift store outfit. I retaliate, and soon all three of us are dripping with each other's paint, slamming into the paper, deliberately rolling our bodies across it. Others have climbed up on the two stepladders and are slashing wild arcs of color across the upper reaches of the paper. Nobody has thrown a bucket yet, oops, yes, now someone has, and a dozen people eating hot dogs and sausages are thoroughly splashed, but they don't care, they go on eating as if nothing has happened. Dancers led by Hannah form a weird conga line that rubs against the hanging paper like a snake trying to shed its skin. All the while the music pulses and booms. I'm dizzy from exertion and excitement.

Suddenly the music stops and the place echoes with silence. Hannah and Ariana each join hands with me and lift my arms skyward. "To our newest dancer!" Hannah shouts. "To our most colorful resident artist!" Ariana shouts as she adds a splotch of red to the front of my torso. Everyone cheers.

I expect the band to ramp up again and look to find Peter when I see a wraith-like young girl, tall and angular, with a soft reddish-brown afro stepping up to take the mike. Without accompaniment, she starts to sing "Amazing Grace" softly. Slowly. Everyone in the place sways. Some people have put their plates and drinks down and are raising their arms and calling out to the singer.

When she finishes, there is complete silence until The Grateful Dadas kick into one of the Dead's most raucous tunes. It's Throwback Saturday Night, retro and weirdly cool, even for this youngish, hip artistic crowd. I don't recognize the song, but it goes on and on and on and on. Everyone's dancing, shouting, grabbing paint and flinging it on the hanging sheets of paper and often on one another. The band plays for another forty-five minutes or so. Peter's son wows the crowd with an amazing solo, channeling Jerry Garcia. They mix in softer tunes that I recognize to give the crowd a break from time to time. After one such soft and almost gentle song, they announce they are taking a break. I see Max heading back out to the parking lot and follow along.

He's ramping up the grill again. Wet towels and buckets hang near an outside faucet. People are wringing out the towels to clean off the paint they have on their faces and arms, or swirling around and letting it all dry.

I go over to Max.

"More food?"

"Yes, we expect late arrivals who come just for the dancing and the free food. It can get really crowded."

"Was that your doing? I mean did you set me up?

Max looks up with a soft smile and a kind of sad serious deepness behind his brown eyes. "We all planned it."

Tears well up and it's not from the smoky barbecue. I go over to Max and put my arms around him. I'm looking down on myself in some crazy way as I initiate this physical expression of love and appreciation.

"You have a story too, don't you?"

Max shrugs and flips the burgers. "Five minutes," he says as he closes the grill top. "Look, I didn't get the money I have, the ability to buy into this place, to live without having to work, because everything in my life was going so great. My dad got lung cancer. He never smoked a day in his life. He got lung cancer and was dead in less than six months. Then my mother crashed and died. Didn't hit anyone, just left the road and slammed into an overpass on a snowy night in the Berkshires. That was it."

"When?"

"Five years ago." Max lifts the grill cover and smoke pours out. "Fuck I burned this batch of fucking burgers." Max shuts off the grill. "Think I'll take a break for a while." As he starts to go inside, he turns to me, "It takes time. It takes even more than time. It takes living and one foot in front of the other and then more living and for me it takes getting crazy and creative and living in this place. Making a new family for myself. I'm hoping you'll be part of it." He continues toward the door and turns back again. "I think Peter likes you."

"Peter?" I'm shocked. Peter is almost twice my age. Well, not twice, but way older. Why would Max say such a thing? *Peter?* I think as I hear the band starting to tune up. I sit outside while the band plays. I open the grill and toss the burned burgers into the trash. By the time I'm back inside, the music is softer and slower. I see Max and Hannah together. Dancing but hardly moving. Holding each other closely. I miss that so much. Peter? I watch him drumming. Light hands, sensitive hands. I like the way he closes his eyes and tilts his head slightly, nodding to the rhythm as he plays. He notices me watching him and winks without missing a beat. It's a friendly, inviting wink, not leering or salacious. I wave timidly. He flips a stick and catches it while playing, showing off. I smile at him but then move away so that I blend in with the crowd. As Max had predicted, the party is swelling, people queueing up for more food and drink. I'm busy for an hour, helping serve up sausages and burgers, and pouring wine and beer into those ubiquitous red plastic cups. It's getting late, close to midnight, but I'm not tired. I'm exhilarated. People come up to congratulate me on joining the Bon Vivants. I haven't joined anything. Just like with the Tribe, I'm not sure about being in a group. I'm not sure about myself.

At one a.m. the police come, but they're friendly and they just ask us to turn it down. They've been here before. One of them even accepts a burger. The crowd begins to thin, and the band goes unplugged, playing an acoustic set to end the evening. It's sweet. They drop the Dead motif and play a slow love song that I've heard on the radio recently. Peter plays with just brushes on a single drum and hi-hat. His hands get even softer. He somehow finds me in the audience, sees that I'm moved by the song, and smiles at me, filling me with a sudden warmth. I don't know if it's sexual or just happiness that someone likes me. It doesn't matter. By two in the morning the party is over for everyone else. People drift away, but I stay up and help Max clean up. We'll do the heavy cleaning in the morning, but we must make sure all the food is put away and the garbage wrapped up in bags "So the rats don't get at it," Max says. I thought Peter might hang around to talk with me, but he packs up and leaves without any further interaction. I'm slightly disappointed. It was so late, maybe he had to go. Maybe he had to get his son home. It doesn't matter. We fill twenty forty-gallon black garbage bags and throw a tarp over them. No longer exhilarated, now I'm exhausted. I say goodnight to Max and crawl off to bed.

In the morning Peter comes back to pick up extra equipment that wouldn't fit in the truck when he packed up the night before. At least that's what he says when he finds me sweeping out the atrium. The paper is still hanging all around from the second-floor balcony, mute testimony to last night's goings-on, but it looks less significant and dramatic in the daylight, without the music and the dancing. The garbagemen have come already and taken away the trash, leaving just some light sweeping and paint, lots of paint, that I don't see how we are ever going to get rid of, but maybe that doesn't matter. Maybe that's the point. Peter loiters by the door and finally asks me a question that catches me completely off guard:

"Which Maya are you?"

"What do you mean?" I ask cautiously.

"It's an unusual name. I looked it up. There are a whole bunch of meanings in different cultures. Are you the Hebrew Maya, which means 'from God'? The Persian Maya, 'generous'? In Sanskrit Maya means illusion, and it's an alternate name of the Hindu goddess Lakshmi. Which one are you?"

It's a clumsy tease, but I go along. "My mother is Russian. Marinovich. I kept her name when I grew up. I like the idea that maybe I'm a goddess."

I give Peter a wondering smile. I'm flattered at how interested he is in me, or least in my name. He smiles and goes on:

"Two more. In Buddhist tradition Queen Maya of Sakya was the mother of the Buddha."

"Oh, great. How do you know all this?"

"I told you, I looked it up. You can find anything on the internet. In German, Maya is short for Maria or Mary. The virgin Maya."

"Hardly," I say, and we both laugh. "Do you need any help bringing stuff to the truck?"

"Nah, I got it. How did you like the music last night?" Peter asks.

"I loved the dancing and the painting, and your son was fantastic, and the band is talented, but I'm not much into noisy rock."

"Yeah, we get that a lot. Most of us are in two or three bands, some of them quieter and more ear-friendly than The Grateful Dadas."

"I'd like to hear that," I say. I like Peter but am uncertain how to act around him. I think about what Max said last night. That Peter likes me. Must be true since here he is. Or is he just picking up equipment?

"Why don't we have a bite next Thursday? My blues group is playing at The Blue Seagulls, a bar restaurant in Oakland. Angela Dawn, the singer from last night, is part of that group."

"How do you know Angela?" I ask, instead of answering directly. I'm sure my ambivalence is obvious.

"She was a student of mine when I taught at Mills College. That's how I met Taisha. I used to be an adjunct there in the music department. A long time ago."

"Sure, that would be great," I answer. I'm not sure what to expect from getting to know Peter. He's already surprising me. He reminds me of an older version of Brad from the Tribe. Someone easy to talk to, someone with wisdom behind his words. Peter leaves and I head upstairs. As I pass Taisha's door on the way back to my room, Jacques bursts out of her door. He nods in my direction, stops and looks in my eyes, makes air kisses barely brushing the sides of my cheeks, French style, and continues to rush away and down the stairs. I look up as I hear Taisha:

"Come on in, girl, let's have some coffee. That man is always late, always in a rush. He should relax, but he's off to prepare the gourmand delights of the day."

As she putters around, I sit on a stool at the island in her kitchen area. Brown bread pops out of her toaster, and we sit with coffee and enjoy slices of multigrain bread with butter and home-made jam, and conversation.

"Was last night okay for you?" Taisha is watching me intensely. "Just checking in."

I laugh out loud. "It was more than okay. It was wild. It lifted me. I'm always wary that my, you know, my darkness might darken everything, for others too. I had a great time. I truly appreciate what you're doing for me. You, you're like my new big sister."

It's Taisha's turn to laugh. Then she turns serious. "Maya, I'm putting together a course in African American literature and Buddhism. I don't have a catchy course title yet, but I know I want it to also be feminist. It's an eight-week seminar course when the new semester starts in September. Would you like to attend, not for credit, just to audit it? It might be of interest to you. It might spark something. There'll be a writing part to it. You should definitely do that part."

"Are you a Buddhist?" I ask.

"Yes, and no. Come, let me show you." Taisha takes my hand and leads me over to a corner of the loft space separated by a shoji screen. Behind the screen, an altar is arrayed on a rough-hewn plank supported by two tree stumps, with pictures, candles, a ceramic figurine of Kuan-yin the goddess in the poster on

Taisha's door, and a polished ebony Buddha, seated in full double lotus, with a thin mustache, a soul patch, and a black Afro. Taisha notices me staring at the statue and says: "An African friend made that for me. Brilliant, yes?!" I nod dumbly. "I was inspired by that book *Monkey* that I gave you." Taisha continues, "I have the great privilege of coming up with my own course content, and of teaching a group of talented young women, mostly women of color. I'm exploring as I do the research. I love Kuan-yin. We all need her compassion. I created this space so I can sit quietly here every morning or come here when I get stuck in my research."

"I'd love to take your course, thanks. Please sign me up," I say.

Having told me what she wanted to tell me, Taisha is ready for me to leave. She's a results-oriented person, always doing. I know that's what makes The Laundry work. I understand it, but it's not part of my nature. I'm more, what, more meandering. Less driven, especially when I'm with people who have more of that productive, let's-get-it-done mentality. It's me. I want to do things, but sometimes I just never get around to them. Maybe that's part of the change I'm looking for in myself. This course Taisha has invited me to is a good opportunity but it doesn't start until after the summer. I have a secret plan for another limit-pushing activity. I'm going to ask Peter to teach me surfing!

The Thursday Peter mentioned comes, but I don't hear from him. Maybe he just expects me to show up at the place he named? I don't go. Am I being old-fashioned? Did we get our wires crossed? I don't know. I don't have his number and can't reach out to him, and I don't want to ask Max for it, so I just set aside any resentment I might have and muddle along.

I'm learning the property management business from Max, part of which is writing letters to tenants in arrears, because as Max points out to me on more than one occasion: "We're not running a charity here." Most people are pretty good about it. I go with Max to a couple meetings with Jacques and the bank that holds the mortgage on The Laundry. They're trying to refinance, but it's tricky. My legal background comes in handy, though I hadn't done any real estate law and anyway the rules are different here in California from back in New England. I'm useful just for being able to wade through the legalese to see what is really being said in the arcane financial documents.

On Sunday I make my weekly call to my mother. She's selling the house in Maine and moving back to Massachusetts, not to our hometown of Nahant, but to be near her sister, my Aunt Sharon, in Lexington. She has stories about how much stuff she needs to get rid of in her life. The plan is to put stuff in storage and stay in an apartment over the garage at Aunt Sharon's. I mostly listen and commiserate. Finally, I tell her what's going on with me. I'm lucky to have landed at The Laundry. I'm taking a course with Taisha. I don't mention Peter because there isn't anything to mention.

"You seem almost happy," my mother says.

The "almost" reverberates, a physical vibration in my spine.

"Almost," I repeat. "Like a spiral, like what kids go through. I remember reading a book, *Your One-Year-Old*, when I had Ella. It was a series, a book for every year, up to teenage, I think. It was about six-month spirals of behavior. Something like that. I never got any further than the first book." There's an awkward silence and then my mother says, "I wonder if they have a series like that for me. Maybe something like *Your Fifty-Eight-Year-Old*."

"I have one for you to read: *Your Almost-Twenty-Eight-Year-Old*."

We both laugh. It isn't a bitter laugh.

Chapter 13 Surfing

Later that same Sunday, Peter calls me. I ask him about surfing. He invites me to go with him on the coming weekend. He doesn't say anything about our missed date, so I don't either. It's as if it nothing had ever been said. There's no party this Friday at The Laundry, so I accept for early next Saturday morning, "when the tide is right for surfing," Peter says. He tells me he can bring an extra board. I buy a modest bathing suit and look forward to Saturday with great anticipation.

When Peter shows up in his pickup with two surfboards in the back instead of musical gear, the first thing he says is: "Sorry about last Thursday. I had family troubles, so my son the guitarist who can also drum sat in for me. I should have called you."

"That's okay," I say, and I mean it. I have no idea what he's talking about and I don't ask. I just let everything slide for now. Am I finally getting to a stable place? I'm quite nervous, wondering what I was thinking when I asked Peter to take me surfing. I'm concentrating on my nervousness and on surfing. I don't want to shake up the emotional undercurrent that's a constant part of me. "Are you sure I can surf? I mean, I've never even tried. I've never done paddle-boarding or anything."

Peter cocks his head to one side and looks over at me. "This was your idea." It is a bit of a challenge, but then he smiles and asks: "Can you swim?"

"Oh, yes, sure."

"Then you can surf."

We get on the freeway toward the Bay Bridge. I ask what beach we are headed to, and when he says Ocean Beach, it takes me back to my first experience of San Francisco.

"You'll be doing more swimming than surfing today anyway. I brought you a wetsuit. Hope it fits. The water is fifty-nine degrees off Ocean Beach. It used to be fifty-five, but with global warming things are changing, and not for the better. Still, you gotta have a wetsuit to stay out there for any length of time."

We cross the Bay Bridge and head out to the beach. We drive right by the Tribe house. For him it's just the quickest way to the beach. I glance at the place as we pass and then close my eyes. *I'll think about that tomorrow*, I tell myself. About seeing Sajiro one more time. To explain and maybe even apologize. I left him in Japan, fled back to the States. Do I owe him a better explanation? Do I have one? Thankfully my fear of the moment is surfing. I bring myself back to the now and listen to what Peter is saying.

"—stay calm and if you get turned upside down, just let the wave motion right you."

"If I get?—"

"I should say 'when you get' because it's going to happen. We're not surfing Maverick or anything. Should be gentle rollers out there today, if the weather report is at all accurate."

I've heard of Maverick, south of San Francisco on Route 1, with its twenty-foot and more waves that

attract risk-hungry surfers from all over the world.
Yeah, we're not surfing Maverick, that's for sure. Peter
parks on the last street before the Great Highway, and
proceeds to strip between parked cars to put on his
wetsuit. It must be a surfer thing. Fortunately, I put on
my swimsuit before leaving my room, so all I have to do
is wriggle into the wetsuit. It fits reasonably well, but
isn't easy to don, sticky and scratchy.

"It'll be better when you get seawater in there," he
tells me.

"Wait," I say. "I thought the wetsuit is supposed to
keep the water out."

"Well, yeah, but you need lubrication. You'll see."
When I'm ready, he hands me one of the two boards
and we start off. We leave everything in the car except
Peter's keys and two towels, me carrying my board
under one arm, a complete beginner. We pass through
an opening in the low dunes and onto the beach. Other
hardy souls are out bobbing in the surf on their
boards, along with locals walking their dogs and
underdressed tourists shivering in the morning fog
which is just now burning off. Like its iconic name,
Ocean Beach is iconic. The beach in the morning has
an unearthly beauty, almost too beautiful, too perfect.
Puffy clouds in an azure sky, long rolling breakers, a
wide stretch of light tan sand up to the dunes. Up the
beach to the north, the Cliff House stands like a
sentinel. I remember my first meal there, the pricey
cioppino, and the fortuitous meeting with John the taxi
driver who brought me to Jane. Now I'm a tourist
attraction.

We wade into the shallows, and then ride our boards over the waves and into the relatively still water past the break point. Then begins my ordeal. Despite Peter's best coaching, I fail miserably, over and over. I get tossed and pummeled like a cat someone has cruelly thrown into a washing machine. Twice I get to my knees, and once, near the end, I stand up and for maybe two seconds I'm surfing, but as soon as I try to look around for Peter, I lose my balance and get roughed up by the agitator again. Meanwhile, in between thrashings, I watch as Peter casually grabs rides, nothing spectacular but with the same lightness and ease that I saw in his drumming. At the end of two hours, I'm as tired as I've ever been in my life, and thirsty perhaps because of having swallowed rounds of seawater. Peter takes both boards for the walk back to his truck. I have a sore elbow and a sore knee but am otherwise unscathed.

"You did well," Peter says as we walk back to the truck, me limping slightly.

"Are you kidding? I was a human pebble out there, getting pounded and smoothed by the wave action."

"You got up."

"Once."

"Many people never even get that far. So, did you like it?"

I don't know what to say. I smile feebly.

"Would you go again, like maybe next Saturday?"

"Sure, as long as they don't need me at The Laundry."

"Cool." We repair to a Chinese restaurant in the outer Richmond where we lunch on spicy hot and sour soup that warms my insides delightfully, and share a strange dish of tofu, fungus, and seaweed that apparently is Peter's favorite. Apparently, he is a regular, because the waiter, a gruff Chinese man, brings the dish without Peter even asking.

Over the next few weeks, Peter takes me surfing several times. I'm not sure if I like it, but I keep at it. There's something about the urgency of being thrashed around by the ocean, by colossal nature, that makes me want to keep trying. There's no time to think about anything except the need to glide on top of it all. It's what I need at this moment in my life. The challenge of the present moment, the sound of the waves, the physical struggle. After our last session, we take off our wet suits on the beach and then both of us run wildly into the surf. It's cold and healing and refreshing. As we run back to the boards and the wet suits and towel off. Peter bends over me and puts his arms around me. He kisses me on my forehead and then smiles and takes my hand in his calloused hand as we head back to the truck. Nothing is said between us, and nothing else happens.

"You've got some things to work out, I take it." Peter says on the drive back.

"I do," I say. "Yes, I do." We leave it at that.

The other best part of surfing is how tired it makes me. When I get back to The Laundry, I fill the tub, soak in Epson salts and crash on my blow-up bed. I'm just thinking that I need to get a real mattress when my

phone pings, and I'm surprised to see a text from Brad.
Instead of texting back, I call. Of all the Tribe, I've
missed Brad. He tells me that the house is closing and
everyone is off to temporary digs until most of them
make the move up to Shasta, to the old rock and
roller's place that the Tribe has purchased. Wednesday
is the final dinner evening before everyone packs up. I
decide to go. It's cowardly in some ways. I'm hoping to
see Sajiro and to have a moment alone to tell him I am
sorry for the way it all ended, so abruptly, but at the
same time be protected from too much intimacy by
having others around.

I show up at the Tribe house late. The place is in
shambles as the Tribe unwinds several years of
residence. The party is sedate and sad compared to the
wild goings-on at The Laundry. Brad greets me at the
door and his first words cut me:

"So, you've become a hedonist? All fine food and
wine, brandy and cigars, music and dancing, eh?" I'd
told him a bit about the Bon Vivants on the phone, and
he must have looked them up and found out more.
He's curious but reserved. As a devoted member of the
Tribe, does he view my actions as a betrayal? I wonder.

"Not really," I say. "It's about freedom, art, and self-
exploration. The part that is really strange is that I've
taken up surfing." I wish I could have some time to talk
with Brad about all I've stumbled into with the Bon
Vivants. How it's helping me.

"How laid-back Californian. Come on in." He walks
me back toward the living room. Before I even enter, I
see Sajiro from across the hallway. He's in his favorite

chair, and there's a young woman sitting on his lap. I turn to leave. "No, wait," Brad says.

"She looks like me," I say, biting my lip hard.

"And you looked like the one before you. What did you expect? Anyway, you're free. It's a good thing. You should be glad of it." Brad's right, I'm free. A weight lifts from me. I have no need to apologize. Just to say goodbye. I stride into the room and immediately catch Sajiro's eyes. Brad must have told him I was coming. He nods and smiles but doesn't ask the woman to get up. At that moment, though, someone calls her name, "Naomi," and she rises without even glancing in my direction and heads toward the kitchen. I walk confidently over to where Sajiro has remained seated. He gestures as if to suggest I could take Naomi's place on his lap, but he's joking, and I know it.

"Hello, Sajiro."

"Hello, Maya."

"How's your mother?" I ask, trying to move the conversation quickly to safe ground.

"She's well. She asks about you frequently."

"Is she moving up with everyone?"

"She'll have a room in the new place, but she'll keep an apartment here."

"Please give her my regards," I say. I want to see Kumiko. On my own terms. Separate from anything to do with Sajiro.

"I will. What can I tell her about you now?" Sajiro quizzes me. A momentary attachment, the old command passes like a wispy cloud that blocks the sun briefly.

"I'm, um, better," I say. Others who knew me during my time with the Tribe are gathering around to say hello. I don't know what I thought this would be like, but it's okay, it's the past, whatever that means. It's good to be saying goodbyes. It confirms that my decision to leave Japan was the best one I could have made. It created a gap that wouldn't have existed had I broken up with Sajiro at the house and had to deal with all the members at the same time.

"Sixty percent? Seventy percent?" Sajiro asks.

"Hard to put a number on it," I say, trying to address the group that is ringing us now. "Are you all excited about moving north?"

"Oh, yes!" says Mariko, the graphic designer. "A new beginning."

"New beginnings are important," I say.

Naomi returns from the kitchen and cuddles up next to Sajiro. I check in with myself. *I'm free.* Just like Brad said. I break off from Sajiro and engage Manami and Chuck in conversation, asking about plans for the move. I'm being polite because I've moved on and have no attachment to the group. I don't stay long. Before I leave, Brad and I go up to his room, which is a total upheaval of books and packing cartons. I want to tell him how I'm really doing, get a weird quote from some famous poet or author, but the connection is lost. We promise to stay in touch, but I'm pretty sure we won't. It's like a clean break for me. When I leave, Sajiro sees me and comes to the door. We say our goodbyes and wish one another good luck.

"Thank you," Sajiro says. "You were a good person to be with for me and I hope I helped you too."

I smile. We bow awkwardly. I think about those times in Oregon, and here in San Francisco, and Japan, and it's all okay. It helped me. It was a kind of sexual healing while it lasted.

When I get back to my place, I text Brad. I thank him and again wish him luck. I ask him to send me Kumiko's contact information because I want to say goodbye to her too. No, I don't want to say goodbye. I want to reconnect.

Chapter 14 Kumiko

My life at The Laundry continues to be a source of easy pleasure and growth. I'm finding some of my old confidence. All the biking and walking is keeping me fit. I'm pretty good at the whole property management thing. The parties continue over the summer, some insane and intense, others more subdued but still uniquely stylish, like the evening when Jacques lights the entire interior courtyard with candles and hosts a sit-down dinner for fifty, with white tablecloths and waiters in tuxes.

One Sunday afternoon, after my weekly talk with my mother, I think about Kumiko. I remember the time we walked in Golden Gate Park and how she knew the old saxophonist playing for dollars. How she learned French while living in Paris. Brad has sent me her telephone number and address. I give her a call. We set up a time for me to see her in her apartment in San Francisco. It's on Second Avenue in the back of a Victorian house owned by an old Japanese friend.

Kumiko greets me and takes me back to her elegant apartment. It's part basement and part fenced-in garden, with flowers everywhere and a stone patio adorned with a low wooden table between two carved Japanese benches. We sit in the garden sipping green tea and munching on Japanese crackers and sweets.

"Almost all native flowers," Kumiko says, and she points out the bright orange poppies, purple lupine, and other plants not now in bloom.

"I'm happy you came to visit," she says. "You needed love at the time you met Sajiro. He loved you too, in his own way. Selfishly, I was hoping for a wake-up call for him. To show him that he's not the complete center of the universe. A mother's foolishness and too much to ask."

I tell her a bit about the Bon Vivants, the parties, the music, the course I am going to take with Taisha. I talk about surfing, and she laughs. I tell her how I've learned that my name has many meanings in different cultures, and that I'm trying to sort it all out.

"Come," she says. I help her carry the tray and teacups back to the kitchen. We go to the sitting area of the apartment. My feet enjoy walking barefoot on the tatami mats. We go behind a simple rice-paper screen that partitions a corner of the room.

"Sit," Kumiko says. I sit on the stool facing an altar. I recognize a poster of Kuan-yin on the wall. When I say the name, Kumiko smiles and says, "It's 'Kannon' in Japanese." On the altar table is a statue of the Buddha. Beads and a candle burning. The writing on the candle is Hebrew, not Japanese.

"*Yahrzeit*," Kumiko explains. "It means 'time of year.' Every year on the anniversary of the death, I light this for my sister. She died when she was only twelve years old. You can buy them on Amazon. You will need to light two."

I take a deep breath and close my eyes. We sit together in silence.

As I'm leaving, I invite Kumiko to the next Bon Vivant event. Peter is going to play with a jazz ensemble a week from Friday. It's going to be a quiet (for The Laundry) event with tables and chairs, a dance area, appetizers prepared by Jacques, and an open mike for poetry. Kumiko nods but it's not clear she'll come. We say our goodbyes.

I get a flyer from Taisha and send it to Kumiko with a note inviting her. The flyer mentions the open mike in addition to the jazz music and suggests that people bring an instrument for a jam session after the band plays. Then I forget about Kumiko and throw myself back into the life of The Laundry. The days pass quickly. Jacques and Taisha want this event to be less a bacchanal and more like the salon that Taisha has imagined from the beginning. There won't be a sit-down dinner and no great quantities of liquor will be served. I'm skeptical that the Bon Vivants can behave themselves and treat the event with the dignity and seriousness that Taisha seeks.

We make our preparations. The lighting is subdued. We hang sheets of paper again, but not for splashing paint onto or running into with human bodies. It'll be a place where people can write their poetry. The white tablecloths come out again. The event's not by invite only, that's not Bon Vivant style, but Taisha is hoping the tenor of the flyer will keep away the hard partiers.

Friday arrives. I haven't been surfing for weeks and am happy to see Peter, who shows up in the late afternoon with just a trio—himself with a reduced drum kit, a heavyset bass player with a standup acoustic bass, and a young African American woman clarinetist, so pale she looks almost albino, with opaque eyes and freckles across her nose. She's timid and doesn't engage with Jacques or Taisha. Afterwards I realize I never learned her name. When the playing starts, it becomes clear that she's the bandleader. The band is set up and starts to play even before anyone arrives. It sounds wonderfully high-brow and elegant. Dinner music with a twist, meandering through jazz classics in a unique style. The bandleader's clarinet never shrieks, and it's not showy. It's captivating. As people arrive, they enter the world her playing creates—no loud conversations, just a quiet murmur like at an elegant supper club.

We're an hour into the party when Kumiko arrives. I'd forgotten I invited her. She's dressed in a simple long black dress and wearing an exquisite kimono-inspired long kaftan jacket with large red and yellow designs. She's brought someone with her. It's the blind black saxophonist from the park! He's carrying his instrument in a case. I'm thrilled, and I go over to greet them and lead them to an empty table. Taisha comes over, sits down, introduces herself, and is immediately taken by both of them. She asks the sax player questions and does the same with Kumiko. This is the kind of cross-cultural gathering that Taisha has hoped for, and I can tell I've gone up a few notches in her estimation. At some point the band stops playing, and Taisha announces that it's time for anyone who wants to read their poetry to stand up.

"Five-minute limit," she decrees. A dozen people queue up by the lone mike that the band has left set up. The poems are a mixed bag—some dreadful, some okay, a couple quite moving. The crowd gives each reader polite applause. No one uses the paint and brushes to put their poetry on the paper. At the end, Taisha looks around and asks if anyone else would like to read. To my surprise, Kumiko stands up and nods to Taisha. She slips the kaftan off her shoulders and makes her way to the space next to the microphone where the long sheets of white paper are hanging. Kumiko stands quietly and then bows formally to the audience. She turns, takes up a brush, dips it in one of the waiting buckets and lets the excess drip off. After a long moment of concentration, everyone is completely silent and focused on her. Kumiko lifts the brush, which is quite large and then moves quickly, slashing several imposing *kanji* in black paint onto the blank paper in three vertical descending lines. There's no dribble or spatter, just radiant black characters, stark against the white paper.

"What does it say?" someone calls out.

Kumiko turns to face the expectant crowd. She looks directly at me for a moment. She walks slowly over to the microphone and says in a strong voice, first in Japanese and then in English:

> *"Goddess or demon,*
> *It doesn't matter. New life*
> *Rising from the waves"*

"What does it mean?" I hear someone ask even though he has just heard a translation. Taisha steps to the mike and says she will have the words written in

English on the paper. "Poetry, especially haiku, requires no explanation. It's all in there. It's all in here." She puts her hand on her heart. "We have to find the meaning in ourselves." Kumiko nods agreement, makes a slight bow towards Taisha, and returns to our table.

"Thank you," is all I'm able to say.

"Thank you for inviting me," Kumiko says.

Jacques comes over to the table, to check on us, to make sure we have everything we need. Hearing his accent, Kumiko responds in French. I tune out and am enjoying the sounds and musing over the whole thing when I hear the saxophonist joining into the French conversation.

The band takes the stage again and invites players to come up and join them, but there aren't many takers. One guy has brought a portable electronic keyboard. He's good, and he fits in playing back-up rhythm and chord changes to support the clarinetist. Another fellow has a couple of African percussion instruments—a thumb piano, a gourd filled with seeds that he shakes in time to the music. After the new people have been playing for a while, the clarinetist comes over to our table and talks quietly with the blind saxophonist. He reaches down and picks up his case, sets it on the table, takes out his instrument, and she leads him up to the makeshift stage.

Suddenly, everything changes. The clarinetist and the sax player exchange riffs, mimicking each other and building off each other's variations. I notice Peter is smiling and concentrating as he focuses and rachets

up his playing to meet the challenge. The energy in the
room is electric. People enter the open space near the
band and move to the music. Kumiko reaches out to
me and we join the movement. It isn't dancing so much
as going wherever the music takes us. "This is *kumite*,
partner practice like in the martial arts. The music is
our partner," Kumiko says.

Kumiko asks to see my room while the music is still
going on and I take her up the back stairs. She looks
around briefly. She even goes up to the loft for a
minute and sees my writing area and checks out the
bed. "Very nice, but the bed is awful. A thin camping
pad with a Japanese futon would be better. Much more
comfortable. Good for your sleep." She's being
motherly, which is sweet, but she is also being a friend
and perhaps a teacher. She takes a card from her
pocket and hands it to me. It's the haiku, as faultlessly
executed as the characters on the sheet of paper in the
atrium, but in miniature. A beautiful gift. I set it on the
windowsill.

"*Arigato gozaimasu*," I say, remembering one of my
few Japanese phrases.

"I have one more thing to say to you," Kumiko
continues in a maternal tone. "It may not mean
anything to you now, but maybe later. It is this. Some
things in this world are more important than relations
with men."

"That's something my mother might say."

"I would like to meet your mother someday,"
Kumiko answers. Then she says: "Your future may
take you away from the world of men, of sexual

relations. Maybe not forever, but maybe for a short time. Maybe for a long time. If it does, let it."

"Okay," I say. Is she talking about Sajiro, or Peter, or me? Does she think I'm going to become a lesbian? I don't know. I'm confused. I really don't understand, and I especially don't know why what she has said is so upsetting. Kumiko pats me on an arm, then enfolds me in an un-Japanese hug. We walk back downstairs hand in hand. The evening had been perfect up until that moment. I know Kumiko means well, but a drumbeat starts up in me that is not from the music. It's the ominous sound I've been running from and want to keep far away from me.

When we get back downstairs, the band is still jamming. It must be almost a solid hour. They have stopped only to confer on what to play next, but even that has been minimal because they instinctively flow together and sometimes simply move seamlessly on to the next part of the music. The atrium of The Laundry is buzzing with creativity. I try to concentrate on the excitement of the evening. I have the right to happiness. I have the right to enjoy men. I've finally contributed something to the fertile originality of the place.

Finally, when the music ends, Peter comes over to sit with us while the rest of the band is packing up. He surprises me by greeting Kumiko in Japanese, but their conversation is in English. I hear the name "Sajiro" in their exchange.

Peter has been talking with the blind saxophonist. "Stefan and I are just setting up some time to get together," he says. "Imagine, I got to play with Stefan Briggs, one of the greats. A legend."

"In my own mind, anyway," Stefan jokes. I remember what Kumiko had said to me about our country not valuing its national treasures. How can it be that a man like Stefan is reduced to playing for change in Golden Gate Park? But for tonight, for this evening, he has been heard and appreciated by an audience and by fellow musicians. Peter is like a star-struck kid around him. It makes me like Peter even more.

"We named my baby Ella after a legend," I say, but the tears start to come and I have to stop. Everybody shifts uncomfortably in their chairs. I manage to get control of myself. "Two legends, actually," I say. "Ella Rosa. Ella for Ella Fitzgerald. My late husband Dan loved her music. And Rosa for Rosa Parks."

"Ella was the best ever. I played with her once, when I was a youngster," Stefan says. "And Rosa Parks, well what can you say. She stood up, or rather, sat down, for us all." I smile and the moment passes.

The shy clarinetist comes by, expresses her thanks to Stefan, and Peter reluctantly takes his leave to bring her and the bass player home. It's late. I wonder how Kumiko and Stefan are getting to their places, and offer to borrow Max's truck to take them back to the city, but Kumiko says, "I called an Uber."

Taisha comes by. She has her hair done up in a Nefertiti-like tower, and truly resembles an African queen. She bows to Kumiko and puts her hand on

Stefan's arm. "Thank you for coming. You made our evening, both of you. Thank you."

The Uber arrives and we walk with Kumiko and Stefan to the door. As we come back into the atrium Taisha puts an arm around my shoulders. "You sure are full of surprises."

The next morning, I sweep and decide how much official paid-for help I will need to get the tables picked up and everything back to normal. Whatever Kumiko was alluding to has a lingering effect on me. I miss Max. He's always been a part of the Friday nights and a partner in the post-party cleanup decisions. I know he's away on family business back in Boston, but I miss him. I plow through what needs to be done.

Over the next weeks, I see Kumiko a fair amount. We have tea and talk. She never refers to anything about men or sex again. I tell her more about my mother, and I go deeper, much deeper than I have with anyone about my troubles. She mostly listens. It's almost like being back in therapy except that we meditate and drink one hell of a lot of green tea.

I go out to dinner occasionally with Jane and Joe and spend more time with Max, Hannah, and some of the others at The Laundry. I'm just trying to have a normal life. I'm still not sure it's possible for me. There's always a river of molten lava, surging below the surface. I just want to stay out of it all, not get sucked down and burned up. To glide, to stay above it, to ride the hot wave.

Peter's been incredibly busy with end-of-summer projects and we haven't had a chance to surf or spend time together. I suspect there are some family issues taking up his time as well.

Taisha is subsumed by course preparations. She'll let me know when the course I'm going to audit will start. Probably the last Monday in August.

I manage to stay above it all. I bike. I walk and finally, when all else fails, I shop. I decide that I'll get a new bed and see if that will help me. Perhaps part of my angst is sleep deprivation. Kumiko goes with me to a shop in Berkeley to help me pick out a futon. She says to go for one three inches thick. I take her advice, but I order a double instead of the single she recommends. Kumiko looks at me quizzically and I think back to her comments about men, but I go with my choice. Later I buy a lightweight double self-inflating sleeping pad with attached pillow online. It's only an inch deep. I want to get away from the instability of the blow-up. My life is rocky enough.

Chapter 15 Endless Summer

Max is planning a pre-Labor Day blowout party called "Endless Summer." Taisha and Jacques are going to be away, Taisha prepping for teaching and Jacques closing the restaurant for a rare break. They've rented a house on the beach in Bolinas. They invite me up, but I decline, wanting to help Max. "Endless Summer" is going to be an old-school rave, with electronic dance music (EDM) instead of a live band, and a DJ Max knows whose playlist is legendary. Max has taken the unusual step of clearing the atrium of everything that can be moved, leaving only the plants and shrubs.

"These Molly people, they get woozy and start drifting around. I don't want them banging into shit or breaking anything."

"Molly?" I ask. I've heard the term.

"Ecstasy. The old 90s club drug."

"Oh," I say. This party is shaping up dissimilarly from Taisha's cultural, artistic affairs. It's not even a Sixties' throwback to the time of acid and experimentation. It's straight-up carnal pleasure, with music. I never did Ecstasy, as MDMA was called back then. A little weed was about as adventurous as I got, and it mostly made me paranoid, so I stopped. "That'll be different." Little did I know.

On the night of the party Peter comes to help set up the P.A. system for the DJ. I'm happy to see him, but still conflicted about where things might be going with him, if anywhere. His family life is a mystery to me, whereas I'm an open book to him. It makes our relationship slightly off kilter, like a wobbly table that just needs a shim under one leg to find stability. We chat briefly, but he's busy with wiring and miking; the DJ has three turntables in addition to numerous other devices. In the rush to get everything ready I lose track of Peter.

Max has put out a quantity of soft drinks but not much alcohol, basically bottles of pink champagne and white wine, sparkling water and juice. When I ask about it, he just says: "These aren't that kind of partiers." But this isn't the 1990s. The people who come are the same crowd that have come to other events at The Laundry—mostly older, with a few young people mixed in. Someone has brought a lemonade punch and set it on a separate card table they'd brought themselves, with clear plastic cups beside it like the kind you see in dentist's offices. It's a hot August night, so I pour myself a glass, drink it down quickly, and go back to arranging snacks on a table, mostly sweet, chocolate-y things, another departure from the salty-guac-and-chips-and-salsa-with-beer-to-wash-it-down appetizers at Bon Vivants parties. On my way back I pass a young man with brown curly hair and brown eyes, who smiles at me slyly. He must be ten years younger than me. I'm flattered and smile back noncommittally.

People begin showing up, and a half-hour goes by. The DJ starts with some soft, slow numbers, gradually building the volume and increasing the rhythm of his offerings. I wish it was a live band. I wish Peter was playing. This pounding, metronomic electronic dance music does nothing for me.

The handsome boy with the high forehead and mop of curls comes by, smiles at me again.

"So, all these people are taking that Molly?" I say, just to make conversation.

"Yeah. You too."

"Huh?!"

"Yeah, I saw you take some," he says. "About thirty minutes ago, you drank that lemonade. Should be kicking in right about now."

"Oh, shit, no!" I shout. "You bastard!" Heads turn, but slowly, like they're underwater. I rush over to the punch bowl, now mostly empty, and notice a sign in front of it that wasn't there before when I took my cup's worth: "DRINK ME!" I start to panic, but alongside the panic, euphoria is spreading through my body, the sensation that the world is perfect. My anxiety is moving way over there somewhere, still there but not touching me anymore. Harmless. I look around. I love everyone. They are all so fine, just the way they are. The music, which had been a mere annoyance while I was setting up the party, now enters my body like a slow liquid fire. I think: *This is the feeling I want for the rest of my life.* I join the mass of bodies swaying and lurching on the dance floor. I let myself relax, as if I had any choice in the matter, and completely go with the flow. The curly-haired boy tries to dance with me, but I'm out of it and don't stick with him. Our slight interaction though, when he slow dances with me for a minute. He wants to grind his pelvis against me, and awakens another thought in my drug-infused mind: *I have to have sex with someone, right now. Where is that Peter?* And suddenly, a gift from God, he materializes in front of me.

"Are you all right?" he says. "Your eyes are way dilated."

I wrap my arms around him and say: "Let's go upstairs to my room."

I take Peter's hand and we go up to my room. Peter looks deeply into my eyes, wraps his arms around me and holds me. We sit on my one comfortable chair for a long time.

"I can't make love to you right now," Peter says. "Not while you're as high as you are. I'll stay with you all night."

That's perfect for me also. My physical attraction remains. I'm open to Peter, to everything. Peter takes me back downstairs and then outside to his truck. We drive away from The Laundry, the party. I have no idea what's happening. I shut my eyes and let Peter take me wherever he's going. We end up on top of Twin Peaks in San Francisco, looking down at the city, the waters of the Bay, the lights twinkling on the East Bay shoreline, and a sky full of stars above our heads. The world is opening in front of me and I'm open to the world. I am safe with Peter. I talk to him about everything that's happened to me and how I'm on some kind of trip that I didn't plan to take—not just the drug that I unknowingly ingested, but a bigger, longer journey. I'm searching. I need to find meaning in my life. Right here, right now, I might find it. There is no time and there is all time. We're still on top of Twin Peaks as the sun rises.

Peter drives me back to his house, a craftsman cottage in Oakland. No one else is home. The house is a delight. I wander around, exploring. Peter busies himself in a kitchen that's welcoming and efficient. A large stall shower is installed at the back behind the kitchen and stairs to an upper floor. Peter makes us a breakfast of eggs and toast and coffee.

"I couldn't make love to you last night though it might have been wonderful. I wanted to. It just wasn't right."

"I didn't even know I was taking the drug. I was just thirsty," I say sheepishly. "I'm still pretty high. Afterglow, I guess."

"Yeah, well, it's irresponsible of someone to put something out there without telling people about it." Peter leans over and kisses me for a long sweet time. He takes my hand and we head to the shower where I luxuriate in the delightful rush of the water on my body. Our bodies.

"Are you getting a contact high?" I ask as we dry off and wrap in towels. Peter's long brown hair back in his ponytail.

"Must be."

Peter gives me a look that I understand. I'm not exactly afraid, but I'm coming down from the drug high and experiencing the return of uncertain reality.

"Look, this won't be the forever relationship we both need and want. I'm older. My kids aren't that much

younger than you are. You're not going to be living in
your room in The Laundry forever or maybe not even
for long."

I nod, I look up into his eyes. I'm grateful for his
reserve and his gentleness and kindness.

"Then there's the now," he says simply.

"There's the now," I repeat and I lean into him as he
leans forward and kisses me softly.

"Is there a big wave in my future?" I ask, my body
against his.

"Let's catch it," is all he says.

Finally, we're upstairs and under the covers on
Peter's wide king size bed. I nestle into his chest and
we lay together as our breathing naturally adjusts to
one another until we are breathing as one. I lift my
arms over my head. His rough hands gently move over
my breasts. His damp hair, loose from his ponytail,
sweeps across me as he kisses me softly and moves
down my body. My arms circle his head. Everything is
intensely in slow motion.

"Is this okay?" Peter murmurs.

Saying nothing, I slide along his body and take him
inside. We stop, then move slowly, stop, then move
slowly. Peter is strong, solid. It goes on and on and I
wonder if I really am still high. Then comes the first of
many quiet explosions. Slow, then moving, slow, then
moving. My explosions of passion do not stop. They
continue until he climaxes deep inside me. We both fall
asleep. By the time we wake, it's afternoon. I have a
slight drug hangover and guilt for not being around for
the post-party cleanup. I'll have to explain things to

Max. Peter makes us a second breakfast—more eggs, more toast, quantities of coffee. We're shy around each other, or reserved, or something. What he said to me last night about this being a relationship that's unlikely to last hangs in the air between us, acknowledged but unspoken. I excuse myself and shower again alone. When I come out, Peter's ready to take me back to The Laundry; he's got things to do and so do I. This is the first time I've been in this kind of relationship, and I don't know if I can handle it, or how. It makes me crazy to think that I probably have no future with this wonderful man, but he's right, and somewhere deep inside me, I know it too. We agree to enjoy the "now" and not worry too much about the future. Easier said than done, but the right approach. He drops me off with a light kiss and a pledge to take me surfing again soon. I hurry inside and find Max still in the throes of the clean-up. He's not happy to see me, but when he hears that I was drugged without knowing it, his anger turns from me to "that little wiseass shit" who brought the punch.

"He put up a sign, but it was too late for me," I say apologetically.

"It's not funny. We would have had serious liability issues if someone had freaked out. You came through it okay, though," he says. I gather he's seen Peter's truck pulling away. "That might be the last Endless Summer for the Bon Vivants at The Laundry."

"Then it wouldn't be endless," I say, and Max laughs his funny laugh, and things are okay again. I offer to finish the cleanup and Max takes me up on it.

He gives me the keys to his truck and asks me to take a load to the landfill, which closes at four on Saturdays. It's all good. When Taisha comes back on Monday, she's heard what happened to me and she's furious, but I assure her I'm okay. She brings me to her place to check me out, though, and makes me a cup of herbal tea that she tells me will help purge any remaining toxicity from my system.

"Class starts tomorrow. You coming?"

"Oh, yes! Looking forward to it."

Taisha smiles broadly, happy that I'm following through. We say our goodbyes. I just want to go back to my place and sleep. I have an ongoing drug hangover, but I should be just about done with that terrible experience.

Chapter 16 Taisha's Class

I wheel in to Mills College through the main gate, consult a map posted on an outdoor bulletin board, and easily find the building where Taisha is teaching. Many of the buildings on campus are constructed in the Spanish style with adobe walls and curved red tile roofs. She's named her course: *Ebony and Ecstasy: Expressions of Nirvana in African American Women's Literature.* It's not as "catchy" as Taisha said it would be, and the word "Ecstasy" throws me for a minute because of my experience last Friday. I can see that Taisha must be a superstar on the faculty. The classroom is packed with eager students. I haven't felt this kind of buzz since I can't remember when. Everyone is younger than me, and many of the students are young women of color whose style, dress, manner of speaking, and most everything else are different from mine. I smile to myself. I don't care about fitting in. I care about the experience. I can't wait to see Taisha in action. She's surrounded by students chatting with her. Many of them know her and have probably taken other classes with her. I take a seat in the back. Taisha acknowledges my presence with a nod, sends the students to their seats, and begins her lecture. She doesn't stay at the front of the classroom; she walks around as she talks.

"What do black people have to do with Buddhism? There aren't many Buddhists in Africa, it's a religion practiced mostly by East Indian immigrants. Africa has rich and diverse religious traditions of its own, many of them. Why not study them instead? Well, Mills College does offer courses in African religions, including Christianity, Islam, and many tribal beliefs, from Yoruba to Igbo. So why this course? This course opened to me because I saw that many African American women authors find commonality with Buddhist tenets. These experiences have found their way into their writings. That's what this course is about. How many people have heard of bell hooks?" Not many hands go up, less than a quarter of the class. Taisha has made her way around the room and is back in the front, where she takes up a marker and writes the words "bell hooks" in lowercase letters on a whiteboard. "We'll be reading some of her work this semester. Anyone know why she writes her name in lowercase letters?" The class is uncomfortably silent. No one knows the answer to this question.

"She's subverting the dominant paradigm. Because she can. It's a form of liberation for her. She's trying to free herself from linguistic straightjackets that define her in ways she won't define herself. Here's a quote from bell hooks I want you to think about as we start this semester: *'If I were really asked to define myself, I wouldn't start with race; I wouldn't start with blackness; I wouldn't start with gender; I wouldn't start with feminism. I would start with stripping down to what fundamentally informs my life, which is that I'm a seeker on the path. I think of feminism, and I think of anti-racist struggles as part of it. But where I stand spiritually is, steadfastly, on a path about love.'"*

I'm in a classroom filled almost entirely with young black women and yet that quote is aimed directly at me. Looking around the room, I can see the intense involvement of the other students. This is a different kind of energy, a different wave. One of self-discovery and finding meaning. I understand why Taisha has urged me to audit her course. It's all in that one quote. Would simply auditing this class prove to be a way forward? Taisha kept saying I was a seeker and here I am, fearing going forward.

After class, I go up to the front to pick up the syllabus and the book list for the course. I immediately notice all the writing assignments interspersed in the materials. Creative writing mostly. This will be interesting.

Taisha comes over and tells me, "You can pop into my library anytime you want. I have multiple copies of the readings. No need to buy books."

The next day, I sit in my comfortable chair reading the first assignment. It's a collection of poems by Maya Angelou. The assigned reading is: *And Still I Rise*. The pain and suffering that inhabits the poem spills over me. I go online and look up more about Maya Angelou. It all sets me to wonder. The pain. The fame. Christian, not Buddhist. Then there's the Maya Angelou quote Taisha has included in the syllabus: "I am grateful to be a woman. I must have done something great in another life."

I spend most of the week reading and doing bookkeeping for The Laundry. I'm happy the party season is over for a while. Fall is a time to focus on other things. Max is busy sculpting. The other creatives are all busy dancing, painting, or whatever, in their apartment studios. Taisha is deep in all her classes. There's an energy and a creativity in the atmosphere.

Peter invites me to a gig he is playing with Stefan Briggs on Friday night at Yoshi's, the famous Oakland sushi restaurant and nightclub that features well-known jazz and blues groups. Both of the Marsalis brothers, Wynton and Branford, have played here. There was a last-minute cancellation and through Kumiko's connections, Stefan is putting together a group to jam and has invited Peter. When Peter gets to my place on Friday afternoon, he's excited. We have a drink and snacks. I decide to wear the black dress with the scarlet roses and the black triangular shawl with dramatic black and white fringes. I pile my hair on top of my head and put on the black and red dangly earrings. Pretty much the outfit I never wore for the first party at The Laundry. My coming-out. Peter smiles approvingly and by five, we are ready to head to Yoshi's.

I'm not surprised that Kumiko is there, looking elegant with her hair also piled up on her head. We laugh when we see one another and compliment each other on how dashing we are. I'm starting to wonder if she and Stefan have more going on than I thought they did.

While the band sets up, Kumiko and I sip saké and eat sushi rolls with funny names like Spicy Geisha, Oakland As, and Jack London. Kumiko comments on its freshness and the delicate flavorings. I tell Kumiko about the reading I have been doing and Taisha's class. She smiles as she listens.

"I've been thinking about what you said to me a while back in my apartment," I say. "About men."

"Sex is so good sometimes," Kumiko smiles. "I still get great pleasure."

"With Stefan?" Kumiko simply smiles and tilts her head to the side.

"With Sajiro, my body came back alive. Peter's wonderful, but we're both realistic about what we're doing." Kumiko again smiles. "Now I'm alive in my body. I want to be alive to something bigger. Now what?"

"What a good question. Keep asking it." Then Kumiko tells me about her recent trips up to see Sajiro and the Tribe. She's going through a transition. I've always spilled out my problems without thought and waited for Kumiko's wisdom. Now I just sit and listen.

"My son, my son is a dreamer. He's not a doer. He likes other people to do things for him. So far that's worked for him. It's not a good life path, if you know what I mean."

I think back to my time with the Tribe, how Chuck and Manami and Mariko and Gloria and the others were always taking care of everything for Sajiro—travel, accommodations, dinners at the Tribe House. Then it was logical, expected, the devotees arranging for the comfort of their leader, but from the distance of time it now looks more like what Kumiko is describing, immature and dysfunctional.

"The new place needs more work than they thought. They have the money now. Sajiro landed a wealthy donor during his stay in Japan, but it'll be some time before they're ready to start having events there. Sajiro has turned his back on the family; questions of lineage will come up."

"Oh, Kumiko!" I exclaim with more emotion than I intend. I don't want to think about the Tribe, but I want to listen to Kumiko. She smiles politely.

"That's not your world. It never was. For me, it's a family matter. I enjoy my freedom here in the United States, but I became a Morioka when I married."

Our conversation is interrupted by the appearance of an MC, a middle-aged Asian man with scraggly white hair and the wispy beard of a Taoist monk, who makes a lengthy introduction extolling the "hidden talent" and "lost years" of Stefan Briggs. It's obvious that the crowd, a mixed group of older black couples and younger white fans, needs no reminder of who Stefan Briggs is or what his legacy might be in the jazz world. I'm secretly thrilled to be a part of this renaissance of Stefan's career. Proud that I made the introduction to Peter. I am also pretty much in awe of the way Kumiko has done the work to make it happen. The band does not disappoint. From the opening notes, it's clear that Stefan Briggs could more than hold his own on any stage, with any players. He's not just a dinosaur. The band does a funky cover of a contemporary song by a young black rapper that's number one on pop charts and on the radio all the time now. I could imagine the light-skinned singer who appeared at The Laundry doing this song, but she's not here tonight. Stefan plays the vocal part on the saxophone, making it growl, whisper, and purr through the changes. Sexy! Peter's absolutely in his element, playing with passion and flair. A new bass player, not the large fellow who played at The Laundry, a scrawny guy instead, with leather boots, leather pants, a leather vest, slouches back on his bootheels while he supplies a generous bottom with a fretless electric bass. A woman keyboardist surrounds herself with a triad of a Fender Rhodes electric piano, a Yamaha synthesizer, and the house Steinway mini-grand, and manages to play them all, spinning on a stool to reach whatever keyboard is right for the musical moment. She's active but not frenetic, matching her playing to Stefan's cool jazz that only occasionally breaks into something wilder and more adventurous, but it's always there, an undercurrent, threatening to roil the musical waters at any moment. Kumiko doesn't perform, though it wouldn't be unheard of to have spoken word, poetry, as part of this performance, even at Yoshi's. She merely nods her head, smiling with satisfaction. During a break, I run into one of the young students in Taisha's class, who greets me with a question:

"What are you doing here?" I can see her surprise. Her question is not an accusation, exactly, but there's a bit of a challenge in it. I explain that my Japanese friend Kumiko has arranged this gig for Stefan. I add that the man I am dating is the drummer.

"Cool," she says. "See you in class." She wanders away without any more interaction.

Peter spends the night with me in my place, but for the rest of the weekend he's busy with his sons and family. I'm happy to be by myself. I spend most of my time reading and jotting down notes. I've raided Taisha's bookshelves and am reading more of Maya Angelou. Many books by Buddhist writers are on the syllabus. If I do the course, it's going to be work. I want to do the course. I'm thirsty for it.

On Sunday, with the time change, it's easy for me to have my call with my mom in the early afternoon. I'm impressed that she's making changes, seeing a therapist, doing some mindful meditation. She says she's inspired by hearing about the course I'm taking and is going to talk to her sister about taking a women-only travel and study course, part of the Road Scholar organization. I tell her that's a wonderful idea.

When I hang up, I look around my apartment. It's time to make changes. I fetch the folding table I set up to use for a desk down from the loft and set it up in a corner. It'll be my workstation for books, laptop, a printer if I can find one cheaply. Back in the loft area I look at the corner under the window and decide it is time for me to make a special place, a place to sit and think and maybe even pray? I think about the altars that both Taisha and Kumiko have shown me and decide why not. I find a platform in the storage room that just fits in the corner of the loft. I cover it with a simple silk scarf.

I need to get out, to move. On the way out, I stop at my dresser and take the locket I've stopped wearing and hold it in my hand. I put it on and decide to start wearing it again. I grab the book *Monkey* and head down to get my bike. I ride over to Alameda. I lock the bike and walk the business district visiting gift shops and buying a couple of picture frames, a three-pack of college lined notebooks. I check out printers at the office store.

Finally, I settle into a spot at a corner table near the window of a place called The Local. It's in an old historic building. In the evenings they have music, but on Sunday afternoons, it's peaceful, perfect. I take out my notebooks, make lists, peruse a copy of the syllabus.

A stylish woman, with long blond hair tied in a loose pile on top of her head, pushes a stroller awkwardly through the door. After she gets her coffee, she sits down at a table next to where I'm sitting. She drinks her coffee and fiddles with her phone. I can see that the baby is probably about a year old. A boy, dressed in blue. A boy with brown skin.

I looked from the baby to the woman and back again.

She smiles. "Sometimes people don't think I'm his mother." I find I can't take my eyes off the infant, who is starting to wake up. Suddenly the woman reaches down and picks up the baby.

"Hey, this is crazy, but my stomach is really off. Would you mind holding him for a minute? I can't get the stroller in the bathroom with me." Without waiting for me to answer, she hands me the baby and runs off to the bathroom.

The baby is staring up at me. I search his dark brown eyes.

"Did you meet my Ella Rosa before you came into the world?"

His mother rushes back to the table and apologizes profusely.

"Are you okay?" she asks. She sees that I have begun to cry.

"I'm okay. He's beautiful." I hold him out and she lifts him from my arms and lays him back in the stroller.

"Thanks so much. Nice to chat." She's out the door, in a hurry to go somewhere. I sit for a long time wondering how I was able to hold a baby and think about Ella with love in my heart.

I stare down at the table and the books, the notebooks. *Monkey* sits on the table untouched. I'm avoiding the book. I flip through it. Read pages randomly. It has nothing to do with me. I decide to head back to The Laundry half-hoping I'll bump into Max or some of the others for a glass of wine or a bit of food. If not, I have food in the fridge and will make do with another evening of reading.

I can still feel the warm baby in my arms.

The class meets Tuesdays and Thursdays at 2:30 in the afternoon. Taisha begins the second class by asking for questions. The girl from the other night at Yoshi's raises her hand. Her name is Nia. She wants to know why we are reading Maya Angelou in a course about black writers and Buddhism.

Taisha explains her reasoning. "We have to start at our beginnings, our roots. For many of us it is the harsh reality of our history as black Americans. Maya Angelou is a vivid example of a woman on a journey, a woman who overcame much and forged a new future for herself."

After class, Nia and I walk out at the same time. We chat about meeting at Yoshi's the other evening. I'm surprised when she asks if I would like to have a glass of wine. Maybe her attitude in the club wasn't a challenge, maybe it was just curiosity. We throw my bike in the back of her SUV and we drive to a local place where we sit out on a patio in the back.

As we order, I take a good look at Nia. She's thin, and shorter than I am, five-four perhaps. Her hair is tight and curly and dyed a blond color that highlights her beautiful brown eyes and round face. She's fit and muscular, maybe an athlete of some kind. I ask and she confirms that she's on crew at Mills. I remember somebody telling me that crew is the sport with the most onerous training routines.

We don't have much to say to one another, so I ask about her name.

"It's a Swahili name and has several meanings, including purpose, resolve, brilliance. There's an Irish version too, but I don't think that's me," Nia laughs.

I tell her some of the meanings for my name, like that I could be a Hindu goddess or the mother of the Buddha. Mother of the Buddha, that's my favorite so far.

We sip our wine. "Are you practicing Buddhism?" I ask.

"I'm definitely looking for something," Nia says. "Just don't know what yet. This is my second class with Taisha. She inspires me and encourages me to do things I didn't think I could do. I'd like to write, maybe teach like Taisha. Live up to the meaning of my name. What about you?"

What about me? Yes, what about me? My altar so far has nothing on it. I tell Nia what's happened to me, my story, and that I'm also looking for something, but I don't know what. I show her the pictures of Dan and Ella.

Nia just sits and takes it all in. Her eyes glisten with emotion. She doesn't say anything for a while.

"I'm really lucky and blessed right now," I say. "The place where I'm living, meeting Taisha, taking her course."

"Let's be study buddies," Nia says. "We can get together once a week or so and go over the lectures and reading."

I nod in agreement. There's no accusation from Nia, no anger, no recrimination, no envy, just tender care and concern. So different from the messy fears of my overactive imagination at the club the other night, when I thought she was being hostile. We finish our wine, exchange a light hug, and set a time for a next get-together. I take my bike out of her car and ride back to The Laundry.

Chapter 17 "A Change Is Gonna Come"

The next few weeks are some of the best I've had since the accident. I see Peter occasionally. It's getting late in the season for surfing, but we get out to Ocean Beach one more time, and I catch a couple of waves and ride for perhaps ten seconds each time. I'm surfing! My sense of accomplishment is way out of proportion to the time spent standing on the board.

"We're going to have to go to Hawaii someday, the birthplace and mecca of surfing, and test out the waves there," Peter says. *Maybe*, I think. I'm comfortable with this casual relationship and not sure I can think about anything more serious than that. I hope Peter is on the same page, but we don't discuss it. We breakfast at "our" spot, and he brings me back to The Laundry. He's kind and gentle, and understanding, but I'm still married in a strange way to Dan and to the family I lost. I'm married to my sorrow and shame at having survived. I don't want to commit to anything more. I don't want to fall in love. All I can manage is the intermittent affair we're having now. Also, Peter hasn't shared everything. There are things about himself and his family life he's never told me, and I've never pressed him.

Max is turning over more and more of the day-to-day property management work to me, but it's not burdensome. I've fixed up my room to the point where it's starting to look like a home, or maybe more like a tiny house because of the limited square footage, but what more do I need, really? I spend my days reading the coursework for Taisha's class. I still haven't started the book *Monkey* Taisha gave me. I don't know why, and even though I'm reading Buddhist texts in the context of Taisha's class, I don't have any kind of formal practice. I go online and read a bit about meditating and decide to try something easy that I find. Meditate every morning for just two minutes. Nothing to think about. Just pay attention to my breathing. I put a picture of Dan and Ella on the altar in one of the frames I purchased. I purchase a jade Buddha and a poster of Kuan-yin. For candles, I have two of the yahrzeit candles Kumiko told me about for remembering. The time for lighting the candles to commemorate the accident is nearing. Still, the altar is an affectation. Perhaps it's just a start.

My first attempt at meditation is lame. Lots of chatter flowing in my mind. I keep at it every morning. I experience at least a moment of no-thinking. Is that what it's all about? Nothing? An interval, maybe a second, where nothing is happening? A moment of emptiness, of peace?

Taisha's class is having an effect on me—making me more aware of the suffering of others, not just the African Americans in the novels we're reading, the horrific period of slavery and the almost-as-bad Reconstruction era that followed, but also all the way up to the civil rights movement and beyond. And even to today, when clearly the descendants of those slaves who came in chains in the holds of ships are still at a disadvantage when compared to their white counterparts. Taisha's class encompasses everyone's pain, not just the pain of African Americans, and it shames me to think how much time I've spent thinking just about myself, my own sorrows.

Monday morning, I get a call from Max inviting me over for coffee. I've hardly seen him these past few weeks and am glad to have time with him. I knock on his door and he lets me in.

"You've been pretty busy lately," I say.

"Tell me about it." Max busies himself with making the coffees and talks about his busy schedule. There is a nervous energy underlying his chatter. He's had a series of shows and been invited to take part in an art symposium on metal sculpture on the East Coast next spring. He even has a couple of major museums considering his works. When he says Guggenheim, he can't contain his high-pitched laugh and slaps his thigh in glee. I must have been imagining that something felt off when I walked in.

I tell him what I have been up to, with Peter, and most importantly with all my reading for the class.

"You've really gone down the rabbit hole on all that stuff," Max says with a smile.

"Yes, and who knows what crazy things will happen next."

"Look, I have something a bit serious to tell you. It's about your work here at The Laundry."

"Yes?"

"Well," Max clears his throat. I can see this is awkward for him. The nervous energy is back in full force.

"We're going to make some business and artistic changes here at The Laundry. I'm crazy busy and want to focus on my art. Jacques, Taisha, also incredibly busy. We want to keep some of the artistic stuff going, but no more open-to-everyone-big-blow-out type parties. On the business side, we're going to get a professional property management company."

Heat rises in me and fear that tears may come. I strive to keep a professional demeanor, but finally blurt out something about how I hope I haven't screwed things up too much.

"Don't even go there," Max says. "You've been too good for your own good. You've shown me why we need to make this change. Too many possible tax and accounting issues, most of which you alerted me to. Liability for some of our crazy parties. The need for insurance, and on and on."

A wave of relief and wonder washes over me: *Why do I always blame myself?*

Max is going on about how they'll pay me my stipend through October and how I can stay in the apartment without rent for a while.

"Hey, it's all good," I say. "I'll just go farther down the rabbit hole with Taisha and my African American classmates."

Max is relieved. He tells me he was never any good at "this personnel stuff" as he calls it.

"I'd have to agree. You are terrible at this."

I laugh. "Look, I'm okay for now. This gives me time for all the reading Taisha has assigned. Time for me to think about, discover, what's next."

Walking back to my apartment, I let this change sink in. There really is no immediate change for me. I guess I can ask my mother for money again if I need to or get a part-time job. I get out my bike for the ride to class. I love my bike. It's kept me in shape. The only driving I have done is an occasional ride to the dump with Max's truck.

I make it to class in plenty of time. Taisha's busy with an electronic device at the front of the room. Nia smiles at me as I enter the classroom. I take a spot not far from her and we nod friendly hellos.

"Okay, listen up," Taisha says. "I'm going to start this class with a blast from the past. Everybody put down their cellphones, iPads, whatever. No internet cheating." A groan from the class. "I mean it. I'm going to play you a song, and when it's over I want you to write down the name of the song, if you know it, and the person who wrote and sang it, if you know it, and hand it to your neighbor, and she'll hand you hers. Then we'll see who knows what about what." With that, Taisha clicks the play button and the opening lines come flowing out of the speakers in a voice like warm molasses:

> I was born by the river in a little tent
>
> Oh, and just like the river I've been running ever since
>
> It's been a long, a long time coming
>
> But I know a change gon' come, oh yes it will

And goes on for three minutes and ten seconds, right to the painful yet hopeful final verse and chorus:

> Then I go to my brother

And I say, "Brother, help me please."
But he winds up knockin' me
Back down on my knees
There been times that I thought I couldn't last for long
But now I think I'm able to carry on. It's been a long, a long time coming
But I know a change gon' come, oh yes it will.

The song reverberates in me. Taisha has once again nailed me. *Is a change going to come?*

Taisha is watching carefully, but no one tries to cheat. They all dutifully write down something on a scrap of paper and hand it to their class neighbor. When that task is accomplished, Taisha takes over:

"Okay, show of hands, how many people have a slip of paper that says some version of *'Don't know'*? More than half the class members raise their hand. Many more than half. Taisha shakes her head in disappointment. "Almost two thirds of you all. Ya couldn't pull 'A Change is Gonna Come' out of that listening? What is wrong with you? Okay, now, show of hands, how many got the title right?" Of the remaining third or so, almost all had figured out the title. "Okay, good. Now, who wrote it, and who sang it? Who had that mellifluous, that heavenly sweet voice? Come on, people!"

I don't say anything even though I know the answer. Don't want to be the know-it-all white girl in the class. I sit back and wait.

Finally, Nia speaks up. "Sam Cooke."

"That's it. That's it, girl. Okay, I don't even want to know how many other of you got that right. It's too depressing. Now, we're going to break into groups and discuss why this song is important, specifically to our class. Got it?"

I'm in a group with Nia and four others. All women except for one handsome, disinterested young man. We decide to all take a turn interpreting the song and telling something about what it means to each of us.

A heavyset young black girl named Michelle addresses me: "You go first, white girl. I'm sure you weren't born in no tent by no river all filled with pain and suffering."

"What do you mean? I don't know about pain?"

Nia puts a hand on my arm, but the next thing I know, Michelle is standing and screaming at me. Calling me bitch and a bunch of other names. Her face is contorted. "You don't know anything. You don't know what it's like when people die around you. When they try to take away your baby."

Before Taisha can even get over to our group, Michelle gives me a hard push that almost knocks me off my chair, and runs out of the room.

Nia tries to say something, but I'm out of the room and running down the stairs after Michelle. I find her slumped in a chair in the lobby, crying. I sit next to her. I can see Taisha and Nia looking down from the mezzanine area off the classroom. I wave them off and keep sitting next to Michelle.

"We're more alike than maybe you know," I say. "What's happening to you?" I ask. "What's hurting you so badly?"

Michelle spills out her story. Her mother has died, and she has a baby, a six-month-old girl. If she can't prove that she can pay the rent in her apartment, they are going to take her baby away. Her grandmother is coming from Florida to help her, but she doesn't have any money and can't help with the rent.

"I'm so sorry I yelled at you and blamed you. You're white and you don't know, you can't know how they treat us."

I tell her she's going to get through this and keep her baby. I tell her I feel her pain, but I don't tell her my story. My pain. When the class breaks up, Nia comes down. She sits with us for a while and we try to comfort Michelle. Taisha lets us handle the situation. I don't see her again that day.

The next morning, a letter arrives for me from the lawyers back in Boston who have been handling the accident case. My fingers tremble as I open it. It's in terse legalese but to the point. A settlement has been reached. I gasp out loud when I see the amount. Even with the lawyers taking their thirty percent, I'm going to be a millionaire, with complete financial independence for the rest of my life. More paperwork is being sent separately for my signature—a final report on the accident and the actual settlement documents. The money will come days after I sign the documents and send them back. I sit with the letter in my chair in front of the folding table with all my books and paperwork. Suddenly, I can see myself sitting there. It's like I've left my body and I'm looking down on the scene. My hands start to shake. I see myself convulsing. Sobbing. My face is unrecognizable. My hair that has grown so long it falls over my face. I lose all track of time. The next thing I am aware of is waking from sleep in my loft. The letter is crumbled and tear-stained on the futon.

I go down to the bathroom and stare at my reflection in the mirror. I keep thinking: *Rich because Dan is dead. Rich because Ella is dead. Rich because they were killed by a stupid drunk driving a telephone repair truck. They're dead and I'm alive? I don't deserve to be alive.*

I make a call to Peter. I don't tell him my news, just that I'm thinking of buying a car and would like his help. We set a time for Saturday morning. I throw myself into my reading and preparing for class. Activity is the only answer. Act like I'm okay. I've been okay. I can keep being okay.

It's Thursday. I can't read or do anything to prepare for class. I knock on Max's door and tell him my news. I don't tell him the amount, just that it's a big number. He's happy for me, though he knows it means I'll be leaving The Laundry soon. I ask him to lend me five thousand dollars so that I can buy a car right away. With his money and the money in my account, I should be able to buy something. He writes me a check without a question. I hug him hard. This chapter of my life has been so important, and Max has been an important part of it.

When I get to class, I notice right away that Michelle isn't there. I make a mental note to ask Nia about her, and the idea pops into my head that when my settlement money arrives, I could help Michelle, but it would have to be anonymous so that I don't come off like the rich white girl fixing everything with money. I try to concentrate as we discuss authors, like the groundbreaking black feminist lesbian poet, Audre Lorde, who said, "When I dare to be powerful, to use my strength in the service of my vision, then it becomes less and less important whether I am afraid." But I'm distracted. My situation is so volatile right now. Everything is about to change. Nia asks me out for coffee after class, but I beg off. I ask her about Michelle but Nia just shrugs; she doesn't know anything. I ride home thinking about Michelle. I've got a whole list of people I could help when the money comes – Peter, Kumiko, and Stefan Briggs. I'm daydreaming so hard I almost get "doored" by a man getting out of a fancy car on High Street.

That evening I call my mother and tell her the news. She's excited for me, but I can hear something in her voice. She's cautious. She's afraid for me.

"Be careful, honey. Money is a tricky thing. Get used to it. Go slow."

"I will, Mom," but I am hardly listening to her. Moving, doing something, anything, is what I am compelled to do. "I'm going to buy a car."

"Do you think that's wise? I mean, the car. You haven't driven much, have you?" She means "since the accident," but she doesn't say that.

"I've been driving Max's truck. I'll be fine." My mother is quiet.

"What about you, Mom? Do you need anything? I'm going to be quite the philanthropist, you know."

"No, I don't need anything, I'm just happy you'll be able to make yourself comfortable. Be careful. Go slow." She repeats.

"I will, Mom."

On Saturday I meet Peter. He looks tired, or stressed, or something, but greets me jauntily outside The Laundry. We drive down to an area in South San Francisco where used vehicle places line one wide street. On the way Peter asks me what kind of car I want to buy. What kind of budget do I have? I tell him I can spend around $10,000. I need to keep some funds in my account for now. What I really want to say is "a Humvee" but that would be crazy, that would be giving in to my fear. "A nice sturdy car," I say. "Good gas mileage. No convertibles. Nothing too sporty." I haven't told him that I could buy a Lamborghini with cash now if I wanted to. It makes sense to me to get an older model car for the moment. I don't know where I'm going to end up, I might not even need a car, but right now I'm giving myself the luxury of having transportation again.

"You can get a decent used car for what you want to spend if you know what you're doing."

"Well, I don't, but you do," I say. We both laugh.

We look at various models, Peter pointing out the plusses and minuses of each vehicle. At the third dealership I stop in front of a bright yellow used Volkswagen bug.

"Now that, my dear, is not a sturdy, safe car," Peter says. Then he sees my face.

I close my eyes and see the car flying through the air. Something like this was our car. Dan's pride and joy. He had restored it a year or two before I met him.

Peter takes me by the arm and leads me away from the car. We keep walking until I calm down. Just when I am about to say that I need to leave and abandon car buying, I see a silver, not-so-late-model Subaru Forester that makes me think of home. I stop in front of it and look up at Peter.

"Reliable car. Good maintenance record. You can always test out the all-wheel drive on a trip to Tahoe in the winter," he says. I see the worry in his eyes, but he keeps on talking, to take my mind away from where I had been headed. "With taxes, registration, and so on, it'll be just under your budget."

We do all the paperwork, I get temporary plates, arrange payment, and set a time to pick it up.

Back in Peter's truck, we drive out to Ocean Beach. He wants to buy me dinner "to celebrate my new purchase," he says. I know he wants to take my mind off things. Take me away from the panic he saw in my face when I stood in front of the Volkswagen. We don't go to the Cliff House. Instead, we park on Fulton and walk over to the Beach Chalet. It's crowded, noisy, pubby, with views of the ocean almost as spectacular as those from the Cliff House, if not from as high a vantage point. I am relaxing, thinking normal thoughts. Like, I'm surprised we never came here when we were surfing. It's more like Peter's style than the Cliff House.

After dinner, we walk along the beach and sit on low dunes in the twilight. I'm thinking about telling Peter my news, struggling with what to say. There's the money, but there's something else. The twilight darkness stirs something inside me, like white towels flapping in the breeze in a frantic beating against blackness. It's the undertow again. I have good reason to fear that I will fall, regress, tumble backwards. The ocean's sound is a drumbeat, beckoning me to a dark place.

Peter leans toward me and kisses me gently on the lips. He pulls me into his arms and holds me there. Instead of being comforted and safe, I panic.

"Maya, I haven't asked much of you. You're so much younger than I am, and you've been through a lot." He whispers in my ear: "But I love you. I want to take care of you."

My body stiffens and I pull away. It would be a betrayal for me to love Peter right now.

"Peter, we talked about this when we started. I can't possibly be in love. Not now. You've been wonderful, but I can't. It's not the age difference. It's, it's, I'm still broken." I see anguish and understanding mingling in his kind brown eyes. He smiles and says, "I take it back," and he holds me tighter and closer and lets me cry against his chest. After a while we stumble up the dunes in the dark of a moonless night. We hardly talk on the way home. Peter drops me off and we make an effort at civility as we part.

Two days later the package comes from the lawyers. It contains copies of reports with details of the crash and injuries. I sign what they need and send it back by overnight mail, but I don't look at the reports. I can't look at the reports. A couple days after that, the check arrives, also by express mail, and I'm a rich woman. It's a cashier's check. I go to the bank, deposit the monster check with a financial advisor who wants me to invest in this and that, but I put most of it into a semi-liquid CD, and the rest in savings, and get a check for Max with unasked-for interest. I pick up the car I've bought, bring it back and park it in the lot behind The Laundry. I tell Taisha about my good fortune and ask her if she could get me Michelle's last name, the name of her baby and her address. I don't tell her why, but Taisha smiles and says she'll make an inquiry with the registrar.

There's a party the next evening at The Laundry, and Taisha invites, me, but I'm no longer part of the crew. I'm going to spend the evening by myself. It's the two-year anniversary of the accident. I buy a bottle of Pinot Grigio, some indifferent takeout Chinese, and plan a quiet, self-indulgently mournful evening. Around eight the music starts in the atrium, but it's not booming like in the summer, just a murmur in the background as I light a candle for Dan and one for Ella and sit cross-legged on a cushion on the floor, wine in hand. With trembling hands, I take up the reports sent by the lawyers. I'm not prepared for what I read. Details emerge that I never knew. I had heard that Ella had been torn from my arms, but oh, why wasn't she in the car seat? She'd been fussy, and I'd decided to hold her, just for a minute, so we'd stopped, and I'd taken her out of the back and held her in my arms in the front. We were just sitting in the car on the side of the road with our flashing lights on. The force of the truck hitting us had ejected Ella from the car. I didn't know that Dan was nearly decapitated in the crash. I'm back there, on that rainy night on that twisty Maine road, and the car is flying. Music is playing, a crappy Europop tune from the late Eighties. Where is my Dan? And where is she, where is Ella Rosa, my darling daughter, my whole life? Maya has Ella, then she doesn't have her. Where does Ella go? Out the window. Into the blackness. It sucks, and my life sucks, and I just want it to be over. I knock over the wine and I don't care. I stand up. I'm dizzy, nauseous, I've lost my balance. Totally.

Ella, Maya. Maya, Ella. Why couldn't I have died when the truck crashed into our car? Ella should have survived and not just in my memory. I lay down, revert to fetal, curl up, and just breathe heavily and slowly, like I am inhaling and exhaling amniotic fluid. That's just practice for breathing real air for the fetus, and I'm already out here, in this toxic reality. I jump up, snuff out the candles, throw on clothes, grab my keys, and rush out. Max sees me and gives me a friendly glance, but I ignore him and head to my newly purchased Forester. I have no idea where I'm going. I know I shouldn't be driving. I only had one glass of wine, but my grief is deep and roiling inside me. I start out too fast and too loose. I head into the city on the Bay Bridge, other drivers honking as I cut in and out recklessly between cars. I don't get stopped. I make my way over to the entrance to the Golden Gate Bridge and pick up Route 1 heading north. I have no idea where I'm going, or why. The road begins the climb over the coastal hills toward Muir Beach, a maddening series of switchback turns on the ascent and again on the descent. I'm taking them more like a skier than a professional race car driver, sliding dangerously and kicking up gravel along the road edge, but I have no fear. I feel nothing.

Near the bottom of the hill, another car comes around a corner too wide. I yank the car toward the embankment on my side of the road, oversteering, and when the car has passed, I try to regain the road surface, but it's too late, I'm skidding and when I overcorrect the car flips on its roof and slides down the hill, finally smashing into a sign on the hillside. The airbags inflate. I pass out. When I come to, I'm hanging upside down, still held in place by my seatbelt. A Japanese monk in a full brown robe is peering in at me.

"Don't move. We've called for help," he says calmly.

"A monk," I say. I'm bleeding from the mouth. My words are slightly garbled. So is my brain. "Are you Monkey?"

"You crashed into the sign in front of the Green Gulch Zen Center. You're lucky, if you'd gone off the road higher up on the mountain, no one might have found you till morning."

"Is the other car okay?"

"There is no other car."

"Oh." I hear sirens in the distance.

"Come and see us when you're better," the monk says. I pass out again. When I wake up, I'm in a hospital bed surrounded by a blue curtain. There's an IV in my right arm. The light hurts my eyes. A black nurse is examining my chart. When she sees that I've woken up, she frowns, an odd reaction, I think.

"Hello, honey. You're one lucky girl. No broken bones. The California Highway Patrol guy said the long skid on the rooftop is what saved you."

"Where am I?"

"Marin General. We get all the crash victims from Shoreline Drive and Panoramic Highway."

"Can I go now?"

The nurse gives me a long look before she answers. "Go? Why would you want to do that? Just lie there and rest until morning, at least. We want to make sure your vitals are stabilized." I drift off.

When I wake again, I'm alone. I hear other people in the room. One of them is moaning in pain. I yank on the tape and remove the IV needle, which squirts liquid onto the floor. A monitor goes off, but no one comes to put the IV back in. I find my clothes in a pile on a chair. They're bloody, but wearable. I catch a glimpse of myself in a mirror on the wall. My face looks like a moonscape, battered and cratered. *Which Maya are you?* I ask myself. I remember Peter asking me some version of that question, about my name and its many possible derivations. I might have known then. Now, I'm at a total loss. Just as I'm about to make my escape, a different nurse appears, probably to check on the insistent beep that's been sounding ever since I took out the IV. She's short, Asian, maybe Filipina, but she looks tough and she bars my way.

"Hey, hey! Where do you think you're going?"

"I've got to get out of here."

"Well, we can't keep you. Don't you want to call somebody?"

"No."

A doctor comes in, and two other orderlies, and a physician's assistant. They all try to convince me to stay, but I insist I'm fine and tell them I'm going to leave. The nurse has me sign some papers that I don't bother to read, releasing the hospital from any liability. Minutes later I step into the harsh dawn sunlight of Marin County, a millionaire without a car, without hope. I start walking down the busy road in front of the hospital. Ambulances are bringing in victims of other accidents, shootings, stabbings. I have no idea where I'm going.

Chapter 18 The Abyss

I don't go back to The Laundry. The cab driver takes me to a place south of Market where they still rent out single rooms. He must have taken a quick look at my deranged state, my bloodied clothing and figured I needed something cheap. Even in the midst of the almost total gentrification of San Francisco by millionaires and billionaires, these places exist. The halls are dark and dirty, my room smells of cigarette smoke and worse, the bathroom is disgusting. I take a shower and find that I'm standing in other people's greasy grey water because the drain is plugged up. I get down on my hands and knees and yank hair and grime out of the drain so the shower empties, agonizingly slowly. There are cockroaches. I spend several days just lying on the bed waiting. I lay under the scratchy blanket. I hardly eat. I rarely bathe because the bathroom is so revolting. I go out for occasional trips for food and then I come back and just lie on the bed and stare at the grimy ceiling. I eat but I'm not hungry. I don't taste the horrible food I buy from the gas station across the street, cardboard burritos with BBs for beans, a travesty here, surrounded by cheap Mexican restaurants and the Mission only a mile way. I'm not starving, but I am wasting away. I hardly move.

People try to contact me—Max, Taisha, even Peter, after all I put him through, but I don't respond to any of them. I've left the world, but I am still stuck in it. I choose this horrible place. The perfect place to suffer. After I can't say how many weeks, I crawl out of bed one afternoon. I need to move again. Like in my earliest days in San Francisco, I walk. I buy a pair of walking shoes and some workout clothes, and I walk and walk and walk. One day I find myself across the street from Jane's apartment. I see her come and go. I see Joe. She's happy. I don't let her see me. When I see my reflection in a store window I cringe—who is that haggard witch? I probably don't even look all that bad. I'm not a junkie, I haven't lost my teeth or hair, but I'm a stranger to myself. I'm nobody. Jane probably wouldn't even recognize me. Max leaves me another message, but I can't be with people who spend most of their time having a good time. *Bon vive!* No, that's not for me.

I walk to the Golden Gate Bridge the next day. Is it even still possible to jump? Do I want to? Next thing I know I am running. I run across the entire span. Then I stand for an hour or so in the middle and peer down at the choppy Bay water, the wind kicking up whitecaps. I'm not really thinking of my death. Just wondering. Detached. Complete separation from myself. The eerie illusion of looking down and seeing myself falling comes and goes, causing waves of nausea. I vomit on the sidewalk. There is nothing in my stomach, but I heave until I have the vile taste of bile coming up deep from my gut. Tourists move around me, disgusted that I'm disrupting their pleasurable walk. I start to run again.

Finally, I'm back in the Marina, contemplating the view of the Golden Gate Bridge from afar. Just like in earlier visits, the sun is low in the sky behind the bridge. The Bay is bathed in a golden glow. My phone rings. It's Kumiko. I don't answer. I stare at the picture of Dan in my locket. His look of happiness and love pierces my heart.

I go back to the SRO shithole, pay up what I owe. Put the few things I have in a plastic bag. I toss the bag into a garbage bin and walk over to Union Square. I buy a travel shoulder bag and fill it up randomly, a dress, underwear, more workout clothes, walking shoes and socks, flipflops. I book a room in the Westin hotel on one of the top floors. The clerk stares at me and I can tell she's wondering if she should call her supervisor. I'm a millionaire. I get a room and spend the next few days, compulsively hand-washing all the clothes I've purchased and hanging them around the room to dry. I order food from room service. It's probably delicious, well-prepared food, but I can't taste. I hardly eat.

On the third day, I go to a fancy hair salon. The haircut is preceded by an ultra-serious, other-worldly consultation about the style I should have. The cost is ninety dollars. If I live, I'll look good. If I die, I'll go out in style. Back in my room, I wash out my hair and put on clean clothes. I sit in the chair staring out the window until I fall asleep in the chair.

Dan and Ella are sitting on a green lawn giggling and laughing. They look up and see me. Ella reaches out to me with her chubby brown arms. Dan smiles.

They're so beautiful. I can't believe I'm with them again. Suddenly the sky turns black and there's an explosion. Ella is flying through the air. As Dan reaches for her, his face takes on an evil grin and his head turns into a snake's head. He slithers along the grass, part man, part snake. I scream but then find myself contorted. I'm hanging upside down in my car, the one I just bought. The one I wrecked. The kind, calm face of the monk is smiling at me through the window. His hand touches my forehead. He gestures that I should follow him as he disappears into the foggy night.

I'm jolted awake. Shivering, I gather everything, take the elevator to the lobby where I check out. It's time. I must leave. I see my reflection and approve of myself. I look rather stylish. Gaunt and battered about the face, but stylish. Which way to go? Over another cliff? Out to the monk's place? Perhaps I should visit there first. Where did he say it was?

My phone rings. It's Kumiko. This time I answer.

"Kumiko, there was this monk. I need to visit him before I can decide what to do. To leave forever or to stay. I can't remember where he said he was from. Right near where I crashed my car."

"Green Gulch Zen Center," Kumiko says. "Where are you? I will come and take you to the monk." Kumiko keeps talking. In my right mind I would recognize that she is trying to get through to me, cajole me. Connect in some way. Instead, I'm impatient and eager to move.

"I'm in the hotel lobby."

"What hotel lobby?"

"The Westin," I say. "But I have to leave. I have to find the monk."

"Maya, listen to me. Take a seat in the quietest corner you can find. Close your eyes and visualize the monk's face. Just breathe and stay where you are."

I go to a corner near the back of the lobby, sit on the floor in front of a chair hugging my shoulder bag and purse. I rock back and forth. I crave movement but do as I was told. I visualize the face of the monk. I can see his gesture from the dream. Asking me to follow him. I remember his brown robes in the wind on the side of the road. I start to pay attention to my breathing. I try the two-minute meditation I had been doing and continue to think about the monk and my breathing. I am talking to myself in a low voice. *Why are you sitting here? Don't you have to go save someone, save yourself? Doesn't matter. Just breath in and out. Hanging upside down. I didn't die, did I? I never die except perhaps I will now. I will make that happen.* Just as I'm about to stand up, I look up and I see my mother's eyes. She is kneeling beside me and has her arms around me. On my other side, is Kumiko. She sits next to me on the floor and puts her arms around me. I start to cry. Not softly. I shake and wail as loudly as I possibly can. Mother and Kumiko simply tighten their arms around me. People are starting to notice. Someone from the hotel desk comes over, concerned but also eager to get me out of the place.

Mom and Kumiko lift me to my feet and I stumble between them as we exit to the street. Max is there, behind the wheel of a late-model sedan, not his old truck. I briefly wonder whose car it is. All three of us women clamber into the back seat, my mother and Kumiko bracketing me in the middle like African elephants guarding their calves. Max drives off.

I close my eyes, let myself be held and drift until exhaustion overcomes me and I sleep in the comfort of loving arms. A shallow sleep. I can hear sounds of traffic, the car on the road. The others must think I'm comatose or in a trance. I'm floating peacefully. I want the ride to go on forever, but doors slam, and we've arrived. When I open my eyes, we're at Kumiko's apartment. I'm put into a low futon bed, a double like the one I bought. Kumiko's bed. Kumiko brings me a strong cup of herbal tea.

"Drink." It's a command. I do as I'm told. I can hear Max's voice in the hallway and suddenly Max comes in and sits on the floor next to me.

"Hey," he says. "You really gave us a scare, you know. I was about to cancel my trip to New York to keep searching for you."

"To the Guggenheim?" I ask. "If you had I wouldn't have been able to live with myself."

Max cackles his strange laugh and reaches out for my hand. "You don't seem to be doing a very good job of that anyway. Pretty terribly damn awful job, I'd say."

I nod in agreement and spill some of my tea. "This stuff is awful. Must be some Japanese herbal remedy."

"I saw the reports. I saw the pictures. Maya," Max continues. "I think, even though you are now wicked rich, you should sue the insurance company for more money for sending you those reports the way they did. There must be some cause of action for that."

"Intentional infliction of emotional distress?" I offer.

"That's it exactly," Max says. "You were cruising, doing okay. What they sent would have derailed anyone. It's no wonder you spiraled out of control. I want to tell you something. Dan and your baby died. The fact that it was gruesome didn't bother them at all. It only bothers you. Don't let it. Maya, find a way. Get your feet back under you or I really will have to stay here and miss my show."

Kumiko and my mother come back into the room. Max gets up awkwardly. They explain that he's driving Kumiko over to Stefan's place where she's staying. I'm to stay at her apartment with my mother.

I drift in and out of sleep for several hours. The tea was strong. Some kind of relaxant. When I finally wake, I go into the kitchen and find my mother heating up chicken noodle soup—right out of a can. Campbell's. She smiles sheepishly.

"I couldn't resist. When you were a kid, you liked this soup and so I just thought—"

I put my arms around my mother, and we stand together for a long while. Then we have some of the soup. It's not Proust's madeleine, but it does bring back sensory memories.

Even though I've slept away the afternoon, I'm exhausted. I head back to the futon bed. I can hear my mother cleaning up in the kitchen and getting ready for bed. I lay waiting, knowing she'll come in to say goodnight. I hear her footsteps. She tucks the covers around me. She sits on a stool next to the bed. Then, unexpectedly, she pulls back the covers she's just arranged, climbs into bed next to me, and puts her arms around me.

We sleep until morning.

BOOK III   BUDDHA

Chapter 19 The Beginning of the Way

My mother stays in San Francisco. She and Kumiko enjoy each other's company. Kumiko takes my mother on outings to Golden Gate Park, Japantown, Chinatown, Nob Hill. Why are they having a good time while I'm still so fragile and weak? I'm like a snail withdrawn and curled up and hiding in my shell. How can they be going off sightseeing?

Kumiko has been my friend, my mentor. I don't want to dilute my relationship and share her with my mother. They make such an odd couple. My tall, elegant, reddish-dark-blond-haired mother. So different from me in coloring. Except for our green eyes. *How fucked up can I be? When these two beautiful women want to help and support me.*

One evening I come out of my room to get something from the kitchen and overhear them talking.

"We can't let her think she's damaged goods and that she won't recover. She will recover. Lillian, I am telling you this from my heart. She is strong." I hear my mother crying and responding in a shaky voice, "Yes, but she still is suffering, still blaming herself. She just can't turn the corner."

"She was doing so beautifully just before. She will become even stronger and more vibrant again. I believe in her power," Kumiko says in a kindly voice.

I quietly shuffle back to my bed. Overhearing them brings tears to my eyes but also makes me smile.

Knowing how much they care, how worried my mother is, how hard it is for them to maintain the artifice that I'm already recovering. I've gone as low as I could possibly go. I have to find a way. A line from a song flits through my head. Something about choosing to live. I will not cause the pain that ending my life would inflict on my mother.

The next day, sitting in Kumiko's apartment and then on a bench in the backyard garden, I finally pick up the picaresque eponymous novel *Monkey* by Wu Ch'êng-ên that Taisha had given me. It's, I don't know if "fun" is the right word, but it makes me think of Taisha and her course, in those last few weeks. I still can't see how it applies to me. I want to talk to Taisha. Soon, but not now. Nobody gets in right now, not my therapist, not Taisha, not Kumiko, not my wonderful, loving mother. I know there's something out there for me, but I haven't a clue what it is, or how I'll find it. This book, *Monkey*, is so odd. The novel is called *Monkey* because the mischievous ape is a way more interesting character than the sanctimonious, holy, and dedicated monk Tripitaka. One passage resonates powerfully with me. After many adventures, fighting demons, monsters, and dragons, crossing high mountains and raging rivers, Tripitaka and his three guardians, Monkey, Sandy, and Pigsy, finally reach India and meet the Buddha, who gives them Buddhist scriptures to bring back to China. Because the supplicants refuse to pay a commission, the keepers of the scrolls secretly substitute blank pages for the ones the Buddha has given them. The pilgrims start their journey back to China but soon after leaving they discover that they've been tricked, and return to the Buddha, who tells them calmly: "As a matter of fact, it is such blank scrolls as these that are the true scriptures. But I quite see that the people of China are too foolish and ignorant to believe this, so there is nothing for it but to give copies with some writing on." Something in this passage is a clue, a key to my future understanding, but like the people of China, I'm too ignorant to understand it.

The book is speaking to me. It makes me laugh. It opens my eyes to things. I am not sure why. I'm not Chinese. The spare aesthetic of Japan appeals to me much more than the rococo Chinese style of shiny gold paint and red brocade everywhere. Yet here it is, *Monkey*, calling to my spirit in some strange way that I don't understand. Once before I've had this sensation from a book. When I was young, I read Tolstoy's *Anna Karenina*, because I thought I should or because it was assigned in a class, I don't remember. Most of it went right over my head, but there was one scene—it's not even an important one in the book—where the landowner Levin is standing in his fields, and all of a sudden, I was no longer reading, I was standing there with Lev, listening to the drone of bees and the soft rustling of the wind through the grain. The impression lasted only a few seconds. *Monkey* is nothing like *Anna Karenina*. Yet here I am, traveling with Tripitaka, enjoying Monkey's antics, on my way to see the Buddha.

Reading *Monkey*, I begin to understand. I'm Tripitaka, not Monkey. Taisha thought that it would illuminate a path for me or that she already saw me on a path. But what is that path? She called me a writer. Is there something else? Something more?

The back garden at Kumiko's is as far as I've gone for weeks. Where is my thirst for movement? Why am I so damn weak? I'm angry with myself. My mother is leaving in a couple days. Part of me wants her to stay. To hold me, to cradle me the way she did the first night.

On Monday morning, the day before my mother is to leave, she and Kumiko are off shopping. I decide to go back to the grubby, sordid single room occupancy (SRO) hotel south of Market where I crashed before. I need to retrace my steps, go back down to the lowest point so I can find a way to climb up. I put on my newest walking shoes, grab some leggings, a tunic shirt and tie a sweatshirt around my waist and head toward the door.

At the door, I turn back. I grab a purse and my wallet and go to the kitchen. I leave a note that says: "Gone Walking. Back Soon," and draw a heart with my initials inside. I head out the door.

I quickly discover how weak I am. Just too tired from all the bed rest to walk far. I catch a bus downtown. Then I walk to Sixth Street. The area of the horrible hotel where I stayed after my crash is completely derelict. There are homeless people everywhere. Why did the cab driver take me here? Was it his fault? My fault? Must be somebody to blame. I stand across the street looking at the place. I notice a group gathered on the corner. They're sharing sandwiches from a bag. The one with the bag is short, round, jolly-faced, white-bearded, a Santa type. He has ruddy cheeks and is wearing blue jeans with suspenders and a plaid shirt. A thin woman in her sixties, also with stark white hair, stands next to him. I keep watching and slowly figure out that this older couple is plain but well dressed and not homeless. After a while, I see what they are doing. They're ministering to the group. They are bringing food and standing around talking with the homeless. I cross over and stand awkwardly next to the gathering. The man notices me but says nothing. The homeless guys are totally focused on the food, intent on watching it come out of the bag and making sure it's dispensed fairly. I edge my way over to stand behind the white-haired woman.

"What are you doing?" I ask her. She smiles gently at me.

"Bearing witness," she says.

"What does that mean?"

"We're just here."

"What good is that?"

"Great question. What is your answer?"

"I have no way of knowing," I say.

"Or not knowing," Santa chimes in. He must have heard us talking. I have no idea what he means. "What are you doing here?" the man asks.

"I stayed here for a month or more. Not sure how long really."

Somehow being around this man is comforting. Like being in a library when the quiet hum of intelligence spreads through a room. He's just "there," like the woman says.

"Who are you?" I ask.

"Eli Ronen. This is my wife, Reva." Eli bows rather than shaking hands, which throws up my guard right away, but I don't react too strongly. I see kindness in the eyes of this man.

"Are you ministers?" I ask.

"Getting warm," Eli says with a smile different from Sajiro's smile or Peter's. Or Dan's. "We have a group that meets in the evenings to study Buddhist scripture and meditate." I notice that unlike the Tribe, no one tries to give me a pamphlet or invite me to the evening meeting.

"Is it like church?"

They both laugh.

"We run the SoMa Zen Center, just blocks from here. We're always there, unless we're out here. Then we're here."

"Okay, thanks," I say. *SoMa Zen Center.* I'm about to drift away when Eli approaches me. I've been through the cult thing with the Lost Tribe, crazy Japanese Jewish clan. I'm not going there again. I take a step back. Instead of trying to lure me in, Eli does the opposite.

"We don't need any new students. You should come only if it meets your needs," he says. I wander away, leaving them chatting with the homeless bunch, a collection of derelicts: junkies, permanently homeless insane people, and immigrants desperate for food. From a short distance, I can't tell Eli and Reva apart from the rest of the group. Their presence lingers around me.

When I get back to the apartment, Kumiko and my mother are in the kitchen.

"Thank you for leaving the note," Kumiko says. "Very good thing to do. So we don't worry too much."

We share tea and sandwiches, and everything is almost normal. My mother and Kumiko are like older sisters together. Connected because of me. My mother is leaving, and I try to act like my old self, whatever that is. I don't want to cause her worry. It's not all an act. Going back to the SRO, seeing the sad and destitute homeless and witnessing the love the couple gave them.

Over the next few days, it becomes apparent my rescuers have a phone tree going. I get calls, there is a pattern. Someone calls, not all on the same evening, but I get a call every night to check in on me. I don't mind. In fact, I'm happy for it. I need the connection, the oversight.

About a week after my mother's departure, Kumiko is off at Stefan's and I decide to visit the SoMa Zen Center for the "evening sit." It's an old school building that has been converted into expensive condos, except for this second-floor space, once the school auditorium. It has a stage on one end, filled with odds and ends—chairs, ladders, a couple felt-covered sound baffles, an obviously broken and disused P.A. system. The room has a beaten-up wooden floor. Maybe it was too expensive to convert, or maybe the builders had to keep it as a public space in order to get their condos built. I don't know.

People are settling in. Some people sit in classic double-lotus, some in half-lotus, some cross-legged, some in chairs. An unseen hand calls the meditation into session by ringing a bell. Eli shuffles out minutes before the service starts. He doesn't sit up on the stage or even at the front of the assembled meditation group, but simply joins the already formed circle. Then we meditate. Or, I should say, they meditate. My attention span is near zero. I find myself glancing around, scratching, shifting uncomfortably. Finally, after twenty minutes or so, the bell rings again. We rise and walk around the room in a queerly formal walk that I try to imitate. Lift up heel, shift weight, slide foot forward, lift the other heel, repeat. After several tries, I get it. This part, walking meditation, resonates for me. It calms me inside. After ten minutes or so of this walking, we resume our seats or cushions for more meditation, and my wandering mind and inattentiveness return. When it's over, everyone shifts to face Eli, so that even though he's still in a circle, he's at the head of the circle, so to speak.

"Welcome," he says. "Your meditation was nice and deep tonight. Who has questions?" He's looking at me, or I think he is, but my meditation wasn't deep, and I'm certainly not going to ask any questions. I'm relieved when a girl on the other side of the room asks about "Ma." I'd assumed that the "SoMa" in the center's name was just the common abbreviation for the area, "South of Market," and undoubtedly it does stand for that, but Eli explains that its deeper meaning is "Sticking (Ma) to our Ancestors (So)." He continues:

"Oh, yes, 'Ma.' 'Sticky Ma.' That's the way we want to meditate. All together, sticking to each other, all finding the deep way in together. Not as ancestor worship. You know the poet Basho's quote: 'Do not seek to follow in the footsteps of the wise. Seek what they sought.' That's true meditation and devotion. Did I answer your question?" Several people around the circle nod their heads vigorously.

Afterwards there's no proselytizing and I don't stay around for long. I don't say anything to Eli or Reva when I leave, and they don't try to stop me or interact with me. I'm back a couple times in the next week. Sitting, walking, sitting, questions. Then I leave. There is no attempt on Reva or Eli's part to engage me further. I relax and just go. My meditation is still scatter-shot and frequently disrupted by a confusing parade of illogical and unrelated thoughts. In one of the question sessions, I hear Eli refer to that chaos of thinking as "monkey mind," and that makes me think of Monkey, the gigantically energetic character of the novel I've been reading.

Kumiko has been checking in on me even though she's staying at Stefan's. She asks me what I'm doing going out so many evenings. I tell her. She smiles and says, "Good. Very Good."

"Is it okay if I sit at your meditation table sometimes?" I ask.

"Of course, please do. Go slow. Slow is good. Deep is good. You must be careful. The abyss, your abyss, is always there. You must keep a part of yourself that is whole and safe, that floats above. That isn't always easy. That is always true. It is true for me also."

I make a pot of green tea to serve to Kumiko as I ask: "Kumiko, is everything okay?" This leads to discussion about the Tribe and about Sajiro. I listen in a detached way. I'm giving and not taking. The Tribe is having difficulties settling into their place near Shasta. Several key members aren't followers anymore because they couldn't leave San Francisco and don't want to live in a remote country area. Sajiro is struggling.

"You know, if you had stayed with Sajiro, our relationship would be so different. Much harder. I might have been your mother-in-law by now," Kumiko says, smiling.

"Yikes! That would have been hard, but now you're so many things to me. Friend, mother, teacher. You've done so much for me. I want to stay here. Are you sure it's okay? Have I pushed you out of your own place?"

"I am having a wonderful time with Stefan," Kumiko replies. "It is such a wonderful excuse to see how we do as a couple, a real couple."

"But what about the financial part? I have money. I can pay you."

"No worry for you. Your mother took care of that for quite a while. You can fix things with her later. You are lucky that even though you are in a time of struggle to regain your true self, you don't have to worry about money."

Her comment makes me think again about sending a check to Michelle and I decide to take care of that when I see Taisha. When Kumiko leaves, I decide it's time to contact people at The Laundry. Max is out, perhaps he's still away. I leave a message and let him know I may stop by and get some of my things, but that at least for now I'll just keep paying the rent on my space. I'm not ready to make changes about housing or cars right now. When I call Taisha, I'm surprised to reach her. We set up a time for lunch at her place. I ask if she'll go with me when I go to my room and just be with me the first time I go back. She agrees without reservation.

On the first day of the second week of my visits to the zendo, I decide to arrive early to see if I can talk to Eli or Reva privately. When I get to the place, Eli is nowhere around, but Reva is straightening the zafus and zabutons for the meditation circle. They're drab gray and dull blue, worn with age, fringes gone, the ridges of corduroy-like material rubbed away, but by neatening them up and plumping them, Reva is making the space a warm and inviting circle.

I ask if I can help. Reva nods. We finish the setup together. When everything is ready, Reva takes me by the hand and we sit at a Japanese table with two cushions in a corner space in the room.

"How are you?" Reva asks.

For several minutes I can't speak. I hold onto Reva's hand and realize that I am holding it as hard as I can and relax my grip.

Reva pulls her hand back and shakes it and smiles at me. It's like Eli's smile, perhaps not as intense, but full of kindness and compassion. "How are you?" She repeats.

"My husband and our daughter died in a car crash two years ago. I just crashed my new car and banged myself up a few months ago. I'm sad and guilty and lost." There, I dump it all out at once. Somewhere deep inside something breaks loose and floats away.

"You are a *vilomah*."

"What's that?"

"There's no word for it in the English language. It's Sanskrit for a parent who has lost a child. Sad is okay if you let it go. Guilty is okay if you let it go. You can't be lost, because, well, here you are," Reva says. She reaches out again for my hand and this time I don't squeeze hard.

As we sit there, saying nothing, a young woman enters. She's a bit round and plump, with shoulder length blond hair. She comes toward our table, and without asking she drags over a chair and sits with us. I'm startled by the intense blueness of her eyes.

"This is Barbara. Perhaps you should get some treatment from her. She does massage and Reiki."

Barbara rises, comes around behind me and puts her hands on my shoulders. "Okay?"

I nod and for the next fifteen minutes I receive the most stimulating, gentle yet forceful shoulder rub I can imagine. Reva still holds my hand. Tears flow, but I don't make noise. I simply receive. After the massage, I arrange for several sessions with Barbara. The physical touching itself is what I long for.

The time for the sit is approaching. "So," I ask Reva, just to be sociable, "Do you have an apartment in the building?"

"We don't live here," Reva says. "We have a place up in Mill Valley."

"Oh," I say, and the thought flashes through my mind that maybe the whole thing is a scam to collect money. A home in Mill Valley must cost millions. As if reading my mind, Reva adds:

"Yes, you'd never know it now, but Eli was a big-time hedge fund manager before he took refuge. The house is all we have left. He gave away the rest. Millions. I don't even know how many. The house will probably go too, in the end, and we'll just move to the streets," Reva says wistfully. She shakes it off. "But I doubt our community would let us starve and freeze."

We stand up together and Reva goes off to get Eli. I take a seat on one of the zafu/zabuton pairs we've arranged. Eli comes out just minutes before the sit is to start. Completely unpretentious, he's wearing a SoMa Zen Center T-shirt and surfer pants decorated with oversized psychedelic pink and orange flowers. He takes a seat next to me in the circle, nods to me but otherwise ignores me. It's not the time for conversation. As soon as the gong sounds to start the period of zazen, I feel the depth and, I don't know the word, the concreteness of his practice. It's like sitting next to a dense block of wood. His concentration is impenetrable. On the other hand, it's like he's not even there, insubstantial. My admiration for Eli Ronen grows exponentially at that moment. I have a new goal. I want to be like that. I want to be not frightened, not even when my mind takes me back to that totally exposed, ultimate fragile moment when everything changed. The moment I'll never understand. The goddess Maya had the power to make weak humans believe in anything, any illusion. My baby Ella could do that too, just by lying there cooing. *That's a real Buddhist thought,* I say to myself, and suddenly, I have an out-of-body experience: I'm thinking about Ella without breaking down. *Is this meditation?* I wonder. Is it what I'm supposed to be doing at this instant? Still, it's a breakthrough for me. I must have smiled or giggled or something, because Eli turns to me in the middle of *zazen* and graces me with another of his all-knowing, hooded-eye, bushy-eyebrow smiles. He nods at me! Can he possibly know? I turn back to the center of the circle, and after a slow second, Eli does the same. When we get to the *kinhin* (walking) portion of the meditation period, Eli falls in beside me, and we concentrate together, harmonizing our steps, our breath, our posture. Walking as one. It's another moment. Eli is acknowledging me, my presence, in the most beautiful and non-threatening way. Maybe it's because of what happened with Reva and Barbara before the sit. I don't know. I do know this: something has shifted.

After the sit Eli gives his dharma talk. It's short tonight. He says: "You can become One with Everything. You can integrate your inner and outer life until there's no difference. This is called 'Living in the Moment,' or just 'Living.'" He stops there and says nothing else. The room remains still for another nine minutes, and then a gong sounds.

The next day I head over to The Laundry to meet with Taisha. Thank God there's no need to recount the whole story because Max has filled her in. Turns out Max is still in New York. Taisha goes with me to my room. The files and papers have been put neatly in a cardboard box. Taisha sees me looking at the box. She shakes her head gently. "No need to go there again. Not now."

"Taisha, I'm not sure what I am doing, but I've started a meditation practice." I tell her about Eli and Reva and the SoMa group. She smiles and gives me a hug.

I go over to the desk and get my checkbook and ask her again about Michelle. I write a check in the amount of $15,000 and make it out to Michelle, write 'Gift' on the bottom, and give it to Taisha. I no longer care what Michelle thinks of me or whether she thinks I'm a spoiled, entitled, privileged white woman. I don't give a shit. All I ask is that Taisha explain a bit about gifting and how she likely won't have to pay taxes on the money, but that she should check with her bank or an accountant or something. Before leaving my room, I go up to the loft and gather all the things on the altar, the little Buddha, the picture of Kuan-yin, the pictures of Dan and Ella, the beautiful scarf, and put them in a sack to take back with me.

We go back to Taisha's apartment and drink coffee and talk all afternoon. It's not all about me. Taisha recounts how the class ended up. What Nia is up to and some of the other students. She fills me in about Jacques, some of the other folks at The Laundry. It's such a wonderful, normal lovely afternoon. I could stay in Taisha's orbit forever.

Back at Kumiko's I set up my altar next to where Kumiko has her altar. I hold the pictures of Dan and Ella and that makes me smile. Yes, smile instead of cry.

Over the next weeks, I spend almost every evening at the SoMa Zen Center. Gradually I gain a centeredness that is new to me. I get to know some of the regulars. I have body work sessions with Barbara that lead to a connection between us. Most of the others are older than I am.

I volunteer to go up to Mill Valley on Sunday afternoon to help Reva get ready for a homeless community retreat in San Francisco. I arrange a ride with Marion Goodman, a professor at San Francisco State who teaches women's studies and sex-based discrimination. Unlike Taisha, who is a dominating force but not an overbearing one, Marion is intense and haughty. At five-foot-ten, with dark curly hair, she thinks fast, talks fast, and dominates any conversation she's in. I'm not exactly looking forward to the drive with Marion but try to stay open to it.

The next morning, I call my therapist Sarah. I leave a message asking her to set up a weekly session with me. As much as meditation is helping, I recognize that

I still need professional help. Besides all the obvious issues I have, I have one other desire—I want my own transportation, but for now at least, I have a terrible fear of driving locked in my body. Later in the day, we text back and forth and set up a time to talk by phone. The only time Sarah has is six a.m. my time on Monday mornings. We agree to start next week.

On Sunday afternoon, Marion arrives promptly at four. She's driving a Toyota Prius, a smallish car that makes me nervous, but I take a deep breath and get in and we're off to Mill Valley. My one-on-one experience of Marion is different from being around her in a group. She still talks fast and is opinionated in the extreme but is also compassionate and interested in hearing about me. We connect on a level I find surprising. I tell her a bit about The Laundry and Taisha, and she mentions that she's been on panels at conferences with Taisha. I can only imagine what a colloquy between these two strong women would be like! We pull into the steeply sloped driveway of Eli and Reva's home, on a winding street tucked up against the base of Mount Tamalpais. The last time I was out this way I was crashing my car and spending the night at Marin General. I'm ahead of Marion as we climb the front steps, and when we reach the door, it opens and I'm greeted by a face that is instantly familiar, even though I've never met the person before. It's the face of country singer and movie star Mike Strong, standing there smiling at me with his Hollywood leading-man looks. Chiseled chin. Scraggly beard. A big man carrying extra pounds. "Hi!" he says. "Welcome." I'm speechless, but Marion slides by me, gives Mike a peck on the cheek, and we enter. I notice one odd thing right away—the smell of cigar smoke. I soon learn that Mike Strong is a respectful and worshipful student of Eli and Reva. He supports the zendo with charitable contributions and raises money by doing events and hitting up fellow celebrities. Eli and Mike are smoking cigars and drinking brandies on the back deck. Reva and a bunch of women make plans for the retreat in the living room. I find it odd, patriarchal, and sexist. I'm surprised Reva puts up with it, but in fact the arrangement suits everyone. When it comes to these events, Reva's the boss. The group of women she's assembled are smart, feisty, independent, and deeply committed to the zendo.

I try to make a contribution to the organizing, drawing on my recent experience at The Laundry, but during a break I can't resist going out onto the deck, with the pretense of getting some fresh air but really to see if I can meet Mike Strong. I wouldn't tell him I'm a fan because I'm not, but I know who he is. Mostly a country singer, but he's also been in films, playing country singers. Eli and Mike are sitting opposite each other in what I would call Adirondack chairs if we were in New England—bulky wooden things with cushions added for comfort. As soon as I pass through the French door onto the expansive redwood deck, Eli jumps up and offers me a cigar, which I decline, and a snifter of brandy, which I accept.

"Mike, this is Maya Marinovich, one of our newest students. She's well along on the path, though she doesn't know it yet."

I don't know what to say to that, so I turn to Mike and say, "Hello." I skip all the big-fan stuff. "How long have you been practicing?"

"Not long enough," Mike says. I sense nothing predatory about him. He's just a kind man who happens to be a movie star.

"What's with the cigars and brandies?"

"You don't approve?" Eli asks. He's not offended. "Yet you have one in your hand. There are no rules. That's the first and only rule. If you have rules you are judging, and if you are judging you're not merging and uniting with the One, you're standing apart from it."

I hadn't expected this to turn into a teaching moment. "Eli is a cosmic clown," Mike says, "and I mean that with the deepest respect and admiration."

"Clown, yes, I'll wear that title gladly. Because clowns put the world in its place."

I take a sip from my brandy and smile at both of them. What a pair! And yet I remember the deep, oh so deep, concentration I felt from Eli in the sit, a depth that can't be faked. The cigars and brandy are for their enjoyment, but there's an element of shock value also. They're testing.

"Why did you say I'm 'well along on the path'?"

Eli looks at me sharply, as if he wants to ascertain whether I can handle the truth. He decides that I can. "Because it's obvious you've learned the first of the Four Noble Truths—that Life is Suffering. Many people never even get that far." Out of the corner of one eye I see Mike nodding.

"I'll take that cigar now," I say, even though I don't smoke, at all. This statement causes Mike to laugh loudly and clap his hands. I must have passed the test. I never light and smoke the cigar, I just roll it around in my hands, smell it, chew the end. Disgusting. After minutes of small talk, I go back inside, shove the cigar in my daypack, and rejoin the women. The break is over, and Reva is speaking to the group:

"The idea is to have a farmer's market in SoMa, but one in which everything is free. It's all about the planning. If we plan properly, it's an easy day. We get restaurants, bakeries, and grocery stores lined up to donate. If we do that, the event will be a success." I love the idea but I'm having difficulty understanding how it fits in with Buddhist practice. Aren't we supposed to just sit and face the wall? Not in Eli's group, apparently. Reva gives each woman a list of places to call and asks me to track the responses in a spreadsheet she's started. *How involved do I want to be?* I wonder. I'm sitting next to a short woman with wavy red hair. Cathy Bishop. Probably in her fifties. She can see I'm awkward and laughs, a warm laugh as she reaches for my hand. "We are lucky to have a young person like you who knows about computers and spreadsheets. Wonderful that you are here."

I learn that she's an independent woman because of a divorce, has almost-grown children, and yet she is part of this group, devoting her time to helping others.

We go for a walk together during a break and I ask her what makes her so committed to the group and the idea of bearing witness.

"Maya, I know your story. There's no way to ever completely get over what you have experienced. I know this."

We walk and I just nod. No tears. I'm not even upset at her talking to me about it. Cathy continues:

"I've been married twice. My first marriage was to a successful attorney. He was ten years older than me. We were very happy. Then he got stomach cancer and after almost two years of fighting it, he died. I found him in the bathroom. He'd taken as many sleeping pills and other medications as he could find and put a plastic bag over his head. It wasn't pretty. He left me a beautiful note that I treasure to this day. I never told the medical people what I'd seen. I think they knew but they went along with it as an accidental overdose because of pain. I was pregnant with my oldest. I got all the insurance money. I had a second marriage that didn't really go anywhere except for producing two more beautiful children. Teenagers now."

We stop a moment. Cathy shakes her head. "How can I let the despair of losing someone I loved destroy me forever? I can't. I go on. Being a part of this group helps me to do more good in the world."

I take Cathy's hand as we walk up the steep driveway back to Reva's living room to work together.

Barbara, my friend and blue-eyed masseuse, is also part of the work group, though she spends an equal amount of time wandering around and giving the odd shoulder massage to as many people as she can. The planning and organizing go well into the evening, and by the end, I'm ready to go home, but more comfortable about being involved with this dedicated band of women who care so much about the world.

I throw myself into the volunteering. On the appointed day, the Free Farmer's Market takes place in a pocket park at 7th and Folsom. It's one of those clear, windy days in the Bay Area when everything sparkles with the fresh ocean light, even the grungy neighborhood south of Market Street. I hand out slightly stale but perfectly good loaves of bread and just-expired grocery items to a wide variety of people, not all of whom look homeless, but I'm not judging them. I'm surprised and happy to see Mike Strong there. A large crowd gathers around him, and he patiently signs autographs while serving out soup. The Free Farmer's Market is a great success. Afterwards, when the people at The Laundry would be popping beers or opening bottles of wine to celebrate, the Zen people just clean up the park and head over to the center for a short meditation. It is Reva who leads and when the meditation is over, it is Reva who speaks, not Eli.

"This has been a beautiful day. We were blessed with an open sky and the chance to be together with open hearts with our community that we have chosen to serve. Your brightness blesses the day of giving."

It is a longish walk back to Kumiko's place. I decide to walk. I want to absorb the brightness and warmth of the sun and the blessings Reva mentioned. *We're all the same, givers and receivers, rich and poor, famous people and street people. Kindness and understanding flow both ways.*

Chapter 20 In Deeper

My meditation deepens. I find I can spend longer and longer in the state of Mu, emptiness, before returning to the everyday world. Eli is always tripping me up, showing me when I'm looking at things from my ego instead of Universal Mind, but he does so lovingly. Practice, like recovery, is not a straight line. It veers, it meanders, but there is progress. It's hard work. I don't do much else except meditate and volunteer. My life is telescoping from both ends, my inner world growing vastly larger while my outer world shrinks.

I have *dokusan* (student-teacher meeting) with Reva, not Eli, and that suits all three of us. It's one of the more formal aspects of Eli and Reva's teaching style, which is relaxed and informal. For *dokusan,* each person sits in an anteroom outside a room set aside for this purpose only and waits to hear a bell within indicating that the next person may enter. The previous student exits through a separate door to another hallway so that there's no crossing paths between one student and another. I later learn that what is said in *dokusan* can sometimes cause great emotion in the student hearing it: anguish, pain, sadness, anger. It's better not to have to see anyone when you leave. For my first experience, Reva sits cross-legged on a cushion, wearing a robe I've never seen. There's a low desk in front of her with a couple of books on it, a lit candle on the back of a ceramic elephant, a couple of scrolls on the walls, and a cushion for me to sit on opposite her. The sessions are like therapy. It's almost impossible to lie when you're trying to do whatever it is I'm trying to do. Reva asks me if I would like to study "following the breathing, counting the breaths," or maybe meditate on a *koan*, or some other technique of one-pointedness, but I tell her that I want to "just sit," the practice I've learned is known as *shikantaza*. Reva questions my choice, but not in so many words. However, I'm free to make this decision. If I'm going to overcome and continue in life, I have to empty everything out and then empty the emptiness. Strip away everything. So even counting my breaths, a standard beginner's practice, is too much "between" for me. I don't want anything between me and Everything. Somewhere in my Buddhist readings I had read a quote from Yasutani Roshi: "The fundamental delusion of humanity is to suppose that I am here and you are out there." That's what I want. No difference between "in here" and "out there."

The months pass quickly. I "take refuge" in a simple zendo ceremony by repeating these three lines:

> *I take refuge in the Buddha.*
> *I take refuge in the Dharma.*
> *I take refuge in the Sangha.*

I know that saying these words does not convey any supernatural power to me. It's more a personal commitment than a prayer. I learn quickly and am almost shocked by how quickly I come to love the Buddha. Surprised that I want to follow the dharma, the irrefutable laws laid out as part of his enlightenment. The hardest one is the last: taking refuge in the *sangha*, the community. Even though Eli and Reva and their students are wonderful, there are dramas and intrigues, as in any group. Whether it's my haunted past or something innate, my advancement is rapid. I spend many solitary hours in meditation outside the zendo, in addition to the regular SoMa Zen Center sits and special events like *sesshin*, intensive periods of almost around the clock meditation that happen every few weeks or months.

One night Kumiko stops by for tea. I tell her about how it's going for me. She laughs and says: "You are rich. Not attached. Not married. You have no boyfriend?"

I smile but say nothing. I haven't contacted Peter.

Kumiko continues: "You are not burdened with family. It is right for you to concentrate. Most others have many problems from life that take away what they can do. Take advantage. You have seen some of the darkest of what life can give. Now you have a chance to experience the glory of life. In Judaism, we talk about Shekhina, the dwelling place of the Lord on earth, it can also mean the glory of God. The good part can come in many ways, many flavors. I think you are open, ready."

Every Monday morning, I have my call with my therapist, Sarah. The sessions provide a different kind of insight. There's so much letting go in the meditation. So much of the unknown. Sometimes I wonder if I will have any true self left. If I will be who I am or if I can even know who I am. Giving up the struggle for a meaningful life fills me with terror and yet at the same time liberates me from the need to be a certain way. Sarah mostly listens.

"How are you sleeping?" Sarah asks the next time we talk. I admit to nightmares, mostly about car crashes. During my waking hours, I'm better and better, but I can't shake the nighttime images.

"You suffered loss and your loss coincided with serious physical traumas. Your body is holding on to that memory and it shows up in your dreams. To heal, you need a practice like yoga, or tai chi or some other martial art. You need to inhabit and explore your body, to move your body."

"I walk," I say. "Miles and miles every day."

"That's great. The massage you are getting is beneficial. Please think about my suggestion of adding another kind of structured movement. Ask Barbara, your massage therapist. She may have some suggestions."

"I will." I do. Barbara suggests simple yoga, which I didn't realize is considered by many to be the precursor to meditation, preparing the physical body for entry into the Divine. I find a basic hatha yoga class in Kumiko's neighborhood and quickly realize how insightful Sarah's suggestion is. My body starts to unclench. I'm learning where my body is in space and not fighting my corporeal presence. It's still hard work, as are the therapy sessions.

As I'm leaving yoga class after the third session, I walk out next to a tall, thin young man. He's extremely fit and limber. In class I'd noticed how he could hold every difficult pose without difficulty. He has a square face, short, bleached blond curly hair, and darker bushy eyebrows. There's a hidden smile behind his eyes. He introduces himself as Jimmy Ueda.

"How can you hold all the really difficult poses for so long?" I ask. "You have incredible balance."

"I do Kiri-Do, a Japanese body movement and martial art, in addition to yoga. My family has a dojo in the avenues, on California near 25th. My mother and father are both teachers. I guess you could say I've been doing it since before I was even born." He smiles a gentle smile at me.

"Do you think martial arts would help me?" I ask.

"I don't know. What kind of help do you need?"

"I'm not planning to be in any street fights. I'm just looking for things that'll complement my Zen practice."

"Oh, then Kiri-do might be just right for you. Kiri-do is, uh, different from other martial arts. Not so martial, even though we do all the kicking, punching, and blocking of traditional karate. Some sword cutting," he adds.

"I'll look into it." I let it drop there and we go our separate ways.

"I've started therapy again," I tell my mother when she calls next. As if it's a room I can enter anytime. As if it's a tap I can turn off and on. As if my whole life isn't a tortured reexamining of everything that has gone before, is happening at this moment, and is to come. *No,* I correct my thinking. *I'm not torturing myself anymore. I don't have a guide and protector like Tripitaka in* Monkey. *I have something even more valuable—a teacher.* Two, in fact. I write about them in my journal and talk about them in my weekly sessions with Sarah, who is pleased. I tell her about the zendo, the house in Mill Valley under the shadow of Mount Tam and the work that the group is doing.

"Even when Eli is drinking brandies and smoking cigars with Mike Strong," I tell Sarah, "he's talking about how they can raise more money to provide more food and shelter to the homeless, cajoling his country-singer friend into hitting up other celebrities for donations. It's amazing."

"There's no higher calling than a life of service," Sarah says, and for an instant the image of Kuan-yin from Taisha's poster flashes through my mind. Then Sarah adds, "That doesn't mean you don't have to be careful and protect yourself. You know the old saying about power. Sometimes the people in admirable positions can fall prey to the corruption that beckons them."

I'm surprised and momentarily put off. Then I think about Sajiro. He helped me break back into my body, but it could have gone differently if I had been weaker in other areas. I've been reading about various Buddhist groups and the many examples of abuse. "Point well taken," is all I say in reply.

The accumulated effect of spending so much time "facing the wall" is hard to quantify, but I am changing—slowly, subtly, relentlessly—even though sometimes the meditation sessions bring things to the surface that are painful and ugly. Reva helps me through those times, explaining in *dokusan* that meditation isn't just supposed to make me happy, it's meant to facilitate the exploration of the artificial construct known as the self. How does it arise? Where does it go? Why am I manically happy sometimes, and radically depressed at other times? In meditation, I begin to see that these are just fleeting illusions that rise and pass away like everything else. If I don't cling to them, they don't hurt me. They can't be me.

I haven't asked for a *koan*, but Reva gives me one anyway. "Think on this poem," she says one day during our one-on-one, "by the ninth century Chinese Chan (Zen) master Linji, translated by Zen teacher John Tarrant:

> *There is a solitary brightness*
> *without fixed shape or form.*
> *It knows how to listen to the teachings,*
> *it knows how to understand the teachings,*
> *it knows how to teach.*
> *That solitary brightness is you."*

I shock Reva as much as myself when I shout: "Yes! It's me!" though her only reaction is a bemused smile. She nods at me approvingly and gestures to the exit door, while reaching for the bell to ring in the next student. "Wait," I say. "You said 'think on it.'"

"Never mind," Reva says. "You're done. Good work."

I laugh and leave.

The next time I see Reva she wants to talk to me privately. I'm thinking back to how happy I was when I had my last meeting with her, but this time it's something entirely different.

"You know Ellen Stewart?" Reva asks.

I nod.

"Well, Ellen is asking if she can have a room at the center. I talked with Eiko Hayashi who is already living at the center as the caretaker. Eiko is okay with it, but also worried because Ellen's condition is up and down. Do you think you could be a friend to Ellen and help me assess the situation?"

"I don't know, Reva. What you suggest, I'm not really being a friend, more like a spy." Reva shakes her head, up and down and sideways, letting her white hair, which is usually up in a bun, flop around her face.

"I know," she says. "It's like being a friendly spy perhaps? I'm just worried about Ellen and don't know what steps to take next."

I volunteer to help Eiko at the center. The first benefit is getting to know Eiko. She's what the Japanese call "Sansei." Her parents still speak Japanese. Her grandparents were Japanese, and they met at an internment camp in Arizona during World War II. As a Buddhist, Eiko has forgiven the world. She has no bitterness. She's devoted to the center. She has money from her family and some financial support, although, I come to learn, they are hoping she will leave the center, find a man and start what they refer to as her "real life" in the world. Eiko laughs as she tells me this background. She already knows my background and tells me so and gives me a very American hug. I can let my story be background, something to live with and, at least in part, get beyond, move past.

We schedule clean-up days at the center and a meeting to review what needs to be done by a contractor.

During the first clean-up session, I make a point of working alongside Ellen, sweeping out the main hall and airing out all the cushions. Ellen is my age, with short curly brown hair, brown eyes, and an olive complexion. Almost my opposite. I'm considered tall and she's just over five feet. I tower over her. At first, Ellen is tight-lipped, sharing little. But as we're beating out some of the cushions at the back of the building and creating something of a dust storm, we both lift up our T-shirts to cover our mouths and noses and take one look at one another and burst out in a furious giggle. That breaks the ice. She tells me she's sorry to hear what happened to me.

"For Christ's sake, does every frigging person in SoMa ZC know all about me?"

"For Buddha's sake, asshole."

And we again burst into giggles.

Somehow our bad language and the giggles ignite each other. Over the course of the afternoon, Ellen shares her story. She wants to be an acupuncturist but is struggling with getting through the required first two years of college. In her teens she was diagnosed with a mental problem and is on antidepressant medication. She's not sure if it's schizophrenia or if she'll grow out of it like some people do in their late twenties.

I see the fear in her brown eyes. It opens me to her. My sadness and suffering are my sadness and suffering. What about Ellen? What about her suffering and the suffering of her parents and family? What about the story Cathy told me about her first husband's cancer and suicide?

When we're finished with the cleaning, the practice hall shines. "Let's do some horizontal meditation and deep breathing," I suggest. We lay out zabuton to make two beds for ourselves and lay down next to one another. After just five minutes of focusing on our breathing, we're both sound asleep. When we wake up, Eiko has a tray, with tea, cheese sandwiches and cookies set on a table.

"The hall looks so clean! How hard you have both worked," Eiko says. We dig into the sandwiches and chatter away.

I want what everyone at the SoMa Zen Center wants: enlightenment, awareness of the true nature of reality, sublime Oneness. Like Eli and Reva, I also want something else: I want my actions to make a difference in the world. Eli and Reva call their practice "Involved Buddhism." When I press Eli about it, he reads to me the words of the Buddha:

> 'I am not the first Buddha to come upon earth; nor shall I be the last. In due time, another Buddha will arise in this world, a Holy One, a Supremely Enlightened One...He will be known as Maitreya which means kindness or friendliness.'

"So you see, kindness, that's the key, it's all about compassion. That's the heart of everything."

"Women, too, I hope."

"Eh?"

"It says 'leader of men.'"

"Hmmm," Eli says, scratching his white beard. "Well, Buddha was a man of his time. He certainly wasn't a feminist. He was initially resistant to the idea of Buddhist nuns, but he soon realized that there was no reason a woman couldn't become enlightened, and he relented. It's true that there were restrictions. We've evolved in the twenty-five centuries since the Buddha lived, and we know now that women are the equals of men. Surely you can see that Reva and I are equals in every respect."

"I should hope so," I say. We both laugh. I think of Kuan-yin, the Bodhisattva of Compassion. She's the one I want to be like. That fits in with Eli and Reva's teachings and the message of Involved Buddhism. The senior students, Barbara, Marion, Eiko, accept me into their "circle within the circle." I must be making real progress. In my reading I learn that there's no timeline in Zen. Enlightenment can happen at any second, even to beginners. When I read about stages of development, I want to pass through them rapidly. I recognize my ego that is involved, but also my will to survive and the challenge to have goodness reign in my heart, in my being. I think back to the afternoon with Ellen, how she opened up. I want to be able to help more people do that.

At my next *dokusan* with Reva, we mostly just sit quietly and meditate. At the end we talk, more like friends than as part of a teacher-student relationship.

"Something happened that surprised me," Reva says, "and made me happy."

I look at her quizzically, wondering what it could be.

"Ellen came and asked me about having sessions with me. Did you suggest it?"

"No, I didn't. I told her about my sessions with you. I spoke rather glowingly."

"The meditation space glows lately. After your cleaning it with Ellen. Eiko tells me Ellen has taken it on and is keeping it up on an almost daily basis. It's a meditation for her."

Over the next weeks and months, I continue my practice. I recognize a pattern has developed. It includes morning sessions writing in my journal. I scribble a list:

- Formal sitting
- Personal reading and meditation
- Monday meetings with Sarah
- Sunday afternoon calls with Mother
- Teas with Kumiko
- Yoga
- Writing

I also write a short To Do list:

- Get back in touch with Jane, Taisha, Max, Peter, Mariko, Stefan
- Next Steps?

At the next informal meeting with Reva, Barbara, Marion and Eiko, Cathy is also present. We have a serious talk about work that needs to be done at the center. I pass around a list.

"This is beyond just cleaning. I think we need a handyman or a contractor."

The other women nod in agreement.

"I'd be happy to make a list and try to project a budget for it. Then we can go over it and see what to do next and if we have funds to do more."

"This is wonderful, Maya," says Reva. "Absolutely what we need and not at all something I am good at."

"I know someone who can probably do some or most of what needs to be done. Shall I get a quote?" I ask.

Everyone nods in agreement.

When I leave the meeting, I am thinking about Peter. About how I haven't contacted him. About how he would be a good person to talk to about the work and if he has time, a good person to do the work. On Monday morning I bring up the issue with Sarah.

"What are you afraid of?" she asks.

"Involvement. Regret. Guilt. The strong desire to keep myself out of a relationship so I can keep going with what's truly important me."

"Quite a list!" Sarah says. "Do you want to stay out of it and above the fray forever?"

"I'm not sure where this is all leading, but I know I need to keep going."

"Well, talking with Peter, explaining, is non-threatening. Maybe he doesn't want to be in a relationship either. Maybe he would just like to know you're okay."

"I need a car," I add sheepishly.

Sarah bursts out in a laugh. "You should get one. Just be prepared for some off-the-chart insurance rates. Take it very, very, very slow."

I'm not sure if she's talking about driving or Peter. I go to my altar and sit. The pictures of Dan and Ella smile out at me. I've added other pictures on the wall. My mother and Kumiko smile out at me, the Golden Gate Bridge in the background. There's even a picture of Peter on the beach, with his long hair pulled back, surfboard by his side, looking quite handsome. I close my eyes and concentrate on my breathing.

I already have my yoga stretch clothes on and just need to put on my walking shoes when the phone rings. It's Peter.

After a tentative and awkward hello, I say: "You must be psychic. I just spent the last hour meditating, but mostly thinking about whether or not I should call you."

"It's been a while," is all Peter says. "How about dinner this weekend?"

"Okay." We set a time and place, Saturday at the Cliff House.

"I'll meet you there," I say. *I need to keep my distance and take this part slow* goes unsaid.

On Saturday afternoon I spend an hour sitting before starting out to walk to the Cliff House. I let my thoughts flow freely. I think about Peter and what's to come. My thoughts are open, easy. I let them come and go. I'm settled in some way. When I get to the parking area, I see Peter leaning against his truck, looking at the ocean. We stand for a moment just looking at one another and then gently we enfold one another in a caring and warm embrace.

Inside we sit in the bistro section. It's early. We get a table right up against the window. We gaze out at the Pacific Ocean. It's hard not to just sit there and stare at the blue that goes on forever. We're also still awkward with one another. I order something called an Ocean Beach Cocktail. Peter orders a local microbrew and a shot of Balvenie Caribbean Cask.

"I didn't know you were a Scotch aficionado," I say after the waiter leaves.

"There are many things we need to learn about each other," Peter says.

The drinks come and we gradually loosen up a bit.

"Peter, dinner is on me," I say. "You know I'm ridiculously rich now."

"So I've heard," Peter replies.

"Let's splurge," is all I say in response.

I order a bottle of red wine with dinner. I'm having salmon. Peter orders an absolutely huge New York steak.

We loosen up completely over food and talk and talk. I know we've been helped along by the drinks and the wine, but how comforting, relaxing, and open we are with one another. We both are responsible and guilty for not contacting the other. Apologies and forgiveness flow in both directions. Peter lets me know that his ex-wife has moved in with him and the kids. She's dying. In the last stages of lung cancer. Hospice has been called and everyone is coping as best they can.

"I can come and help," I offer.

Peter looks up, surprise in his eyes. "That would be wonderful." I remind myself to follow up. If I'm going to become a compassionate person, I'd better start now.

The details of meeting at the SoMa Zen Center are worked out and even the idea of him helping me again with the buying of another car.

"A tank might be in it this time," Peter teases.

"I'm okay now," I smile.

"Yes, I can see that. You are different."

"Yes, I am," I say. "I need to continue on my new path. I hope that's okay."

"Of course it's okay," Peter holds my hands in his rough strong hands. "It's more than okay. For both of us, for now."

At the end of the next formal sit, Eli speaks about the timing of awakening. "There are no rules. A person might meditate for fifty years and never fully experience enlightenment. Or someone could walk into the zendo one day and become enlightened as they step across the threshold." I think on his words. It's what I have been reading and thinking about. I wonder again if it's my ego that's pushing me, but I've been on a pretty powerful trajectory, a path catapulted by my personal tragedy. I've moved beyond everything in my life being based on the death of Dan and Ella. I can sit with that and my suffering in a place of stillness, without breaking down. Increasingly I'm stronger both in body and in spirit. My sense of compassion is rapidly extending beyond myself and my personal misfortune to encompass the whole world.

I think back to my dinner with Peter. I had volunteered to help take care of his ex-wife who is dying of cancer. The next time I talk to him about the work he's doing on the zendo, I make a date to visit. On Saturday I show up at Peter's cottage, where I once slept off a molly hangover and made love with Peter. Peter's ex Adrienne is not in the upstairs king bed. She couldn't make it up stairs. Peter has set up a pallet for her in the living room. I'm shocked when I see her, wretchedly thin, with grey skin and yellow eyes. She's far gone, near death. I find the inner courage to approach her and ask questions, but she's too tired to converse. I rub salve on her swollen feet and hands, give her sips of water from an infant's sippy cup. Soon after I arrive, she falls asleep. I wait a couple hours but she never awakens, and Peter, grimly determined to see it out, tells me I should leave. He accompanies me to my car. He whistles and manages a weak half smile when he sees the fancy car I have leased. "Guess we'll go car shopping when this is over, he says."

We don't hug or touch except that as I am about to get into the car, I take his rough, strong hands in my two hands. His pain shoots through me. I close my eyes.

Peter leans over the open window to the car as I sit in the drivers' seat. "The kids are taking it pretty hard. She and I haven't been together for a long time, but this seemed like the right thing to do."

It is the absolutely right thing. So very hard, so very right. I think, but I don't say anything.

Adrienne dies within days. After that I don't see Peter for weeks. When he comes back to work again on the zendo, he's quieter, more focused than I remember. Like Peter, maybe even with Peter, I am going to continue on the path of compassion. My heart-mind is opening.

Chapter 21 Zen Body, Zen Mind

The next time I do yoga, I see Jimmy again and am impressed by his physical agility, grace, and balance. I remember what he said about studying a martial art of some sort. Over the next several weeks, I start looking into martial arts. As helpful as I find yoga, the nightmares have persisted. Maybe something more active and rigorous would speed things up, dislodge the body memories of nighttime car crashes. Something tells me it might also augment my development in meditation. I'm never sure what drives me but with the help of my Zen teachers and my therapist Sarah, I'm coming to trust and believe in myself and I follow my intuition, my instincts. It's San Francisco—with a cornucopia of offerings available—tai chi, karate, aikido, tae kwon do, as well as lesser-known practices. I try classes in different forms but nothing fits. Tai chi is too passive, karate too focused on combat and self-defense. I continue my long walks, and on a sunny Sunday afternoon, I find myself in front of the Kiri-Do dojo on California Street. With a start I remember that this is the family dojo of my new friend from yoga, Jimmy. A large poster covers the window.

Need to Change Your Life?
Try Kiri-Do (The Way of Cutting)
The Martial Art for Personal Transformation

A jolt runs through me as I read the words. That's me: I need to change my life. I'm on the path already. Maybe Kiri-Do is what Sarah was getting at when she suggested a body-centered practice. At the end of the next yoga class, I approach Jimmy and ask about beginners' classes.

"We're all beginners. We always will be. You should just come. We all practice together. Are you free Wednesday night? If you are, come by. I'll be there too."

So here I am showing up for class on a drizzly San Francisco Wednesday night. I'm wearing grey sweatpants and a long-sleeved white t-shirt. The dojo is a nearly empty room with a scuffed and worn wooden floor and a *tokonoma* altar in one corner. Everyone leaves their shoes and street clothes in the outer entry way. The first thing I notice is that there are few students, and they're all in incredible shape. A youngish woman welcomes me. She's not Japanese, but she's dressed in a white martial arts outfit I later learn is called a *gi*.

I'm surprised when Jimmy comes out. He's wearing a white uniform, white special shoes, and a white skirt-like covering that makes him loom large. When he sees me, he smiles broadly and nods in my direction. The class is about to start. Jimmy has everyone form a circle.

Jimmy leads warmups, a series of increasingly strenuous stretches, starting at the top of the head and working down to the lower part of the body. It's not too hard. I'm getting a bit comfortable. We reform the circle at the end of warm-ups and have a short standing meditation. An older Japanese man walks out from a back room. He's shorter than Jimmy, and has the square body of a martial artist, compact, muscular, with short-cropped gray hair and glasses. His face is severe, with none of the easy warmth Jimmy projects. He notices me right away and comes over to me while the rest of the class waits on the side. Jimmy hurries over to make an introduction.

"Father, this is Maya, a friend of mine from yoga class. Maya, this is my father, Mr. Ueda. In class we call him Sensei."

Sensei nods. "Hello, Sensei," I say, and I bow, something I learned from my time in the Tribe.

"Please just follow. You are not expected to know what to do. Jimmy will be near you."

What happens next surprises me. There are a series of partner exercises that include leading and following and jumping. Lots of jumping. After twenty or thirty minutes, I am completely exhausted and surprised. I thought I was already in pretty strong shape, but these exercises are something else. Also, there is something to the way we are touching one another. Holding out our hands to support the person doing the jumping. Jimmy comes by to be my partner toward the end of the break-out session and I follow as best I can. When I lead him, I notice how the slightest movement on my part sends him jumping up almost to the ceiling. I try to pull back my energy, but he just smiles at me and continues.

We again stand in a circle for a brief calming meditation. We do some strange movements accompanied by sounds. I continue to do my best to follow. The rest of the class is more technical. As far as I can tell, it's basic karate stuff, except the students aren't sparring, there's no headgear or padding, and when they do partner practice, they don't strike each other. I try to follow Jimmy's father, the teacher, but it's hopeless. He doesn't explain anything and pays no attention to me. I'm supposed to copy what he's doing, without any instruction. Oh well, I think, waiting for the class to be over so that I can leave and never come back. A funny thing happens toward the end of class. We take up wooden practice swords. I notice that each of the students has one of their own, carefully wrapped in cloth scabbards or *furoshikis*. Jimmy gives me a loaner. We follow Sensei in a series of cuts. Jimmy comes over to correct my form because I'm holding the sword upside down, but in my defense it's hard to tell, since the thing, I learn, is called a *bohkutoh* and is just a straight, heavy piece of hard wood that barely resembles a sword; it has no curve and only the hint of a blade edge, though it does have a rough point which keeps me from holding it by the wrong end, thank goodness! The funny thing is, I like it all—the sword, the cutting, everything!

After the class, Jimmy comes over to ask how I am and what I thought. The other students are filtering out of the dojo, bowing to the Sensei and bowing at the entrance before turning to leave. I intuitively understand that they are appreciating and acknowledging the sacredness of their practice space.

My time with the Tribe and in Japan taught me at least that much.

Just as I am about to leave, Jimmy's father comes over to the two of us.

"Why are you here?" he asks. It's a challenge. I wonder: *Did I do something wrong. Have I presumed too much in some way I'm unaware of?*

The question takes me by surprise. I don't have a quick, easy answer. Sensei is silent; he's not offering anything. He waits. He expects an answer. I think about it. Hesitantly I start to give a response:

"I'll tell you why I'm here. I love the *zazen*, the sitting that I'm doing at the Zen Center. I love the *kinhin*, the walking meditation. I have terrible nightmares; my therapist told me it's from my worst memories locked in my body. And, sometimes I get so restless that I just want to—"

"Scream—" he says.

"Yes."

"So. I see. Scream, right now."

"What?"

"Go ahead. Scream."

I look at Jimmy, but he's stepped back and is letting me have this moment with Sensei on my own.

"Scream what?"

"Anything. 'Yes!' 'No!' Your scream is a meditation also."

"I don't know," I say doubtfully. Okay, I'm not completely ignorant. I've heard of Primal Screaming. It's so unlike anything Eli and Reva are teaching me.

"There are many ways," Sensei says. "Even within Zen. Many ways. You have to find your own way within the No Way."

"No Way?"

"Exactly." And he opens his mouth and lets loose a yell that roars around the dojo until I think it's going to shatter the windows that rim the upper level of the room.

"Try," he says. "First, go deeply silent. Then, scream!"

"Ah," I say. 'Go deeply silent' is a clue. I kneel down, make myself small, concentrate my breathing, empty my mind. I go toward the place that I've been seeking these months in the zendo. This time when I get there—instead of grasping to stay in it and immediately losing it, always fleeting, never settling in—this time I jump up and give out a shriek that comes from the depths of my being, from the inside of a smashed car, from the newfound power I have found through meditation. I start to cry, but then I stop.

Sensei smiles for the first time and says in a kind, almost gentle voice: "You have pain locked in your body. I'm glad you are here even if it is for a short time."

Can he see the pain I am holding? Can he see the hot molten river that still flows somewhere inside me? The one I've tried and am still trying to bury. To escape. Can he see the pain from the accident? The part Sarah says is locked in me?

"Now, try running around the dojo screaming."

"Wait, what? Why? What for?"

"To free yourself, of course. Sitting is good, standing is good, walking is good, all will get you where you want to go. You have good teachers at the Zen Center. Now try. Cut! As if you have a samurai sword in your hands, the sharpest blade imaginable."

"Cut what?"

"Cut everything. The air, the walls, the sky. Me. Yourself. Scream!"

I have no idea what I'm doing but I try again. And again. And again. Each time, Sensei exhorts me to try harder, express myself more and more. Finally, I get frustrated and angry, and I run around the room like a crazy woman, yelling, "Yes!" and "No!" randomly, hating the teacher, hating this foolish exercise. When I stop, I'm crying. As before, I stop myself, a new thing for me. Before I can say anything, he says: "Better." That's all. It's just a moment, but in that instant of complete release I see possibilities.

At the next meditation session in the zendo I mention my first Kiri-Do class experience to Reva. She knows of the Uedas and approves of the idea of me taking up another practice.

"It can only help," she says.

I also mention my new sword practice during an early-morning session with Sarah. She also approves, using almost the same language as Reva: "Perhaps it will help."

I make Kiri-Do a regular part of my routine and go to class weekly. I even get a *gi* and a basic wooden sword, *bohkutoh.* I notice the students treat these plain swords with utmost respect as if they were sacred objects, keeping them in their coverings except when using them, and bowing after each use. I'm never going to be a master swordsman, but the one-pointedness, the intense focus and concentration required is certainly good for taming my erratic mind. It's deepening my *zazen* in ways that I can hardly understand. I learn the basic cuts, and I enjoy the way the combination of the gently strenuous yoga and the outright arduous Kiri-Do classes complement each other.

A couple of months go by. One day after yoga class, Jimmy mentions that there's a special Kiri-Do event planned for the weekend and asks if I would like to go.

"What is it?" I ask.

"It's called *takigyo*. Waterfall training. Up in Marin. My father will lead it. If you want to come, show up at the dojo on Saturday morning." I'm noncommittal with Jimmy. The idea brings back memories of the hike up Tennessee Valley with Sajiro. I think about it and decide I shouldn't let the past influence the future. *No regrets*, the Buddhist texts say.

On Saturday, Sensei takes a vanload of students up onto Mount Tam. We drive halfway up the mountain, park in a lot near Lake Lagunitas, and hike up an almost hidden path. I soon learn why the trail is avoided by most hikers. It's steep and slippery. Water runs down it, making footing treacherous as it parallels a runoff stream, sometimes crossing it. High up on the mountain we come upon a waterfall, the rivulet spilling over a ledge more than twenty feet up, into a shallow pool. It's a magical place, a hidden dell of wondrous natural beauty, sheltered and tranquil, the water splashing into the pool musically. Sajiro's words about the ocean view at Tennessee Valley come to me unbidden: "This is always here."

"Here," Sensei says. We all take off our daypacks and the others start to change into their white *gis*. No one cares about modesty, so I strip down with the rest and put on my *gi*. Sensei stands at the edge of the pool and chants a prayer, intermittently clapping his hands. A senior student informs me that this is a supplication to the water god to keep us safe and not send anything over the fall onto us while we're there. "It's a Shinto thing," he says. I shrug off this oddity and watch as Sensei enters the water first. He stands under the plunging cascade, takes the horse riding stance, and executes *tsuki* punches, each time emitting a shout which reverberates over the sound of the water into the surrounding silence of the forest. When he's satisfied that the falls are safe, he leads us, one by one under the waterfall, senior students first, and leaves us there for as long as we can stand it. Before the first person goes in, he says: "In Japan the water would be much stronger than this, and much colder, but for American students this is a good first time for *takigyo*."

Some people last only seconds, others revel in the pulsing crashing liquid beating down on their heads. Some simply stand there, and others perform imaginary sword movements; and no one takes their sword into the cataract even though people have brought theirs with them. When my turn comes, I'm shocked by how cold the water is, and I think that I'll stay in for only a second or two. I find myself standing straight and still. I lift my hand up and reach up into the water that's crashing down and cut forward with my arms. It's the movement I did from the balcony a long time ago, when I was planning to jump and end my life, the time when I turned away from death and towards the struggle to find a way to live.

When I step out, hands reach out to assist me. I stand by the dark wet rock next to the falls and support myself with one hand. I look at my white hand against the dark shining wet black rock. The rock is me. I am the same as the rock. We have become one.

On the next Wednesday, as I enter the dojo, I'm shy for some reason. The waterfall training humbled me and at the same time ignited a fire inside me. How can standing in cold water ignite a fire? How can my white hand be the same as black rock? How can black rock be me?

Jimmy starts the class by asking us to form a circle. This time we sit in *seiza* position on our knees with our eyes closed. There's an obvious space in the circle and I'm expecting Jimmy's father to step into that space and meditate with us. Instead, a tall blond woman quietly slips into the circle, wearing the white skirt that I have learned is called a *hakama*. I immediately recognize her as Jimmy's mother. She is the Sensei's wife, and the Sensei this evening. She has curly blond hair that frames a round beautiful face. When Jimmy ends the meditation, we all bow toward her.

She steps into the circle and asks us to hold hands, to let the energy of the circle pass through us, through the left and to the right. I'm surprised at how the circle comes alive, pulsating, swaying as one. When we start the class, we again do more cutting movements. The difference is that we do them slowly as if we are cutting through a thick liquid. We end up reaching to *Ten* (Heaven) and slowly cutting down. This is *my* movement, that I've done instinctually. It is the movement that saved me from jumping. It is my waterfall movement. It's wonderful to follow this strong woman. The entire class is free hand. No swords, but plenty of movement, plenty of cutting using our hands and arms, with many different partners. The end of the class is simply running and cutting with our arms for a long time. Energy comes and goes, surges and ebbs until I am in a trance of movement and meditation.

At the end, Jimmy calls us back into a circle for meditation.

"Jimmy, your mother is amazing," I say after class. He leads me over to introduce me, and I have a sensation of surrender. I've found another teacher, another woman to help me find my way.

I never miss a class of Kiri-Do. My sword work becomes more assured.

Similar to my experience in the zendo, I surpass some students who have been practicing much longer than me.

"It's not a competition," Mrs. Ueda tells one student who is peeved that I'm progressing so rapidly. "It's not a competition with anyone except yourself. Remember that."

My posture changes. I notice that when I walk down the street, people are, if not truly afraid of me, then respectful. I doubt a mugger would ever pick on me, I'm projecting too formidable a presence, without doing anything martial whatsoever.

Then one day it all ends suddenly.

In class one Wednesday evening, Jimmy's father is watching me in partner practice with another student, Paul, a guy I don't know well. Paul is a lanky white guy, not so much muscular as lithe, stringy, flexible, and quick. We're practicing timing and cutting techniques. We have to catch the other's movement. Beat him or her to the punch so to speak. Sensei stops us almost immediately after we change roles. He gives me a funny look. I can't read it. Is he going to praise or criticize me?

"Do you want to defeat and humiliate your opponent?" he asks. "Do you wish to be victorious and ego proud? No! You want to lead them into *mu*, emptiness. Suck them into the vacuum space where there is no ego. Can you do that?"

He gives me that look again, and this time I think I understand. It's a test, like the first day when he made me run around the dojo forever. I stand with my eyes closed for a long while. Sensei's eyes are on me. Paul is waiting. To do what Sensei is looking for, I must connect with Paul in some way that I haven't yet. I must find his center, cut it open, and let it expand. I have an instantaneous momentary vision of the poster of Kuan-yin hanging on Taisha's door in The Laundry. Unbidden, the phrase "kill him with kindness" comes into my head.

I face Paul again, look at him as deeply as I know how, really examining him, his strengths and his pains. He looks away at the last instant before we bow. Then, each time he raises up his sword, I slash across his body in the space he's opened up. I'm shredding him with each cut. In some weird way as I'm cutting Paul, I'm revealing myself also, opening up my shell and letting inside and outside merge. I finish the round and bow deeply to Paul, who also appears to have been strongly affected by the experience. He walks away with a slightly stunned expression on his face. Sensei approaches me. He doesn't bow, which would be totally out of character, but he cocks his head to one side and says:

"For you the sword is a step on the path. For me, it *is* the path. It is my life. Different paths. I'm glad ours crossed."

I bow, holding back tears. Sensei is dismissing me. He knows I'll never study sword long enough or hard enough to follow his path. I can't let anything, even the practice of Kiri-Do that I enjoy so much, get in the way of my true search. We both know this is my last class. As Sensei Ueda says so wisely, I'm on my own path and must follow it.

Chapter 22 I Meet the Buddha

It's May. I'm walking in a part of the park way out on the avenues, where one wouldn't expect buskers; but here is one, a thin brown man of indeterminant ancestry—Mexican, or East Indian, or Native American. He's wearing a straw hat, a colorful yellow and orange shirt with mirrors sewn into it along with delicate embroidery of paisley-like swirls in blue thread. He has a smallish accordion slung over his body and hanging down loosely in front of him. He isn't playing as I walk by, paying him absolutely no mind, until he addresses me when I'm past him:

"Hello there, pretty Pilgrim."

I turn but don't backtrack, wanting to keep distance between me and this stranger who accosts me on a secluded path in the park.

"I bet you call all the girls that," I say.

"No. Only you."

"Who are you?"

"Zandro Pandi at your service."

"How do you—" I start to ask, but he puts a finger to his lips to silence me.

"Pilgrim, you have journeyed far. You may ask me questions about yourself, your quest, but not about me. You are close. I am here to help you over the finish line, so to speak."

My rational mind is saying to start running. Get away. I stand still. I can't move. The line between heaven and the earth is coursing through me.

"Why did Dan and Ella have to die?" I blurt out. It's at the root of everything else that has followed, and despite all my experience and all my study, I still don't know the answer. He responds immediately while I stand there open-mouthed. No one else comes along on the path.

"Life is suffering. Losing one's spouse and child suddenly is a terrible suffering. Your suffering comes from wanting things to be as they were, which they can never be. Quench the desire, stop the cravings. Don't seek anything. Give it all up, let it go, relinquish it. Live right. Dwell in Oneness. That's enough."

"Sandro—"

"Zandro. Zandro Pandi."

"Zandro Pandi. Who are you?"

"Pilgrim," he says. "Do not ask about me, ask about yourself."

I ignore this warning and keep at it: "You sound like the Buddha. Are you the Buddha?"

"I might be. How would you know?" I don't know. I am unknowing. Zandro Pandi smiles at me, and everything is falling away, everything is passing. I have no thoughts, no words, for the sensations. No me. All One. I am vanishing, my Self a mere echo receding into silence. After a long time, I don't know how long, I ask:

"What should I do next?"

"Nothing."

"Nothing?"

"What does it say in your favorite book— 'It is such blank scrolls as these—"

"You're freaking me out."

"At least that wasn't a question. Good. Okay, if you need me to say something more, it's this: Stay on the path you have made for yourself. Keep meditating."

"That's it?"

"That's all there is. Your *shikantaza*, 'just sitting,' is good. That's why I'm here. You called me."

"Can I come visit you again? Will I find you here?"

"Oh, Pilgrim. I am everywhere and nowhere. Mostly nowhere. You don't need me. You are me."

"Can I meet Kuan-yin also?" I ask. Zandro Pandi only gives me that forever smile again, and a second satori—a second wave of utter Oneness that washes over me, cleansing and emptying my mind. All that remains is—nothing. Just Zandro Pandi's smile, as vast as the Universe. After I don't know how long, maybe an instant, maybe forever, I hear him noodling on the accordion keyboard, getting ready to strike up a song.

"Oh dear, I think your shoelace is untied," he says.

Reflexively I look down at my shoes, almost simultaneously remembering that I am wearing slip-ons, and when I look up again, I am alone. My ordinary mind begins to seek its level again. Have I been hallucinating? I thought I was getting it together. Have I instead lost it completely?

I walk slowly over and sit on a large boulder next to the path. I close my eyes. Life is radiating inside me. The sun is warming me. Zandro Pandi is not a park weirdo, and I'm not losing it. I've had a satori. Can it be that I've met the Buddha?

Suddenly, I'm once again outside my body looking down on myself. This time, I'm not seeing a creature racked with grief and pain. I'm seeing a calm being who knows who Zandro Pandi is. He's the Buddha. So am I. I start to walk again. I can walk almost without looking. I could walk with my eyes closed. I stop by Stow Lake. Then I have another satori—it doesn't matter if my meeting with Zandro Pandi was real or not. I'm not afraid. I look back and see my suffering and tragedy. I look forward and see death. Without fear. Everything is One. Dan and Ella are still with me, will always be with me.

I wander around the park in a daze for the next several hours. I wonder: *Is my therapist Sarah Kuan-yin? Is my one-time friend Jane? Sajiro's mother Kumiko? My own mother? The women at the SoMa Zen Center?* I look at every woman who passes by, examining each one for signs of holiness. I see it in all of them. Every single one.

I'm so excited I start running, and almost knock over a Chinese lady on the path, who scowls at me. I stop and kiss her on the cheek so fast she can't stop me.

When I show up at the zendo that evening, Eli takes one look at me and quickly asks a senior student to lead the sit. He and Reva disappear, and when they return, they've changed into full Zen robes, rich brocade fabrics with flying birds sewn into them in silver filigree. Eli is even wearing an elaborate headdress that covers his ears and looks like a football helmet. I've never seen them in anything except street

clothes. It's a revelation, and a marker of their standing
in the greater Zen community, of which I'm only dimly
aware. They take me back to the *dokusan* room, and,
highly unusual, both sit with me. Nothing is said for
long minutes, as we gaze into each other's faces. I don't
have to tell them what happened. Many minutes pass.
The sit ends in the zendo hall and we can hear people
dispersing, but we have not left the places we took
when we entered the *dokusan* room. Finally, Eli clears
his throat and, in a voice choked with emotion, says:
"At this moment, I would normally confer oral
transmission of the dharma on you, but clearly, that
has happened already."

"Yes," I say. Then I say: "I'm on the path you and
Reva have shown me. I'm going to follow Kuan-yin. I
want to live a life of service. In what way, I can't say
yet."

At this, Eli and Reva rise as one and approach me
and give me great hugs. "I predict one day you'll have a
zendo of your own," Reva says, holding my hands in
her hands and smiling through tears. Everything has
changed, and yet nothing has changed. I go home that
night, make myself a cup of chamomile tea, go to sleep,
wake up, myself, Maya Marinovich.

There's one person I must see right away. On that
Saturday morning Kumiko picks me up and we drive
over the Golden Gate Bridge through a fog so thick we
creep along at twenty miles an hour until we burst
through on the other side of the bridge into blazingly
clear sunlight. We're following the path I took that dark
December evening when I wrecked my car, out of Mill

Valley up the Panoramic Highway, and then onto
Shoreline Drive, Route 1. When we start the downhill
on the other side of the coastal range, I squirm in my
passenger seat, but Kumiko is going much slower and
much more carefully than I was on my wild ride. How
did I ever even get as far as I got that night without
crashing sooner? The view opens, and we catch
glimpses of the Pacific Ocean at the end of the valley
below, shining blue and inviting. Near the bottom we
pass the spot where I ended up, saved by my rooftop
slide and the sign along the edge of the road. We pull
into the entrance to the Green Gulch Zen Center. I
notice the sign has been repaired with a new post. I
haven't made an appointment or inquired about which
monk had come out to rescue me. We find the welcome
center and a bookstore-gift shop and ask some
questions of the young woman at the reception desk.
She disappears into a back office, where we can hear
her making phone calls. When she returns, she asks
us to walk around on the grounds and then wait in the
Wheelright Center just opposite the bookstore. She
hands us a map, and we do as she asks, touring the
grounds, which are elaborate. There's a long narrow
zendo, a tea house, a yurt, dorms and residences,
many other outbuildings, and cultivated farmland, as it
is a working farm. After a while, we enter the
Wheelright Center, a comfortable conference room with
picture windows to take advantage of the views. There's
no one here. We wait. In the past, I might have been
anxious or nervous, but now I sit equitably, while
Kumiko walks around looking at the books and

pamphlets on the conference room tables. When the monk enters the room, I wouldn't have recognized him, partly because the last and only time I saw him I was hanging upside down in my overturned car, and partly because he looks like all the other monks we've seen since we arrived: shaven head, brown robe, straw sandals. He recognizes me. He bows. He speaks first:

"Welcome to the Green Gulch Zen Center. My name is Tezuka. We've met once before, under different circumstances. My, how you've changed."

I smile. "Yes. I'm right-side up now."

"Indeed. May I ask how you came to undergo such a rapid transformation?" I understand his question. It's been barely six months since I was a would-be suicide on the roadside outside the center.

"I have good teachers." The monk glances at Kumiko wonderingly, so I explain my connection to the SoMa Zen Center and Eli and Reva and give the monk a brief summary of my recent personal history. The monk nods approvingly as I describe my shikantaza "just sitting" practice and touch on breakthroughs I have achieved.

"I met the Buddha," I say casually, an inexplicable statement that doesn't surprise the Green Gulch monk. He doesn't react at all to this outlandish claim. Total equanimity.

"Why have you come to see me?" Tezuka asks.

"To thank you. I might have died if you hadn't come out."

"Perhaps. You have made good use of your 'second life,'" he says. Tezuka looks at me calmly, just as he did that night on the road. "Would you like some tea? We're just about to start *chado*."

After the tea ceremony, Kumiko drives me back to her apartment. I sit in the car for a moment with her.

"I am so happy and proud. I kept saying that you should take it slowly. I was wrong. You are a lucky one. You have entered your new life quickly. I know you have been working hard, but many people try and try and work hard and still don't reach anything approaching what you have reached. My blessing on you."

"Thank you. For everything," I reply. We sit for another moment, holding hands and then I get out of the car.

The following Sunday, I call my mother at my usual early afternoon time.

"Maya," she says. "There's something I want to tell you and I am afraid to bring it up."

"What is it, Mom?

"I had a dream. I didn't want to tell you because it might trigger more upsets, but it was so vivid."

"Tell me."

"In the dream you're sitting with Dan and Ella. It's like one of those professional family photos, you're all dressed up and posing for the photographer. So beautiful and happy. I woke up crying, but the tears were tears of joy."

"Thank you, Mom," I say. "For telling me. That's a beautiful dream. I have a picture like that right on the shelf where I meditate."

"Mom, there's something I want to tell you, but I'm not sure how to say it. It's about my meditation practice and things that have been happening of late." I take a deep breath. "It's about the deep level that I have gotten to."

"Something has changed in you," my mother says tentatively.

"It's more than that," I reply. "I had an experience. I know it sounds crazy, but I met the Buddha in Golden Gate Park."

"Maya, are you sure you're okay? Do I need to come out there? Call Kumiko?" There is concern and motherly angst in my mother's voice.

"Kumiko knows. You should call her. I probably shouldn't use this term living in California, but it's a seismic shift for me. Please don't worry." I don't want to leave my mother hanging with my news, but I figure it'll all come out as things move forward. "How about you Mom? How's it going?"

To my surprise I learn that my beautiful mother has started to go out on dates. We giggle and laugh about some of her experiences.

"I'm in absolutely no hurry, but I'm having fun again. I figure I deserve a bit of that too."

"Of course you do. Just stay safe and remember how much I love and appreciate you."

When I hang up, I can't stop smiling and feeling love, for my mother, for myself, for the whole world.

There's one other person I need to tell what has happened. On Monday morning, I open with Sarah in a new way.

"Okay, Sarah, are you sitting down?" I ask. I proceed to tell Sarah about my experience in almost the same way I told my mother.

"Maya, are you okay?" Sarah sounds both excited and concerned. "How do you know what you're talking about is real?"

I tell her what I told my mother. "I can tell. People around me are confirming it. My teachers at the meditation center saw it right away. My life has had a major shift. I still need to study, to continue to meditate, do yoga and many other things. But I'm better now. I truly am."

Then Sarah surprised me.

"I wish I could be there with you. I wish I could give you a hug right now."

"Sarah, I wish you could too. Are you okay with continuing our talks for the next few months? It'll help me settle into my new situation, give me a different perspective on things."

"Of course." We end the call soon after. I'm surprised and relieved at how easy it was to tell my mother and my therapist what has happened to me. I finger the locket and the gold pendant Jane gave me. I trace the shape of the Japanese lettering. *Ichi-go Ichi-e. One life, one chance. One chance meeting.*

Chapter 23 The Cloud Nine Ball

I try not to change much in the way I'm living my life. I go to meditation and yoga, I have *dokusan* with Reva, I volunteer. I see Kumiko and talk with my mother and my therapist. After hearing Eli recite the Buddhist maxim "even an ant treasures its life," I extend my empathy to all sentient beings and become a vegetarian. No more ham or bacon in Timberbeast breakfasts or meaty burritos for this girl. The biggest change is that I'm happy and I want to share my happiness with everyone. Some people find that obnoxious. In a meeting of the senior student group, Marion makes a catty comment implying that she doesn't think I really had the experience I describe.

"A homeless man with a funny name and an accordion, he was the Buddha?"

I hadn't said Zandro was homeless, but he might have been, like those souls Eli and Reva feed every day, who teach us so much by their humility, compassion, and love for each other. Marion's remark doesn't bother me. I can't say that I earned enlightenment. I probably didn't. I'm not judging me. I don't judge anyone or anything anymore. Or I try not to, anyway, although I'm still human, still susceptible to human faults and foibles. It has just been my great good fortune to have glimpsed the Oneness of Everything in all its glory and ordinariness.

Most of the rest of the group are supportive and encouraging. Their acceptance helps me make a decision. I'm going to throw a party, at the party place, The Laundry, and I'm going to invite everyone. All the people from the SoMa Zen Center. All my friends from The Laundry: Taisha, Max, Jacques. Students from Taisha's class. Lost Tribe people, Chuck, Mark, Brad, Manami. Kumiko. Stefan. Sajiro. Peter. My therapist. My mother. John the taxi driver. Jane and Joe. Jimmy Ueda and his parents. The lawyer I worked for in Boston. I want the party to be a thank-you to everyone who helped me along the way and a chance to introduce them all to each other. Why I think this is the right thing to do, I have no idea, but once I set it in motion, it takes on a life of its own quickly. Max loves the idea. "A dress ball!" He comes up with the official name of the party, the one that goes on invitations I send out: "THE CLOUD NINE BALL!" Okay, it's goofy and it has only the most tenuous connection to my life, but what the hell, I go with it, because it's loopy and fun and that's what I want this party to be. We pick a date far enough in the future that it will give time for people to make plans.

My partners in organizing the party are Kumiko, Taisha, and Max. My idea is to have everything catered. I want Jacques to relax and enjoy himself. There'll be a band and a dance floor, and an open-mike time later in the evening for people to join in to play music, read poetry, dance, whatever.

I meet with Eli and Reva and confirm the date will work for them.

On Sunday, during my conversation with my mother, I say: "Mom, I think you should come out and check on me."

"Are you okay?" She immediately sounds worried again.

"I am more than okay. I am having a party and I want you here."

"You brat, pulling my chain and scaring me."

"Mom, I'm still your sassy daughter. Seriously, you can stay with me at Kumiko's apartment. I'd like you to be here for a while. Maybe help with the last of the preparations." I tell her the date and she marks it down in her day planner.

On Monday morning during my telephone conversation with Sarah, I ask her about it. She notes the date as well and says something I never expected: "I'll clear my calendar."

I hear from Taisha that Michelle has used some of the money I gave her to secure an apartment for herself and her daughter. She's going to come to the party. I'm thrilled. It turns out I don't have to do much work on The Cloud Nine Ball. The folks at The Laundry are old hands at party-throwing, and they're happy to celebrate me. I let them. Perhaps it's just the way things are happening, but everything that was stuck before is flowing now. No impediments. The greater world is still in turmoil, with droughts, plagues, wars, unstable political leadership, deteriorating climate, but my corner of the planet is radiantly peaceful and pleasant, a huge change from the past two years.

While the party prep is going on, mostly being handled by Max, Taisha, and some of the others at The Laundry, I spend most of my time with Eli and Reva helping them organize a retreat. It's to take a group of children of the homeless to a place that Mike Strong has arranged, a ranch and vineyard up in Sonoma owned by a wealthy friend of his, Doug Kimball, who made his money in high-tech and then bought himself this country place and retired to it as a gentleman farmer.

After a week or two of getting everything set up, we show up in a rented school bus with thirty children. Most of the kids touch a cow for the first time. They run through rows of planted grapevines, play hide-and-seek among the towering trees of a eucalyptus grove.

At the end of the afternoon, the children take a swim in a spring-fed pond on the property. They spend time jumping off the dock, seeing who can make the biggest splash and the most noise. It's nerve wracking and we watch them carefully. I'm already planning that we need many more chaperones and supervisors for the next outing. We purchased a change of clothes, pajamas, and flip-flops, and a bag of toiletries with a new toothbrush, toothpaste, a comb and a brush for each child. Cathy Bishop oversaw the purchasing. She pulls in with a van loaded with all this stuff at the end of the swim. The kids wash up in the outside shower, wrap up in beach towels that they will take with them and then they go "shopping" at the van. For some of these kids, this may be the first washing up they've had for many weeks.

In the evening we roast hot dogs (tofu dogs for the Buddhists,) cook 'Smores over an open fire, and drink outrageously expensive wines from paper cups. Mike Strong is there and sings old cowboy tunes for the kids: *The Streets of Laredo, Red River Valley, Get Along Little Dogies*. Some of the kids are scared by all the open space, their lives up to this point having been confined to shelters and the street. We had planned to have them sleep in tents, but that turns out to be too much like their living situations in the city. Doug and his wife Karen graciously open their home and the intended tenting experience turns into a campout in their spacious living room. Doug, a nerdy guy as high-tech CEOs tend to be, lean and fit thanks to daily sessions with a personal trainer, with aviator glasses and an almost Prince Valiant bowl haircut, is awkward with the kids but tries hard. His wife, a former model, blond and also Hollywood-movie-star fit, is naturally comfortable and helpful, and by the end of the evening a couple of the younger kids are sleeping in her arms on the wraparound sofa.

Mike plunks himself down next to me on a window seat and holds out a package. It's wrapped in a dark purple Japanese cloth. *It's a furoshiki* flits through my mind and I smile that I remember the word.

I open the package and lift out a gleaming bell-metal bronze bowl and a wooden mallet. Separately wrapped are a pair of miniature cymbals tied together by a leather strip.

"These are some things that have helped me in my meditation," Mike says. "They're Tibetan singing bowls and cymbals. The sounds really help me. Of course, I like sounds."

I look at Mike. He smiles. I'm still not entirely comfortable with Mike because he's so incredibly handsome and because I'm so aware of his fame. I take a deep centering breath that puts these thoughts out of my mind. I concentrate on the gifts that I'm holding in my hands. I look into Mike's eyes. "Thanks. I'll study how to use them," I say. "I hope they can help me the way they've helped you."

At that instant I feel Mike's pain. He's handsome, famous, and like all of us so fragile and has suffered so greatly. *From what?* I wonder.

On the bus heading back to the city at the end of the retreat, Eli sits next to me. "We've got to do more of this," he says. A sudden thought enters my head: I wonder if there's a connection to be made between the Tribe, who have a splendid place for this kind of thing although much farther north, and the SoMa Zen Center. The kids are exhausted but happy as we return them to their parents, a group nervously waiting on a street corner in the Mission. Some will sleep on cardboard beds under plastic sheeting in Golden Gate Park tonight, others in crowded, dirty depressing SROs like the one I inhabited. *We'll do more*, I think.

The next morning, I sit in meditation for a long time. Something needs to be cleared out, refreshed, forgiven? I rise above my nattering mind just enough to listen in. *There's so much suffering, so much work to be done. I don't deserve my advancement. How can I spend money on a frivolous party? Who do I think I am?*

Elevated? What a crock. I am so scared. Scared of what? The party? That my grief and pain will surge back up and reclaim me? I half-open my eyes and see the purple *furoshiki* next to the meditation altar. With shaking hands, I unwrap the bowl and the cymbals. I close my eyes and take up the cymbals. I brush them gently together. A high airy chime circles and spirals and lingers in the air around me. I see Mike Strong's smiling face. I take up the bowl and not knowing how to use it, I strike it just one time. A broad clear sound surrounds me.

Thank you, Mike. What a beautiful present and what beautiful timing. I've come through, at least for now.

The next Sunday I drive my newly leased bright red Toyota Highlander to the San Francisco airport to meet my mother who is going to be spending a few weeks with me. The party is in just one week. I am stunned by the number of people who are coming and wildly appreciative of how Max, Taisha, and others have organized it all. Food, music, the whole thing.

When my mother's luggage is safely stowed in the back of the car, she comments on the size and luxuriousness of the car.

"It's just a leased car. I needed something safe. I've been working with Reva and Eli, carting lots of kids around and I need to know that they're safe too. I'm still seeing my therapist Sarah on the stuff that is stuck in my body from the accidents. Guess what?" I add. "Sarah is coming to the party."

My mother just nods and smiles.

"Are you okay?" I ask.

"Overwhelmed and happy."

"Tonight, we're having dinner at my apartment. Kumiko's apartment. Kumiko will be there, and Stefan." I find myself chattering away about rooms at a hotel reserved for out-of-town guests, the various people who are coming. All the help I have gotten with arranging the party, until finally, I just stop talking and we cruise along 280 in silence and into the city and wind our way through Golden Gate Park to the apartment.

Kumiko comes out and greets my mother. She bows formally and then laughs and throws her arms around her. The four of us have dinner, saké, sushi, tempura, many delights, some prepared by Kumiko, some from Japanese restaurants in the neighborhood.

Later that week, just two days before the party, I have a *dokusan* meeting with Reva. When I show up, I'm surprised that Eli is there also. We sit in silence, and then Eli says:

"We're both happy to celebrate with you at your party this weekend."

Reva chimes in: "Yes, what a treat to meet some of the people who have been part of your life. Mike says he's coming."

"How wonderful!" I notice the larger Tibetan bowl on a shelf in the corner of the room and remark how he gave me one to help me in meditation.

"That saved his life, I think," Reva says. "It helped him through some dark years."

I notice she is saying years, and not just times. I can see in their eyes that they want to tell me something, so I say, "Yes?"

Eli clears his throat. He puts his hands through his wild white hair and rubs his beard. He sighs.

"Maya, this is said more as a friend than a teacher. It is wonderful that you want to share your newly found insights, your happiness, your joy. People will love you for it and some may be jealous and hate you for it." He gives a light laugh. The laugh of experience. "The party will be a fine place for sharing joy. Be aware, the kind of experience you have had, your enlightenment has opened you up in ways you will discover as you go forward. You may see and even experience what others around you are seeing and experiencing. It may be happiness, but it may also be deep suffering and pain. It won't happen all the time."

I close my eyes and go back to Mike giving me the gifts. His pain.

"Yes, I think it's happened to me lately and it happened even before, when I hadn't begun meditation." I'm thinking of Mike, of Michelle, even of Sajiro. "Thank you for being such good friends and wonderful teachers."

"We don't have all the answers," Eli says bluntly. "We're not above the suffering. We live with it too."

It's Reva who says: "When you take on the pain of the world, it doesn't mean you suffer all the world's pain. Who could do that? It means you vow to lessen that pain."

"I understand," I say, and then I giggle because that sounds so pretentious. Eli and Reva both start to laugh too, and then we're all three laughing. We just laugh and laugh.

The day of the party my mother and Kumiko disappear, leaving me alone in the apartment so I can't help in any way with the party prep. It's clear the party organizers don't want my help.

I sit for a long time in meditation, but excitement and restlessness intrude so I head out for a long walk in the park. I go over to the conservatory and walk around, admiring the roses, hydrangeas, and dahlia all in bloom. I walk around Bunny Meadow and think about the time I met the Tribe there. When I get back to the apartment the Dynamic Duo—as I've taken to calling Kumiko and my mother—are there waiting to dress me for the party. For a minute I fear Kumiko is going to put me in a Zen monk's robes, or worse, in a kimono, but instead they bring out a gorgeous ball gown of a kind I've never worn. The hem touches the floor. The dress is a V-neck, sexy and revealing with a full, layered skirt. The color is a deep red. As I put the dress on, I wonder if it's too sexy. Kumiko holds out a puffy-sleeved jacket of the same deep red color and material. "Kind of like Cinderella, don't you think?" I say, but when they lead me to a mirror, I think, *I look amazing!*

"Shoes?" I say. "No ruby slippers?"

"That's Dorothy from Oz, silly, not Cinderella. Hers were glass."

The shoes they give me are my own, sparkling black slippers, for comfort, and in any case my feet can hardly be seen beneath the wide skirt that hangs full length. Kumiko does wear a kimono, a dazzling, colorful one I've never seen before, and even *geta*, the notoriously difficult to walk in wooden clogs, but she does so effortlessly. My mother opts for more casual dress. She's wearing an off-white pants suit with a midnight blue silk sleeveless top. Her dark reddish-blond hair is piled on her head, which makes her look even taller than she is. She's the height of casual elegance. She wants to be comfortable. I don't blame her. I don't blame anyone, for anything. We three ladies pile in the car. I laugh as I struggle to tuck the full skirt around my legs. Stefan has been picked up already for a sound check with the band.

The car pulls up in front of the entrance, and as I step out of the back, I laugh. There's a red carpet, god knows where Max got that from, and a porkpie-hatted photographer pretending to be a paparazzi and taking my picture with flash. I stride into the atrium of The Laundry, waving my right hand back and forth perpendicular and sideways like the Queen of England, which gets a laugh.

The room is packed. The band starts to play. Max and Taisha are on the stage in front of the microphone. Max is wearing tight black jeans, a T-shirt, and a dark red tuxedo jacket with wide black lapels. Taisha almost matches Max, though she towers above him, tall and elegant in a shiny and tight long dress. She sports a matching tuxedo jacket. The guests are invited to mingle as hors d'oeuvres and drinks are offered by waiters carrying trays. I see and greet so many people. Jane and Joe come by to say hello and share hugs. I hardly recognize Melissa, the lawyer I worked with in Boston. She's wearing a slinky dark green gown. Her tall and ample body make a striking contrast to the way she looked in her up-tight lawyer outfits. Her red hair is longer than I remember and instead of being pulled back in a severe ponytail, it curls down onto her shoulders. She hugs me and laughs at my outfit. "Save a dance for me," is all she says.

"It'll be like Christmas!" I laugh.

When I turn away from Melissa, I find myself face to face with Sajiro. He's dressed simply in jeans and a Tribe T-shirt. He smiles at me, but what I receive is his sadness and pain, which has been more apparent to me with everyone of late. Each person's suffering is different. I know a bit of the source of Sajiro's pain. He kisses me on both cheeks, and we bow to one another. He drifts off to a corner of the room where many others of the Tribe are gathered. They lift their glasses to me, with smiles.

I see a woman that I'm sure I should recognize. She's short and plump with a full head of dark and grey hair in contrasting streaks. Natural. She's wearing a long simple black dress and a lovely, flowered silk shawl falls off one shoulder. *Oh my god*, I think. It's Sarah, my therapist. When she reaches me, I burst out in a laugh.

"Sarah, you look beautiful. I didn't know it was you at first."

Sarah just smiles, a full smile, not her thin, reserved therapist's smile. We gaze at one another for a long while and then share a long warm hug.

"Let me introduce you to my mother and some dear friends," I say, and I lead her over to the table where Kumiko, Stefan, and my mother are sitting.

My heart is full, but after another half an hour of greeting and mingling and being congratulated by people, *for what?* I find myself thinking, *for having survived? for having overcome my own craziness?* I need to escape. Just then, arms encircle me. I turn to find myself face to face with Peter.

"How beautiful."

"Please come with me," I say.

We skirt around to the back stairs and up to my room, which to my surprise is open and untouched. Peter takes me by the shoulders and looks into my eyes.

"Are you okay?"

"I'm wonderful. Just overwhelmed."

He takes me in his arms and holds me.

"Please come find me whenever you need to. I'll be up onstage with the band most of the night."

"I will."

"Not just tonight. Whenever, always."

"I will," I say as we leave the room and head back down to the party. It was only five minutes, and just a long hug, but Peter has given me the strength and support that I needed.

Jimmy Ueda has sent his regrets; he's going to be teaching at a workshop on the East Coast. But when I look up, I see Sensei Ueda and his beautiful blond Sensei wife. He's in a tuxedo. She's wearing an outrageously lavish silk and taffeta ball gown that would not be out of place in Buckingham Palace. They stand at the entrance to The Laundry as if waiting to be announced. I see Kumiko hurry over to them, lead them in, and seat them with her and Stefan.

Max and Taisha are up at the mikes rolling out a next phase for the party. Open mike. They announce that there will be two sessions of this with some dancing and more music from the house band mixed in. "Anyone who might like to perform with the band is invited to do so," Max shouts. "The band will back you up any way they can." Stefan and Peter and all the talented musicians are more than up to that task.

First up is Michelle, the girl from my class. She thanks Taisha and me for all we have done to help her. She says she wants to sing two songs.

"This one is for Maya. She helped me when I was too proud and unhappy to even reach out." She looks over at Peter and Stefan and the group. "I'm kind of nervous and scared. I've mostly been singing in church and these are church songs, but this is still a stretch." I can hear the nervous tremor in her voice.

"You go girl," Stefan calls out. Though he doesn't really know what is coming. Michelle starts to hum so they can figure out the key and the song that is coming. The keyboardist smiles and starts a wonderful introduction to the song as Michelle starts to sing "Lean on Me" changing some of the lyrics to say, "You just call on me sister, when you need a hand." Her voice grows and fills the room. When she finishes, there's a moment of shocked silence and then wild applause. Michelle waits for the crowd to go silent again, and then says:

"This one is for Taisha." Michelle laughs with a grin. She hums again and begins, *"I was born by the river in a little tent, it's been a long time coming, but I know a change gonna come."* At the end of Sam Cooke's mournful protest song, the applause is muted, almost worshipful, as if people were in a church and wanted to be respectful.

Others get up to speak, but after Michelle, no one wants to sing. Just as Taisha is about to step to the mike again to call a break in the action, Mike Strong walks up to the mike. He's kept a low profile up to this point, with his cowboy hat down over his face, sitting at a back table trying to make himself as inconspicuous as possible. He picks up an acoustic guitar and looks over at the band. "You guys are incredible!" he nods to the band, "and Michelle, well, I hesitate to follow such a talent, but I wrote this song, just this past week for my friend Maya. It's called "Pretty Green-Eyed Pilgrim." By this time there is a rustling in the room as some people realize who Mike is. He starts to play, and everyone leans into the music. After a long instrumental introduction, Mike begins to sing:

"I couldn't sing a song that day
You saw the sorrows in my heart
We walked along that sacred way
The path that has no end, no start.

Your green eyes burning through my haze
Told me: "We're all pilgrims on this quest,
Go live your days, go live your days,
Go do your best, go do your best."
After the first verse the band joins along. It's more folk than country. It's like an old friend sitting around with his guitar, entertaining us. When he strums the last chord, the applause for Mike is quiet, like we were all in his den and he's just, you know, hanging out with us. "Well, I've been told to announce a break for a while for some more dancing."

I intercept Mike as he walks back toward the table where he's been sitting at the back of the room. We stand facing one another for a moment.

"Thank you." I bring my hands in together in front of my heart and bow.

"Thank you for understanding some things I thought almost no one could see in me," Mike replies.

My mother is moved to tears by the song. She approaches us. "Thank you for that beautiful song. I'm Maya's mother, Lillian. I can't believe how you captured this beautiful daughter of mine in that song."

"Thanks," Mike smiles down at Lillian. "She's quite a young woman." He says this while still looking at me.

"You must have some experience." Maya's mother smiles up at him. "Have you performed much?"

"Oh, I'd say, yes, quite a bit actually."

The quiet dance music has started up with a slow song from the '70s. One of the young band members starts to play and sing a version of Eric Clapton's "You Look Wonderful Tonight."

"Maya, I think I should take your mom for a spin." He turns to Lillian, "Would you like to dance?" he asks as he opens his arms and sweeps Lillian onto the dance floor.

After the dance, my mother heads back to the table where Stefan, Kumiko, and I are sitting with drinks.

"What a talented singer and handsome fellow," Lillian gushes. She's a bit tipsy. "I really enjoyed dancing with him. He must have performed as a song writer and singer."

Kumiko and Stefan laugh and explain exactly who Mike Strong is. The Grammys, the platinum country albums, the movie roles. Lillian laughs along with them.

Still a little tipsy, Lillian sees Mike standing off to the side. I've left Stefan and Kumiko's table and am standing next to him. We're both watching the party. She sidles up to us.

"Hi, I'm a bit embarrassed because I didn't know who you are. My friends have filled me in. Hope I didn't offend you."

"Well, I'd say it's like jumping into a cold mountain lake. Bracing, even shocking, and refreshing. It does someone like me good, you know. To remember just how small that lake is, and how short a distance you have to go to find someone to whom all that doesn't mean a darn thing. Just to be a regular person. Ready for another?" And he again nods to me as he takes my mother's hand and leads her back out on the dance floor.

Taisha comes by. She's like the proud mama. "You go, girl." I stop her before she moves away.

"I've started writing."

"I knew you would. I told you."

"Yes, and guess what the book is called? *More Monkey!* It's about a modern pilgrim who goes on a journey, searching for truth and enlightenment."

Taisha takes me by the shoulders and stares into my eyes. "Did you meet—you did, didn't you?" I smile and say nothing. "I look forward to reading your book," Taisha says with cool love, and backs away from me as if bowing in *gassho.* I wave to her to stop. We both laugh.

I see Max standing with a proprietary look on his face, like a maître d' surveying his domain. I go up to him and take his hand.

"Think it's time for a dance." I slip off my puffy-sleeved jacket.

"My goodness, you look ravishing without that jacket. You've been working out! Is it safe to dance with you?"

I just giggle and we go out onto the dance floor where some down and dirty rock and roll is being played.

While we're dancing, Zandro Pandi walks into The Laundry with his accordion slung around his neck. A slight shock wave strikes me.

"Max, I need to stop for a minute."

My Heart Leaps Up. Zandro's eyes find me immediately and I stop mid-step. He waits until the band finishes the song and then walks up to Peter.

How I wish I could hear what they are saying to each other!

Peter raises his hand for attention and announces: "We have a special guest tonight who would like to play a song for Maya. Please welcome Zandro Pandi." My first thought is I'm the only person who knows who he is, but immediately I realize that's not true. Anyone to whom I told my story will know. Kumiko. The monk Tezuka, who came, to my surprise, and in street clothes. Therapist Sarah. My mother. To almost everyone else, Zandro will look like a down and out musician who wandered in off the street. Out of the corner of one eye I see Eli and Reva talking excitedly to each other. I see Marion staring at me open-mouthed.

Zandro steps up to the mike and says, "Congratulations, Pilgrim!" Then Zandro begins to play his accordion, the epic opening of the Beatle's "All You Need is Love" that starts quirkily with notes from "Le Marseillaise." The band joins in quickly, the electric guitar player and an electronic keyboardist both trying to reproduce the comical brass sounds in the original. Zandro looks directly at me when he sings: "Nothing you can do but you can learn how to be you in time, It's easy."

When he gets to the chorus, he shouts one word:

"Everybody!" and the whole party sings, "All you need is love!" I see people crying, laughing, hugging each other. It's a total love fest. Mike Strong is onstage strumming and singing his heart out. Stefan is riffing sax lines, trading off with the guitarist, and the two of them are jamming up a storm of sound.

When the song ends, Zandro speaks into the microphone. He says just two words: "Party on!" and walks out. People part like the Red Sea to let him by. I don't follow him, because I know what will happen. Sure enough, Marion chases after him out the front door of The Laundry but soon returns looking stunned. I overhear her telling Eli and Reva: "He's gone. He vanished! I was right behind him!"

The party goes on late into the night.

Chapter 24 Gone Beyond

Six months have passed since the party. December rains are pouring down outside my window. It's morning and I'm having a temper tantrum over nothing. A heel has come off a shoe I'm trying to put on. I almost never wear shoes with heels. Now I remember why. I'm irritated over the inconvenience. I'm late for an important meeting with a wealthy non-profit donor to the SoMa Zen Center, and I'm dressing up for once. Most of the time these days I wear T-shirts and cotton string pants.

Why did this have to happen today? Why am I having a fit? I shouldn't be acting like this. Angry over a damn high-heel shoe. I throw the shoe against the chair and start to laugh. *No, but human beings have fits all the time. I'll do what I can.*

I stop for a moment and gaze out at the rain, then I reach for a pair of low, stylish, water-proof boots that go with the skirt I'm wearing. I close my eyes to center myself and the last lines of the Heart Sutra glow in my brain, bathed in light: *Gone, gone, gone beyond, gone completely beyond, Awake, Hallelujah!*

I laugh, look at my reflection in the mirror. I like what I see. I peer down at my clunky yet hip shoes, grab a raincoat and umbrella, and head out into the rain—Maya Marinovich, widow, vilomah, millionaire, Zen student, martial artist, sometime surfer girl, pilgrim.